HYACINTH
girls

HYACINTH
girls

LAUREN FRANKEL

CROWN PUBLISHERS
NEW YORK

Published in the United States by Crown Publishers, an imprint of the Crown Publishing Group, a division of Penguin Random House LLC, New York.
www.crownpublishing.com

Crown is a registered trademark and the Crown colophon is a trademark of Penguin Random House LLC.

Grateful acknowledgment is made to Faber and Faber Limited for permission to reprint 8 lines from *The Waste Land* by T. S. Eliot, copyright © 1922 by T. S. Eliot. All rights reserved. Reprinted by permission of Faber and Faber Limited.

Library of Congress Cataloging-in-Publication Data
Frankel, Lauren, author.
  Hyacinth girls / Lauren Frankel. — First edition.
      pages ; cm
  ISBN 978-0-553-41805-7 (hardcover) —
  ISBN 978-0-553-41806-4 (ebook)
  1. Teenage girls—Fiction. 2. Bullying—Fiction. I. Title.
  PR6106.R4529H93 2015
  823'.92—dc23
  2014028591

Printed in the United States of America

Jacket design by Melissa Faustine
Jacket photograph by Lisa Kimmell/Getty Images

10 9 8 7 6 5 4 3 2 1

First Edition

For John

"You gave me hyacinths first a year ago;

"They called me the hyacinth girl."

—Yet when we came back, late, from the Hyacinth garden,

Your arms full, and your hair wet, I could not

Speak, and my eyes failed, I was neither

Living nor dead, and I knew nothing,

Looking into the heart of light, the silence.

Öd' und leer das Meer.

—T. S. ELIOT, "THE WASTE LAND"

Prologue

On a chilly October morning I watched them put Callie's face on a billboard: two men in hard hats hoisting the vinyl sheet on a rope through the air. I chewed gum in my parked car, the traffic whizzing by me, as the sheet billowed and flapped in the wind like a huge dark flag. I wanted to be the first one to see her, so I'd driven over early, making promises to myself about how I was going to be. Focused. Resilient. Like nothing could touch me. I wouldn't reach for the tissues in my pockets, and I wouldn't start wailing in front of the highway.

Up on the scaffolding, the men were moving faster in their high-vis jackets, wrestling her picture into the frame, using sticks to press it smooth. My view was clear, but I opened the door, wanting to see without glass between us. And then I just stood there on the side of the road: she was completely transformed. Callie was fourteen years old. I'd known her since the day she was born, but even her freckles seemed unfamiliar, magnified so many times. Her hair looked shockingly bright, as if dyed to match the sun, and her green eyes were wide open, gazing out across our town. This was on the corner of Whitefield Road, about a quarter of a mile from the high school, not a picturesque stretch of Pembury (no stone walls or steepled churches). But it was a road that everyone used, commuting to work and to school, so I knew they'd struggle to avoid her unless they opted for the bumpy old B-roads.

I'd been fantasizing about how they'd react, seeing her here for the first time. The people from our town, adults and children alike. Floods of tears, of course. School buses flooded with tears. Spontaneous candlelit vigils and rallies on the grass below. Other times, in angrier moods, I imagined more satisfying repercussions. Cars crashing during the school run, scalding lattes dropped onto crotches, girls screaming at their parents to please take a different route. Maybe one of the guys from her list would suddenly stop in his tracks, and fail, in his astonishment, to notice a speeding truck. Then I imagined people from out of town, visiting for Thanksgiving, who'd ask uncomfortable questions after noticing her picture. "Well, she went to Adam's school," the mother would say, and Adam would lurch up from the table. Then his mother would glance at her lump of turkey and try to begin again. "I guess you didn't hear what happened." And everyone would put down their forks.

The man who designed the billboard recognized her as soon as I showed him the photo, the effect of constant news coverage since it happened in September. She wasn't smiling in the picture. There was a crease of tension between her pale brows. I'd taken the shot last summer after the trouble had already started, although I didn't see it at the time—I was blissfully unaware. Vision doesn't have to be about clarity, and on the day that I took the picture, we were sitting in our landlady's garden, enjoying the heat on our skin. The stalks of lavender were thick with honeybees, and a sparrow twittered in the bushes, and I could see the little hairs sprouting on Callie's bent knees. She stretched her arms above her head, flexing her slender fingers, and when I lifted my camera I told her to say cheese. She didn't smile. I hardly noticed. The billboard designer clicked his keyboard and Callie's picture filled his screen.

"What would you like the sign to say?" he asked.

"Do you know your children?" I said.

"Are you asking *me*?"

"No. That's what I want on the billboard."

Do you know your children? The words were printed to the left of Callie's face. Not a very subtle question, but the right one, I had thought. To some it would feel like an accusation: *Do you know what they've done? Do you know what else they're capable of?* To others, a warning: *Do you understand it could've been them, with their faces up here on the billboard?* Sometimes I wondered if the words were meant for me alone, a reminder of my own failure. I had never been a great one at connecting the dots.

In fact, in one of my old stories, a story I'd often repeated to Callie, I told how I believed I was possessed when I was twelve years old. I had been going through the usual preteen troubles: crazy hormones and strange compulsions, an overwhelming sense that I was losing control. So I had decided that these things weren't me—something *else* must've got *inside* me. I looked at the symptoms and explained them to myself this way: I had been possessed by a demon. I needed to be exorcised. I begged my best friend Joyce to take care of it, and she had agreed in her canopied bedroom, chanting and singing, tapping her mouth like an Indian chief. Joyce's imagination was stronger than mine, and as her friend I never doubted it, so when she said that the demon was gone, I was relieved and utterly grateful. Callie sometimes teased me: *You know you weren't really possessed, right?* And I smiled and nodded, but I'd been absolutely certain. I had looked at the clues and believed I understood. I'd done that all my life, drawing the wrong conclusions.

And with Callie it was worse, because I was convinced that I knew her. I thought I could trace her life through a thousand remembered moments. Here she is, pink and puckered, wrapped in newborn swaddle, while Joyce announces blearily: "Rebecca, I'm a mother!" Then there's the puffy-cheeked toddler singing songs and grinning, the little girl chattering about earthworms on the sidewalk. At ten she announced that she was going to be a biologist. At eleven she convinced me to be a vegetarian. I knew every one of her preferences, from shampoo to music to fruit. I washed her underwear and listened to her nightmares. I watched her fall asleep hundreds of times. I felt her presence so close. I knew her habits so intimately. I thought I could understand her, and I thought I always would.

But I couldn't even understand myself. I didn't know how I'd react. After the billboard went up, I didn't feel much satisfaction. The words seemed empty beside her oversized face. Do you know your children? How could anyone know? If these kids didn't know themselves, how could they give their parents a clue? Was I really trying to help them or was this just a final fuck-you? A hostile outburst from a troubled woman. I caught my reflection in the glass, eyes baggy, hair tied back—the smell of the hospital still clinging to my coat. What kind of person was I to make such a gesture? A meek dental hygienist. A woman who baked PTA cupcakes. A friendless thirty-four-year-old who was raising her best friend's daughter. I looked up at the billboard, wondering if this was really justice. They might still see Callie however they chose. Some might say the bitch got what she deserved. Others would see her as a victim. Maybe a few would be amazed that this could happen in our town. But she'd watch over them now, she'd be there and they'd have to remember, on late-night drives and morning commutes, heading to football games or dances, her skin dazzlingly illuminated by the bright bulbs of light.

To really explain everything I'd need to go back at least six months, to that day last April when I got the call from Callie's school. But there'd also be stuff I'd want to leave out, particular things I wouldn't like to tell. For instance, the silly little daydream I was having before the principal called. My fantasies weren't particularly racy, no torrid scenes involving latex and drills. In fact, they were altogether chaste, with scarcely a kiss exchanged. What they *were* was retro. Boring and anti-feminist. I'd lean over to clean a patient's teeth and imagine his proposition.

I called them "gateway men" in my head, choosing the ones who looked skinny and anemic. Men who lived alone in five-bedroom houses and worked all hours at their city jobs. He would be fed up with microwave dinners and greasy overpriced Chinese takeout; what he really, secretly desired was a good home-cooked meal. In my mind it would start accidentally, our eyes connecting above my surgical mask, our arms brushing together as I tore off some floss. Then electricity, ka-ZOW! Like we'd always been waiting for this moment, and here was my door—my gateway—to a whole new life. My heart would pound as he leaned forward, and right then he'd ask me: Did I know anybody who could be his live-in chef?

At that point in my life I was teaching myself to cook. My goal was to master one new technique each month in our small rental kitchen. I wouldn't have had the time to do this, but luckily I suffered from insomnia, so most nights I'd find myself drowsily lining up ingredients and preheating the oven. There I destroyed piecrusts and pastries, deflated umpteen soufflés, repeating the steps over and over, reaching for eggs and more butter. But I loved it. I loved the moment when my body and mind were completely absorbed, when I forgot about who I was and just focused on the mixture. Fingers sensitive to the texture of dough, eyes attuned to the sheen of egg white, hand stirring automatically as the bubbles began to inflate. My anxieties disappeared when I concentrated fully, as if each uncontrollable variable could be mastered with enough attention. When my dishes finally came out perfectly, like the photos in my cookbook, it was more than just an accomplishment, it was proof of something bigger. If I worked hard, followed directions, and focused intensely, things would be okay: they'd turn out the way I'd planned.

That afternoon, last April, my fantasy was chipping along nicely. My patient wasn't wearing a wedding ring, and nothing about him screamed pervert. He had good shoes and good insurance, which signified a good job. And I started imagining my audition, the first meal for him that I'd cook. I settled on a hearty vegetarian stew, not too spicy. He'd ask for seconds, thirds. Then he'd make me a generous offer. Callie and I would move in to his house, which would have all the modern conveniences, a sunny kitchen with marble counters, a six-burner cooktop, and a top-of-the-line mixer for making homemade bread. He'd tell me he wouldn't be around much, but to cook whatever I wanted. Callie and I should make ourselves at home, and of course her friends could use the pool.

In reality, the man was talking. He asked if he could spit. After he'd leaned over the bowl, I asked if his teeth felt very sensitive. There was some uneven wear I'd noticed and I suspected nighttime grinding, which was more common these days. Dr. Rick blamed it on the recession. We started talking about fitting a night guard, and then more generally about relaxing. Meditation, yoga, something to relieve his stress.

"I find cooking relaxes me," I said, and he raised his eyebrows in a friendly way.

"Have you ever tried a lavender cupcake?" I asked. "Lavender's very calming."

He shook his head, and I really liked him: this man with his sallow, unhealthy complexion. Teeth chipped and imperfect due to his clenched, stressed-out jaw.

"I could bring you the recipe," I offered. "They're actually low in sugar."

"Oh. No. I don't really cook."

I pictured his kidney-shaped pool, and how we'd laugh someday about this moment, and screw political correctness. I wanted him to save me. Why should my fantasies be politically correct? Nothing in the world was ever equal. I was raising a kid alone on my hygienist's salary, and he had money to spare and too many bedrooms to ever use. I just wanted to not have to worry, to have time to play around in a kitchen, to know that everything didn't rest on me—a life like so many others had.

I hadn't buzzed for Dr. Rick yet, but the door was swinging open. Before I could continue with my patient, our office manager handed me the note.

Callie's school called. You need to call back ASAP.

Then I was standing in our office's sterilization room, clutching the phone to my ear, taking short, quick breaths as Callie's principal spoke. Words. More words. Mostly incomprehensible. The tang of antibacterials was filling up my nostrils.

"Traumatized," the principal told me. "The other student was trau-matized."

I'd left my patient with Annette, and my legs were still trembling. I'd had the daylights scared out of me with this unexpected call. I'd been picturing terrible things—a harrowing ride to the hospital—but this was something else. A scenario I couldn't follow.

"Ink?" I repeated.

"That's correct—in her face. And her blouse was ruined."

When a school principal explains that your girl has thrown ink in someone's face, there are probably certain things that you're not sup-posed to do. You're not supposed to break down in tears, divulging your personal problems. You shouldn't act like the mother of a crimi-nal, angrily insisting, "She could not have done this!" And you probably shouldn't get so defensive that you ask what the other student did to provoke her. But when it happened to me, all my shoulds went right out the window.

"No, no way. Callie doesn't fight with anyone. There must be some mistake. What did this girl do to her *first*?"

"Nothing." The principal said it like I was scum for even asking. "She was just working at her desk when Callie attacked her."

Callie and I shared a seven-hundred-square-foot apartment. We shared meals and gossip and jokes, and after her latest growth spurt, we'd even started sharing shoes. At home, she'd swing her leg over mine and offer to do my nails, fussing over the cuticles, insisting I try deep purple. She was always a deeply agreeable person, fun and affectionate, corralling her friends for a group hug, jumping in the air when you had good news.

"But Callie's so gentle," I said, and then I started giving examples. Spiders behind the toilet, beetles inside the screen door, half-dead flies drowsing on the windowsill. Callie scooped each of them up and shuffled to the front door, where she released their bodies in the open air. "A pholcid," she announced. "Daddy longlegs." She'd once been stung on the palm by a wasp she was trying to liberate, and as she ran cold water over her hand, she worried: Did wasps die after they stung you?

"It's our policy to meet with parents before taking disciplinary action," Mrs. Jameson told me.

And that was when she said it. Bully. Bullying.

We lived in a small town. Pembury, Connecticut. A place that was once all farmland and livestock, but that was before my time. It was now the land of mini-mansions and cafés, gift shops and boutiques; there was even a French bakery that sold tiny pastel macarons. It was the dream of small-town life with fresh air and rolling hills and cows grazing in the fields that had attracted so many bankers and CEOs to this Connecticut valley, yet it was because of them that so much had changed. They bought up the old farmhouses and renovated them to include skylights and game rooms. They ate at the new ethnic restaurants and enrolled their kiddies in the expensive baby gym, and all along they believed that they were giving their children an old-fashioned upbringing. I'd come here with the same idea. I'd heard about the schools, the woodland trails, and the incredibly low crime rate, and I wanted all of that for Callie. But I'd grown up in a small town, too. I should've remembered the downsides.

When Mrs. Jameson said "bully," I could imagine the way this would stick to Callie. The whispers among parents, the icy looks around town. *Bully* was like a code word. A signifier of family dysfunction. A child who'd turned inhuman after being spoiled or neglected. Even school shooters were given more leeway: *it wasn't their fault, they'd been bullied.*

And if this was how Callie was going to be known, her life was about to change. Certain kids would avoid her. Teachers would eye her suspiciously; they'd mark down her papers without realizing their bias. She would be discussed, dissected, and I would be, too, because what kind of household produces a girl who bullies?

As I pulled in to the lot behind Callie's school I was still hoping for a simple explanation. She'd spilled the ink by mistake. She had tripped and fallen. I wanted her life to be easy, her problems laughable—like the ones I used to watch in a 1980s sitcom. There might be a bad first date. A haircut catastrophe. Maybe a time when she tries alcohol and decides it's not for her. I wanted dilemmas that we could solve easily in thirty minutes or less. Audience applause. Cheerful theme tune and closing credits.

The school's double doors swung open and students started flooding across the lot, swinging bright satchels, laughing, texting. I watched as the flow of children increased before finally slowing to a trickle of stragglers, boys carrying hockey equipment, a teacher patrolling the bicycle racks. The car door opened, and then Callie, Dallas, and Ella squashed into the backseat, all sugary fumes, hair sprays and lotions, colorful eyeliner and tangling limbs. They'd been best friends since first grade and were closer than sisters. I'd dubbed them the Siamese Triplets when they were kids, after they'd tried to braid their hair together so they were attached at the head, blond strands ripping as they yanked one another down. They were usually gossiping and giggling as they slid their backpacks to their feet, but today they were silent; they weren't even texting.

"Did somebody call you?" Callie asked, fingering one of her rubber wristbands. Each contained a message about animal rights. There were orange paw prints on the one that she rubbed.

"Mrs. Jameson," I said simply. "She told me about the ink."

It was a surprise to watch my ordinarily stoic thirteen-year-old start to crumble. "I can't believe this. I wasn't even near her." She slumped forward suddenly, hiding her face in her lap.

"Robyn is such a liar!" Dallas leaned forward across the seats to talk to me. "She's *always* bothering Callie. She follows her around like she's crazy obsessed." Dallas had been elected head of student council two years in a row, and she spoke with the directness of someone used to being heard. She shook her hair in disgust—it was almost white, like a child's at the end of a long summer—and then she prodded Callie on the back. "You should tell Rebecca what she says to you."

"What does she say?"

"She says stuff about Callie's mom," Dallas said while Callie rubbed her face against her pink skinny jeans.

Before I could absorb this, Ella was nodding. "Robyn did it to herself. She squirted it all over herself."

Callie sniffled miserably into her lap, Ella wrapped her arms around her, and I searched my purse fruitlessly for a package of tissues. I'd never even heard of Robyn, but Dallas was happy to fill in the details: Robyn Doblak wore mega-tight clothes. She liked getting *attention*. She probably used the paint to get everybody looking. Dallas gestured to her own chest, moving her hands up and down with great bouncing motions.

"Did you see her do it?" I asked Ella.

Ella's short hair flopped across her forehead as she nodded, arms still around Callie. "She put the paint all over herself."

That was when I realized. The principal had it wrong.

"Mrs. Jameson said it was ink, not paint."

"It was paint. In our art class. The teacher went out of the room, and Robyn squirted it all over her chest."

Callie lifted her small wet face; wisps of gold hair had come loose from her ballerina bun and liquid liner trailed toward her ears. Dallas handed her a package of tissues printed with cartoon cats, and we all watched while she blew her reddened nose. The girls looked concerned. Callie looked devastated.

"Miss Dimmock hates us," Ella said. "She's never liked me or Callie. That's why she believed Robyn instead of us."

"But everyone *knows* Robyn's a liar," Dallas said. "She has *issues*."

"It's because Callie never tells her to go away. She's too nice to her," Ella agreed.

They began to come up with explanations. Maybe Robyn was trying to get Callie's attention with the paint, and when it didn't work, she blamed it on her. Or she thought it would be ultra-hilarious to get Callie in trouble. As her friends continued to hypothesize, Callie balled up the tissue in her fist. She bit her lip, shook her head. I reached between the seats, patting her knee, wanting her to know that I'd never doubted her at all. Then Dallas tapped her on the shoulder. "You know what I think? I think Robyn's in love with you."

"Don't worry," I promised. "I'll take care of this."

That night, Callie told me what Robyn had said about her mother. We were sitting cross-legged on her bed beneath the photos she'd taped to her wall. I glanced at a picture of Callie's mother at a pumpkin farm. I'd taken the picture. Callie had been four and we'd watched the farmer making cider.

"She said that she died so she wouldn't have to look at me."

Callie spoke in a rush without pausing for breath, and I thought of the way the counselors used to explain it. A child's grief might take a vacation, but that didn't mean it was finished. It always lurked beneath the surface, waiting to come back.

"That's not true," I said. "You know that's not true!"

Callie nodded. Robyn just thought it was funny.

"I would completely understand if you did throw paint on her for saying a thing like that."

"I didn't, though." She tugged out of my grip.

Right then I imagined Robyn as the worst kind of child. A girl who'd never lost anything, who lacked empathy and depth. I'd read about kids like that, whose emotions were actually dying. They spent all their time online and forgot that humans could feel.

"There must be something wrong with her to say such a nasty thing," I said.

Callie reached for a pinecone on her bedside table, turning it over in her hands. Whenever she needed comfort you'd find her outside. She collected twigs, leaves, and tiny bird skeletons, stashing them around her room like they were deeply precious. Callie poked her fingers inside the pinecone's ridges, then fixed her green eyes on me. "Can I stay home tomorrow?"

"Hon—"

"They think I did it." She shuddered. "They'll all think I'm horrible."

"Nobody thinks that. They probably think *she's* horrible."

"I can't go back." She suddenly pressed the pinecone to her lips. "I can't go back with everyone thinking I did it."

I sifted my brain for advice. What level of outrage would help her? Even after all these years, I often felt like a bumbler. I could dole out sympathy all night and it might not make any difference. I looked at Joyce's picture on the wall, hoping for inspiration.

"What do you think your mom would do?"

Callie shrugged and shook her head.

"People talked about her, too. Remember how come? After those boys in our junior high tried to throw me down the stairs."

Callie didn't answer, although she knew this story well. We used to act the whole scene out when she was a little bit younger. Callie would deepen her voice the way I'd taught her and narrow her eyes at our imaginary tormentors. She once cracked the wooden coffee table when she jumped on top of it during a reenactment.

Callie finally spoke. "She changed what everyone saw."

I met Callie's mother when I was twelve years old. I was about to be thrown down the eighth-grade stairwell in my first week of junior high.

Over the summer, my cousin tried to prepare me because he'd been through it, too. Curtis used to come home with black eyes after disputing a certain small-town rumor. "If they talk shit about Grandma, don't get mad or deny it," he said. "Just find out their names and I'll take care of them for you."

Curtis's girlfriend listened to this advice skeptically as she rubbed sunscreen over her freckles. "Why don't you just knee them in the balls?" Lara said. "Kick them where it counts."

Lara pounded the sunscreen bottle against her palm: no one would call *her* grandma a whore.

"She's not fighting." Curtis squeezed my scrawny shoulder. "Rebecca's not a fighter."

But when Curtis went to the beach snack bar, Lara made me get up and practice. She showed me how to aim for their weak spots, kicking her strong, hairless legs in the sand. "He's worried about you," she said. "He thinks they'll eat you alive."

If Curtis thought I was going to get eaten he didn't say so, not even on the first morning of school, when he put his hand on the back of my neck. "You've got an invisible force field," he said. "And that's me. Okay?"

But when I ended up in the eighth-grade stairwell the force field didn't seem to be working. Something bounced off the side of my head. "Tell your grandma thanks for last night."

A boy had thrown a penny at me and it disappeared among the moving bodies. I didn't aim for his balls, but I spoke loud enough for people to hear.

"Congratulations. You have AIDS," I lied, obviously not thinking very tactically. Announcing my grandma had AIDS wouldn't improve my reputation.

"Oh, shit. Silibetti got AIDS."

"Chris, you got Grandma AIDS!"

This is where I would've liked to walk away, having dissed Silibetti, but Silibetti wasn't done. His hand clamped down on my arm, and then he grinned for just a second.

Guys aren't supposed to hit girls, especially not small ones who still sleep with teddy bears, but Silibetti lived by a code that was different from most. My face stung from the shock of his hand. Then his friends grabbed me around my knees, laughing as I struggled and flailed in the air.

I don't remember screaming as they lifted me up at the top of the staircase. I was too busy trying to grab the railing as they bounced me up and down. My fingers kept slipping off the bars, sweaty and useless, while they held my legs out behind me like I was flying through the air.

"Wheee, Superman! Haaa, wheee!"

And I could already feel the jolting impact, the way they'd let go and I'd plummet down.

"Satan!" a girl's voice rang out. "Praise my Satan brothers!"

If I wasn't still bouncing I might've seen her purple polo shirt, her blond ponytail bobbing as she pretended to bow. "Sacrifice her soul," she cried, as I felt something hot trickle down my face.

I suppose nowadays to get the same effect you'd have to pretend to be a terrorist, start screaming about jihad and the infidels to create such instantaneous alarm. But in 1987 we were all scared of the Satanists—they were the ones on the evening news, infiltrating schools and churches, posing as pastors and preschool teachers, abusing kids in the sewers.

The crowd murmured and fell silent. The blood drained out of my arms. I felt the moment when I would fall rapidly rushing closer.

"Shut the fuck up, little girl!" That was Silibetti.

"We'll throw you over, too."

Apparently the girl just smiled. "Praise Lucifer."

That was when they dumped me on the floor, letting me slump down by their feet. They didn't throw me over the railing but instead went after her. I tried to remember Lara's coaching. I kicked at their ankles, and then I felt a small hand swiping across my face.

The girl had touched me. I saw my blood on her hand. She held it up at the boys and started to chant. "DIGAdigaDIGAdigaDIGAdigaDIN! LucIFerLUCiferLUCIFER COME IN!"

Her voice vibrated through my body, shaking me to the core, and the boys didn't grab her or throw her over as she rocked back and forth. Her voice was dark, complicated, and kids started pointing at her, and then at Silibetti, too, like they were both part of some blood-drinking cult. Was Silibetti afraid? Did he know he'd been branded? He called her a crazy bitch as I gave one last kick. Then the bell was ringing and people were trampling past. They stepped on my feet and fingers, and I felt groggy, unsteady. I decided I'd stay on the floor. I'd take a nap on the cool gray tiles. Soon Curtis would find out what happened and I imagined he'd leave high school to come here and get me, speaking in the soft voice he used when our moms were asleep. Then he'd offer to carry me home, and I'd twine my arms around his neck, and he'd say it was all a bad dream. I would never have to go back.

There was a girl's face in front of me. I realized it was her.

"Do you want to go to the nurse?" she asked sweetly. "I think they busted your lip."

I stroked Callie's hair as I finished with the familiar words. "They called her Joyce McFrenzy, Evil McFrenzy, or EMF for short. People claimed she'd summoned the devil and levitated for a full minute over the stairs. I once asked her why she was willing to do it just to save somebody she didn't know, and she gave me this grin. 'I knew we were meant to be friends.'"

"And then you were hyacinth girls," Callie said.

"Yes," I said. "We were."

All My Interactions with Robyn Doblak, #1
For Rebecca/From Callie

I won't count all the times I saw her in art class.

I'll just start with the first time we talked in school. We probably wouldn't have even met if I didn't have to see Miss Baranski. You know, she never said anything useful—she wasn't a REAL psychiatrist. It was always just *How are you feeling? How are things at home?* She used this fake soothing voice and I always gave the same answers. *Good. No problems.* But the worst thing about it was she was always running late. You had to wait outside her door, and sometimes people saw you, so you had to lean against the wall to keep your face hidden . . . or stroll back and forth to the water fountain, like people wouldn't guess what you were doing there.

ANYWAY, it was right before Christmas, I could hear the chorus practicing "Frosty the Snowman," and I'd been waiting for Miss Baranski for the last ten minutes. Robyn was waiting, too, humming along with the music. Then she noticed one of my wristbands. "Pit bull awareness?"

It wasn't like when you met Mom. It wasn't some amazing scene. I wasn't saving Robyn and she wasn't saving me. I was only killing time. I started to explain.

"There was once this pit bull who saved thirty peoples' lives. But all anyone thinks is they're these vicious crazy killers."

"Thirty people? How did he save them?"

"They got stranded in a flood and this pit bull—she brought them food."

She nodded and I looked at the foil trees stapled to the wall. I would give Miss Baranski two more minutes and then I was taking off.

"My dad wanted me to get a dog," Robyn said. Then she started touching her silver headband. She said her mom changed her mind because dogs were too much work. I already knew that her dad was dead. I'd heard about his leukemia. Pretty much everyone in school heard about it when he died in seventh grade. What I didn't expect was that Robyn would start crying. Right there, out in the hall. I probably should've knocked on Miss Baranski's door, but I didn't think of that until later. I just started talking about whatever popped into my head. I told her about the imaginary dog I had when I was little and how she used to chase me around the house. I was just trying to make her laugh and I started talking louder and louder. "Imaginary dogs are great," I said. "You can get a whole pack of them. And the best part is they'll attack whoever you want."

I did a little growl and Robyn finally smiled. Her mascara was running so I raised my hand to her face. I used my sleeve to wipe it and Robyn let me. She seemed really thankful, but embarrassed, too.

2

The next day, I met with Callie's principal. Mrs. Jameson was a large, distracted woman whose makeup had melted into a thick soup beneath her eyes. Her jewelry hung sloppily into her cleavage and as she offered me a seat she called me "Mrs. McKenzie."

"I'm actually Rebecca Lucas," I corrected her. "I'm Callie's guardian, not her mother."

"Pardon me," she said without warmth, and I wondered if she'd even bothered looking in Callie's file. How could she miss that one of her pupils had no parents? She made a notation on a loose piece of paper as I settled into the plastic chair. There was a single leafy plant on her desk and a framed landscape on the wall, but the room felt dead, as if she'd intended to decorate and had given up early. Mrs. Jameson looked at me intensely, her eyes crossing a little behind her glasses, searching my face for something. Guilt, deceit. I'd arrived late, trotting through the halls, perspiring and uneasy, gulping down air that smelled of new computers. I already sensed how this would look. I'd got trapped in unusual traffic—a vintage tractor show was on that weekend—and for ten minutes, I'd been delayed behind a steam-powered tractor. The gargantuan machine belched smoke, chugging along at twelve miles an hour, bullishly refusing to let anyone pass.

"Tractor show?" Mrs. Jameson repeated doubtfully, as sweat pooled inside my blouse. I offered a second apology and then proceeded with Callie's defense.

"I was shocked by your call yesterday," I said. "I'd never had a call like that before in my life, and I knew before I even spoke to Callie that she couldn't have done it. She's been extremely upset by what this girl said—"

Mrs. Jameson cut me off, looking down at the loose paper on her desk, a hint of disgust tugging her coppery lips. "I'd just like to start with the incident report," she said, and then she began to read in a disappointed tone. "The student Callie assaulted was working at her desk when Callie approached her and called her 'Bullets.' She then threw ink on the student's shirt and hair—"

"It wasn't ink," I interrupted. "It was paint, and Robyn actually put it on her own shirt to get attention."

"I understand why you'd like that to be true, Ms. Lucas. But I'm afraid that you're misinformed."

I began trying to make Callie's case then, telling how Ella had witnessed everything, while Mrs. Jameson responded with icy, noncommittal phrases. *I see. That's what she told you. Mmm. Mmhmm.*

"You don't think it's possible Robyn did this to herself?" I asked.

"It's not rational."

"It is if she wanted to get Callie in trouble. If she did it out of spite."

"I want to be clear," Mrs. Jameson said curtly. "I take any kind of bullying seriously, but what happened yesterday was particularly disturbing to me. The student was distraught." She gave me a woebegone look. "One of our teachers had to sit with her for an hour trying to calm her down."

I pressed my elbows against her desk, staking out a little piece of territory. If I wavered for even a second things could devolve quickly. I might offer to pay for Robyn's shirt. Or promise to question Callie further. But I had to remember: a crying girl proved nothing. That was the thing about modern parenting: kids were treated like ticking time bombs, as if every misery or setback could trigger their own self-destruction. Mrs. Jameson was behaving as if Robyn was permanently damaged, but that just showed a worrying lack of perspective.

The night before, I'd gone downstairs to talk to our landlady. Mrs. Romero had raised her own kids in Pembury, so I was hoping for some good advice. In the eight years we'd lived on the second floor of her house, she'd never once raised the rent, and when I brought down the monthly check, Mrs. Romero always gave me a gift. If she didn't have a cake or casserole ready, she'd grab a box of cookies and hand it over as if this was what I was really paying for. But when she opened her door last night, I realized we wouldn't be talking about school. "There's a new one, Rebecca," she said, and then she went to retrieve the letter. It was postmarked from York Correctional Institution, and had my name on the front. Mrs. Romero checked our mailbox daily so that Callie wouldn't find one. Most of the letters were addressed to me, but a few had been sent for Callie. "You're never tempted to read one?" Mrs. Romero asked, and I shook my head. I always burned them. After Callie fell asleep, I torched it in the sink. Now, if Callie's principal was disturbed by a little paint, how would she feel if I brought up murder? If I pointed out that *real* tragedies happened all the time?

"Do you know what Robyn said to Callie?" I asked instead. "She told Callie that her mother died so she wouldn't have to look at her."

Mrs. Jameson looked down her nose at me as if I'd made this up on the spot. "Did Callie report this? Did she tell her teachers?"

"I'm sure she did." I feigned confidence. "Yes, of course."

"Well, I haven't heard that before, and I'll certainly look into it, but I do have an impartial witness who spoke to me about what happened yesterday. And according to her, Callie's been bothering this student for a while."

"Who was the witness? Do you mean the alleged victim?"

"I don't give out student names, but there was a witness other than the student who was assaulted."

"You have *one* witness out of a whole classroom of students? I'm guessing this isn't an adult. There wasn't an adult in that classroom." My hands were starting to tremble, so I shoved them under my thighs. "And what about our witness? Ella *saw* Robyn put the paint on herself."

I forced myself to look her in the eye. Mrs. Jameson tugged at the collar of her low-cut blouse as her jewelry swung drunkenly above her cleavage, and suddenly I realized what all the makeup and jewelry and cleavage were about. She wanted kids to like her, to think that she was cool. *That Mrs. Jameson, she's okay!* And why would she want that? Because she'd once belonged to the same tribe as me: the awkward kids, the unpopular ones. Maybe she'd been bullied herself. That was why she trusted Robyn over Callie. That was why she would harbor a grudge against a kid who was naturally popular and pretty.

"You've already decided Callie's guilty without any kind of investigation," I continued. "You're assuming that because she's popular and this other girl isn't that she's the one with the power and she's the bully. But that's an old-fashioned idea and it isn't very helpful."

Mrs. Jameson looked stumped for a moment, but then she began the "I'm just like you" speech that I often used myself. She had a daughter, too, and it was tempting to overlook certain things. Girls often had a difficult time admitting they'd behaved poorly, but if we didn't acknowledge their bad choices, we'd have trouble guiding them in the future.

"Mrs. Jameson," I said sharply. "Callie's lost both her parents. Now imagine that this girl was lying about you. Imagine that your reputation was getting dragged through the mud."

Before she could respond, there was a knock on the door. For just a millisecond I saw a look of relief cross Mrs. Jameson's face. The school secretary stuck her head in. "Sorry. Can I just borrow you for a sec?" Mrs. Jameson stood up while I squeezed my fingers together—taking a deep, shaky breath once she was out of the room. I remembered what Callie had told me earlier, how Mrs. Jameson sometimes embarrassed herself in front of the whole school. Callie knew I wasn't naturally confident, so she'd brought it up over breakfast, perhaps to give me a boost before our meeting today. "She gets on the loudspeaker, you know, in the middle of class," Callie said. "And she'll start to make an announcement but then she forgets what she wanted to say." She described the long, painful silences—the umming and ahing—and the way her class would burst out laughing while the teacher rolled her eyes.

I could hear Mrs. Jameson speaking in low tones outside the door, and suddenly I remembered the incident report. Why *couldn't* I read it? If she was so certain, why not share it? Unless she knew that her details were wrong and the report was full of misinformation. I slid my hand across the desk, glancing over my shoulder. It had been written in pencil, marked with scribbles and cross-outs, with a doodle of an owl in one corner of the page. I skimmed through it quickly, reading about the red ink and Miss Dimmock, Callie and Robyn, and then I saw a name I didn't recognize: Lucinda Berry. *The witness,* I thought, but I couldn't read any more.

Mrs. Jameson was bustling back into the room, thanking me for coming in. She didn't sit down, but gave a tense smile, avoiding my gaze. She said she'd investigate further and give me a call. Then she stood by my chair as if preparing to march me out. Another parent might've remained seated until things were fully settled. They might've mentioned lawyers and lawsuits with cool hostility in their throat. But I hadn't transformed so much in one day. I swallowed my objections and headed for the door.

"I feel all chattery," Callie said that evening, as she huddled on the sofa, wrapped in a blanket.

I'd told her that even if she was suspended, she wouldn't be punished. She and I would know it was a farce and spend the day out having fun. We could go on a day trip to New York. Or drive up to Boston. We could stop by the vintage tractor show, eat blueberry pie.

"I don't know why this is happening." She shivered. "I think I might be cursed."

"Don't say that. You're going to be fine."

"I don't ever want to see her again. I bet she wants to kill me."

"Robyn's not going to hurt you." I tucked in the edge of Callie's blanket.

"What else did Mrs. Jameson say?"

"Well, she claims there was a witness."

"She does? Who?"

"I . . . I'm not sure."

"Great. Now two people hate me."

"Callie, girls can be jealous."

"Did she say it was a girl?"

"Well, not exactly."

Callie turned and looked into my eyes.

"Was it Lucinda?" she asked. I made a face and shook my head. But Callie could read me sometimes, and she knew she'd guessed it right.

"I am cursed," she moaned. "This isn't getting better. She's going to do something worse. I know she will."

"What do you think she might do?" I asked, rubbing her arms to warm her up.

"I don't know." Callie's teeth clacked together. "Just something bad. I don't know."

*

Callie was born lucky, that's what Joyce said. Even though Callie's father was already married and asked Joyce not to have her. Joyce was nineteen when she got pregnant, studying pre-law at college, but when she learned she was expecting she decided to drop out.

When I first met Callie all I could see was her vulnerability. The flaking skin on her scalp, her delicate curling feet. She seemed so defenseless, but as I visited from week to week, I could see there was strength in her steady gaze, in the speed that she grew. She laughed and smiled. One week she couldn't roll over and the next week she could. One week she couldn't grasp a rattle, and the next week it was tight in her fist. She unfolded herself for us a little more every day.

Joyce moved home with her parents to raise Callie, and I saw them on the weekends. But despite her claims of good luck, Joyce had started to seem depressed.

"If she says 'antiseptic' one more time," Joyce muttered as her mom left the room, "I'll kill myself."

"Don't kill yourself," I said. "You can always come stay with me."

"Sure. A baby in the dorm. A screaming baby on the keg."

"Once I start working, we'll get a place together. Okay?"

It was the first time I'd said it, and Joyce didn't respond. I'd taken it for granted that she'd want my help, but we had never discussed the details. I let the subject drop, but the next time we talked on the phone, Joyce was the one to bring it up.

"When we move in together, I think we should decorate our place like a jungle," she said. "Leopard-skin couch. Fuchsia walls."

There was a deliberate jokiness to the way she said all this, like she was afraid I hadn't been serious. She didn't have to worry. I knew exactly how to play along.

"We'll get zebra-print sheets and snakeskin pillows."

"Hang mosquito nets from the ceiling?"

"And stick an elephant in the corner!"

We began to make plans that seemed more and more real. There would be a house near a park, swimming pools in the summer. We'd pick pumpkins at a farm for Halloween and give Callie her first taste of apple cider. We'd teach her to sled and ice-skate, to jump double Dutch, and there would be chalky hopscotch squares all over the driveway. I knew that there would be sacrifices, but that was almost the best part. When Joyce was around, selflessness would be easy.

After I graduated, I returned home to Cansdown, found a job in a dental clinic, and saved up to rent an apartment for the three of us. Within a few months, we'd found a small two-bedroom in Honey Hill, the center of town. Joyce and Callie took the larger bedroom, while I took the smaller. She put a potty on our bathroom floor, set up a play area in the living room, and filled up the refrigerator with snacks and juice boxes and the cheese slices Callie would roll into tubes before eating. In the morning there were songs in front of the TV, shrieks, small socks pulled over small feet, the smell of apple juice, puzzle pieces shoved under the couch. I was still very young, but suddenly I felt settled, full of responsibilities and adult knowledge. I watched how Joyce handled her daughter, playful yet firm, unself-conscious, and I tried to imitate her. I learned the names of stuffed animals, how to slow down a tantrum, bedtime rituals. Each night, Callie sat on the edge of the bathroom sink, and I hummed the tooth-brushing song while Joyce got out the paste. At three years old, Callie already had her own little quirks and habits, her own sensitive, formidable personality, and when I saw her chuckling, or patting her own arms, or babbling nonsense to herself, I knew that Joyce had been right. Callie was born lucky, and it was up to us to keep her that way.

*

I burned the soufflé I tried to make that night. It was cheese and broccoli, so it stank up the house. I could still smell its charred odor in my hair when I took the call from Callie's school the next day. My hands were clammy as I waited for the news, but then Mrs. Jameson surprised me. A group of students from Callie's class had come forward unexpectedly. Each one had sworn that Robyn put the paint on herself.

Paint, I thought triumphantly, not ink at all.

Mrs. Jameson was remarkably unapologetic. "The interesting thing is," she said, "the student who originally reported the incident came to me today and told me she'd been wrong. She said she'd made a mistake. I thought it was quite a coincidence, everyone coming out with the same story like you said."

Her voice was skeptical, as if she was planning to tell me that everyone was lying except for precious Robyn.

"Well, I'm relieved that you listened to them," I said harshly. "And I hope you'll hold these girls accountable for the lies that they've told."

"Yes," Mrs. Jameson said. "Thank you for your help."

We celebrated together. After dinner, I took Callie out for ice cream and we sat on a wooden bench, licking our cones. She poked holes into her strawberry scoop using her tongue and snorted as she wiped pink ice cream from her nose. "I hope you write this down," I said. "Because it's so unbelievable and dramatic." I crunched my cone, shaking my head. "You've got the villain pretending to be a victim. The dim-witted queen who almost allows a great injustice to occur. And then the condemned heroine who's saved at the last moment by a righteous crowd. Pretty incredible. Don't you think?"

"Like a fairy tale," she said lightly. "Oh, dreams can come true."

I wrapped my arm around her freckled shoulders, and the easy sugary feeling lasted until later that night when the phone started to ring. I was already in bed watching a cooking show on TV. "Can we talk?" the woman asked. It was Cerise Doblak. Robyn's mother.

"I've decided to pull Robyn out of school," she said tersely. "I don't know if you're aware of what Robyn's had to endure over the past few months, but we just can't take it anymore."

I quickly muted the TV, feeling unfairly ambushed.

"Robyn used to have friends. She used to be happy. But some of the girls came up with the delightful idea of taunting her about her breasts and now she can't even walk into a classroom without being barked at like a dog. It's sickening. And Callie's little stunt the other day was the absolute last straw."

There was a gulping silence on the line, the sound of a woman coming unglued. I tried to maintain my composure.

"She used to be happy—" she said.

"I'm sorry she's unhappy." I took a breath, propping myself up against the headboard. "But whatever she's told you about Callie, it isn't true. Callie wouldn't hurt a fly. It's been difficult for us to understand why Robyn's making up these stories."

Cerise gave a horrifying snort of laughter. "Making them up? Has it ever occurred to you that Callie is lying?"

"Everyone came forward to defend her after *Robyn* lied."

"That was a great stunt. Getting everyone to lie. Getting everyone to blame Robyn."

I imagined Cerise's spittle drying on the mouthpiece of her phone. I wondered if she was maybe a little unbalanced.

"This isn't some conspiracy." I lowered my voice. "The class came forward because it was true."

"They've all turned against her." Her voice broke. "They hate—"

"She bothered Callie before," I said. "She's said terrible things about Callie's mother. She told her her mother died because she couldn't stand to look at her."

"She never—" Cerise began. "Robyn wouldn't."

"Maybe she needs help."

"She wouldn't say that," Cerise protested. "Her own father passed away."

"A therapist, maybe."

"Robyn can be immature. She doesn't always notice when she's irritating people. And I should've been more careful about her clothes, but I know she's not lying. I know when she comes home crying, telling me all the things they've done to her . . ." Cerise's voice changed then; it became fast and spiteful. "The truth is, Callie targets her. She masquerades as this perfect girl, but she's cruel underneath. She humiliates Robyn and I fear for her future. That kind of person, that kind of—"

I don't remember hanging up the phone, but suddenly her voice was gone. I unmuted the TV and stared at the screen. Like mother, like daughter. They both needed help. Bipolar, schizophrenic, messed-up people. I left the phone off the hook so she couldn't call back, but my stomach bubbled with acid and I clutched it in pain.

Callie was in the kitchen. She stood beneath the small yellow light in bare feet, staring into the open cupboards. She had opened all of them. A bag of pretzels was on the counter.

"Cal? Are you okay?"

She turned to me, her hair loose around her shoulders, her eyes squinty with surprise. "I forgot it was my turn to bring snacks in for science."

"You'll never guess who just called me," I said, holding my stomach. Callie's lips parted as if she was trying to take in more air, and then she leaned against the counter, knee bouncing up and down. It bounced faster and faster as I told her that Robyn was leaving.

Callie wrapped her arms around her waist, and her face looked a little green. "They'll say she's leaving because of me."

"They won't. They defended you."

"But it's all too drastic. I can't believe she would leave."

I watched Callie's face. Did I wonder? For a second.

"Her mom said you guys make fun of Robyn's chest."

"Her chest?" Callie echoed, her knee suddenly still. She tipped her chin upward, and I saw water brimming through her lashes. Then she grabbed the bag of pretzels and hugged it to her.

"They called her Bullets," she said, gazing at the floor.

"They did . . . not you?"

"They called her stuff," she stammered. "They said stuff."

"But not you?"

"No, I would never."

"Did you try to help her?"

"I wanted to," she said. "I knew I should, but I didn't know how. I just . . . couldn't."

All My Interactions with Robyn Doblak, #2

For Rebecca/From Callie

I'm counting IMs, okay? I'm just going to print them out for you.

IM Dec 23 2008 20:03:16

19:54:21

robynroarxo: Callie? Is this you?

19:54:54

LithoCALpus: Hiiiiiiiiiiiiiii?

19:55:12

robynroarxo: It's Robyn from school 😊

19:55:27

LithoCALpus: Hi Robyn

19:55:59

robynroarxo: So ever since Friday I've been reading about pit bulls. I keep telling everyone they're not psycho killers!!!

19:56:20

LithoCALpus: Mega. Thnx!

19:56:48

robynroarxo: just cuz a few go psycho doesn't mean they're all that way

19:56:59

robynroarxo: it's just their owners that make some bad.

19:57:46

LithoCALpus: yup, some people DEFINITELY shouldn't be ALLOWED to own dogs

19:58:07

robynroarxo: I know, and cats too. My aunt has this cat who's totally EVIL.

19:58:27

robynroarxo: so anyway I was wondering where you got yr pit bull wristband.

19:59:02

LithoCALpus: Hold on a sec. I'll find the link.

19:59:14

robynroarxo: cuz I wanna get one too.

19:59:40

LithoCALpus: Pitbulllove.com

19:59:55

robynroarxo: thx and sorry about Friday I'm not usually such a mess!!!

20:00:35

LithoCALpus: no worries I get it.

20:00:47

robynroarxo: Christmas SUX w/o my dad

20:01:01

LithoCALpus: 🙁🙁 TOTALLY

20:01:13

robynroarxo: Your mom's dead right?

20:01:50

robynroarxo: Sorry don't mean to be nosy

20:02:06

LithoCALpus: No it's okay . . . My mom AND my dad

20:02:50

robynroarxo: Urgh 😖 sorry

20:02:58

LithoCALpus: Don't worry

20:03:10

robynroarxo: anyway merry sucky Christmas

20:03:16

LithoCALpus: thx. You too.

3

Contrary to what Callie had feared, nobody blamed her when Robyn left school. Robyn disappeared quickly, without fanfare, group hugs, or contagious tears, and according to the Siamese Triplets, hardly anyone noticed. One week Robyn was there, splattered with red paint, and the next week she simply wasn't. There was nothing for them to do but get on with their lives.

Callie graduated eighth grade with first honors and an award in science. The ceremony was held in the school auditorium and they put on one of those sentimental slideshows that makes everyone weep. I spotted Callie in different pictures, smiling out among a sea of children, posing on the playing field, arms wrapped around her friends. The music soared as the pictures flashed past, exhorting everyone to remember, remember before it slipped away. Some of the kids started sobbing into one another's necks. Our last time in middle school. Our last time in this building. Our lockers, our lunchroom! Oh my God, we're gonna miss it so much!

I'd bought matching necklaces for Dallas and Ella even though they cost more than I would usually spend, and as we arrived at Dallas's graduation party I was happy I'd stretched my budget. Dallas lived in an enormous white mini-mansion, complete with Greek columns. It was set back from the street on a wide lawn dotted with weeping trees and stone paths and tall, bushy clusters of yellow and purple flowers. It was only four o'clock, but already the circular driveway was packed with cars, and we had to find a space on the edge of her neighbor's lawn. Music drifted from the backyard as Callie strode confidently ahead to the wooden gate, which was draped with roses and honeysuckle. To one side, there was a table that had been piled with gifts, and then a collage covered with pictures of Dallas. Dallas in riding gear. Dallas in front of the Eiffel Tower. Dallas with her arms around her two best friends. Callie added our gift to the pile and rushed out into the yard, toward the roses and the gazebo and the barbecue smoke.

For months I'd been hearing the backseat gossip about this party. Dallas's mom had bought tiki torches to light around the pool. She'd hired someone to repaint the cabana and restain the decking. She'd arranged an ice-cream sundae station (even though Dallas complained that ice cream was babyish). Dallas's father was a well-known radio host, and Dallas was always teasing us about which celebrities might show up. I'd never even been to one of Editta's parties before, but Callie had reassured me about a hundred times that while the kids would dress formally, the adults would look casual. She'd picked out the plain black linen blouse and flat sandals that I now wore, and as I looked out at the crowd I was relieved to see she was right. Adult men wandered around like giant toddlers, wearing long baggy shorts that showed off their pudgy legs and bright polo shirts that stretched across their bellies. Meanwhile, their daughters stood together in little flocks, glossy and delicate, preening in high heels and golden earrings. The girls froze occasionally, as if startled by the giant toddlers, but they were just posing for a camera's flash, a snapping cell phone. I watched Callie in her electric-blue sheath as she embraced Ella and Dallas. Earlier, she'd asked our landlady, Mrs.

Romero, if she could take a white rose from her garden, and now I saw why. Even among all the elaborate hairdos and tiaras, the Siamese Triplets stood out. Dallas had a fat gardenia above one ear, Ella wore a white orchid, and Callie had threaded her rose into the braid that circled her head like a crown.

I began to wander over to the deck, where I could see Dallas's mom. Editta was waving her hands frantically—either trying to shoo away a wasp or experiencing a hot flash. As I climbed the steps, Editta continued flapping her hands, an irritated expression plain on her face.

"Editta," I exclaimed. "It all looks gorgeous!"

For just a moment her irritated look passed into blankness. Then she smiled vaguely and stilled her hands. "Hi, hon. So glad you could make it."

Editta leaned forward for an air-kiss. Her face was sultry and tanned and only slightly piglike. In the nineties (in another life, Editta said) she modeled swimsuits, although I couldn't imagine she was ever one of those fun, frolicking-in-the-sand kind of models, but rather the moodier sort who leaned against rocks, looking disdainful and pouty. Now a mother of three, she carried herself with the puffed-up grandeur of an opera singer.

"Look at the chairs!" I enthused. They were artfully draped with fabric and flowers, and stout white candles flickered on a nearby table.

"Yes," Editta said, as if she hadn't noticed until now. "How's . . . how's your work?"

"Oh, same old same old. Lots of whitening treatments now that it's summer."

I was used to blank stares and vague responses from Editta, so I wasn't surprised when she failed to respond. She had trouble focusing. Her eyes were always darting away, distracted, so I'd learned a few techniques over the years. I made a habit of asking her lots of questions in a loud, engaging voice. I exclaimed enthusiastically at everything she said, and when all else failed, I asked about her horses.

"Were you up all night, getting ready for the party?"

"Yes," she said finally. "You have no idea."

I nodded agreeably: *not a clue.*

"It's been a nightmare," she said through her teeth. "From beginning to end."

She told me that the caterers had brought in *store-bought* biscuits. And the tarts they had made were too soggy to eat. I tried to appear sympathetic and alarmed.

"What kind of tarts?"

"Rhubarb," she said. "And they thought we wouldn't even notice."

Editta threw a dismissive look at all the beautiful food, the stuffed figs and skewered watermelon, the chocolate-covered strawberries. I knew this was how she'd ended up living the way she did. Every detail mattered to her. If it was me, I wouldn't have minded if the caterers put out cheap biscuits. I would have been too busy taking notes on how they'd created such a feast. But Editta maintained a constant vigilance— rejecting carpets with the wrong fibers, curtain rods with the wrong filigree, shower handles with the wrong finish—so her family could live this elegant life.

"Imagine," she said. "They thought I wouldn't care!"

She abruptly excused herself, muttering about a quiche, and I wandered across the lawn, toward a tree covered in climbing roses. Nearby, girls circled together like garlands in the afternoon sun. They bent to examine a shoe, casually adjusted earrings, leaned carelessly on one another's arms.

Alison, Alison!

Lilla smooch.

Randomness on the blog.

Such a prink! Bomb!

I couldn't understand them, but I watched as they crowded around to examine a phone, ate off one another's plates, danced and squealed and touched one another's hair. The thrill of connection, the easy intimacy—they seemed deliriously happy. I wished I felt the same. From a distance, I could see Callie lift the gold heart around her neck before letting it drop. The girl beside her suddenly jumped in the air and landed safely, grabbing Callie's arm.

Down at the pool, boys bobbed among the tubes and rafts in the unclouded water, while a group of girls stood to one side. As I lingered, I noticed that the girls looked about ten years older than the skinny, hairless boys. The girls held themselves aloof, even as they drew closer to the pool, aware of their hips and angles and fluttering lashes. The boys started throwing a football back and forth, pretending they didn't notice the girls, while a mom, oblivious to the sexual tension, ran alongside the edge of the pool, shouting to the boys as she took their pictures. One boy drifted lazily on a yellow raft, soda in hand, smiling beneath his sunglasses as the ball whizzed overhead. "Powder puff!" a girl shouted, and then another jumped back as if afraid of getting splashed. The ball whizzed closer and closer to the boy on the raft while the mom took pictures and the girls sipped their drinks. I could see what was coming a moment before it happened. The ball caught the boy's hand and his soda went flying. The boys all hooted as the soda's brown contents spilled into the water. "You got him, Jimmy!" the mom yelled, taking another memorable picture.

At just that moment, I saw Ella's mom coming toward me. Ali Brooks managed the careers of some of the country's top filmmakers, and she'd once brought Callie along to a shoot where she ended up eating pizza with Steve Buscemi. "We've been so crazy busy," she gushed, as she lifted her oversized sunglasses. She wore one of her perfectly tailored shirtdresses, cinched with a quirky belt, and I wished, not for the first time, that we were real friends. We drifted over to a pair of loungers while Ali told me about funding a client's documentary.

"But what about you!" she exclaimed. "I've been dying to talk to you about that nightmare girl in their class." Ali's collarbone poked out beneath her tanned skin, and she leaned in closer like we were best buddies. I couldn't resist. I began telling her everything.

"You mean Robyn?" I said coyly. "Oh, Robyn was terrific."

"I heard the mother called you up."

"Cerise." I drew out the name ominously. "She wanted me to know that Callie is evil."

"Incredible!" Ali's earrings swayed against her cheeks. "The nerve of some people!"

"Well, I could see where Robyn gets it from. I actually felt sorry for her, with a mother like that."

"She never should have called. It's completely out of line."

"The thing is she acted like she was doing *me* a favor. Warning me about Callie."

"Ugh, you know, you can't tell people how to raise their kids."

There was an awkward pause as we both remembered that Callie wasn't my kid. I smiled and cleared my throat, pretending I hadn't noticed. "And the thing is *her daughter* is the one who needs help."

Ali nodded vigorously, the cords on her neck stretching. "If she called me up like that, I would've just lost it. I would've laid into her."

"Well, I hung up on her. I couldn't stand to hear her voice."

We continued to chummily insult Robyn's mother until I noticed Ella making her way around the pool to us. She wore a white dress that showed off her narrow waist and swimmer's arms. "Mom, I need the clips," she said, stopping in front of us. Her eyelashes were caked in fine purple sparkles, and her angular jawline had a pearly glow.

"You look so adult, Ella. I almost didn't recognize you."

Ali grinned at her daughter. "I know! How elegant is she!"

Ella lifted one foot with an exaggerated kick so I could admire her high silver shoes.

Ali pulled a bag of hair clips out of her bag, handing them to Ella. "I was just talking to Rebecca about your good friend Robyn."

"Ugh, ugh." Ella shuddered. "You said it was just like that movie."

"Oh, yeah. *Single White Female.* Hopefully Robyn didn't kill any puppies."

"She might've killed puppies," Ella said. "Urgh, nasty. She was so needy, trying to dress like Callie."

I hadn't heard that before. I asked Ella what had happened.

"At first it was just little stuff—the same bracelet as Callie—but she got all stalkery, wearing the same kind of clothes."

Ali caught my eye, realizing this was news to me.

"Hopefully it's all in the past now." Ali patted my arm. "She had a little crush and it's over." She turned to her daughter. "It's lucky you girls could be Callie's witnesses."

Ella mashed her lips together. "We couldn't let some creeper ruin her life."

Ella spoke with such revulsion that I almost felt uncomfortable. But then I reminded myself that this was loyalty at fourteen. Feeling like your minds were perfectly connected, every problem shared between you, her enemies were yours, and you even dreamed sometimes the same.

I started thinking about Joyce and how we'd tried to give ourselves ESP, sending our thoughts out like arrows into each other's brains. We were thirteen years old when we sat knee-to-knee on Joyce's denim bedspread, eyes squeezed shut, focusing on our thoughts. If we wanted it enough, it had to happen. If we truly believed, it would come true.

"You're thinking about hate," I told Joyce. "You hate Phil Collins."

"I do," Joyce whispered. "But that's not it."

That was our hyacinth-girl summer, when Joyce showed me that scrap of poetry, and read it aloud in a wistful voice. "'They called me the hyacinth girl,'" she read. "'Yet when we came back, late, from the Hyacinth garden, / Your arms full and your hair wet, I could not / Speak, and my eyes failed, I was neither / Living nor dead, and I knew nothing.'"

Joyce clutched her neck as she said "could not speak," and we mulled over the riddle. We didn't know who the hyacinth girl was, or what had happened to her exactly. But there was something romantic and chilling about the images that sprang to mind. We decided to splash water on our hair, so it dripped messily down our T-shirts. Then we wandered around Joyce's yard, picking weeds and dandelions, pretending to weep, mourning the things we hadn't yet lost. We were hyacinth girls, our arms full of flowers. We were heartbroken victims, but this game soon grew old. We needed more action, more violence, so we decided the hyacinth girls would become heroes. "We'll use our ESP," Joyce said, and this made the whole thing much more satisfying.

Joyce and I set about creating people who needed to be rescued. We imagined stolen babies in dirty diapers, little girls trapped in wells. We made up whole armies of victims to defend, as well as enemies who attacked us, their dastardly plans binding us closer together. We were shot, strangled, locked in tiny boxes. We were thrown off cliffs, only to be saved by our hyacinth partner.

We should've known how it would look, running around, screaming our heads off, but we were so engrossed we didn't know we were being watched.

Curtis was leaning against the chain-link fence, doubled over laughing. Worse, his girlfriend was there too. Lara grasped at his arm.

I didn't need to look at Joyce to know that she was mortified. I'd frozen when I saw them, my arms still high in the air.

"Damn," Curtis gasped. "You girls under attack?"

Joyce mumbled something behind me. And I dropped my arms to my sides, kicking at the dirt, ashamed of our child's play. But then Lara seemed to take pity on us, socking Curtis in the arm. She managed to keep a straight face as she asked if we wanted to go to the beach.

Lara let me practice my ESP on her later, and she was the perfect candidate. I pictured her thoughts like fluffy white clouds that I could reach out and grab. "You're hungry . . . for french fries." "You want a butterfly tattoo," I announced. And no matter what I guessed, Lara winked and announced that I'd nailed it.

Lara was fifteen that year, the same as my cousin. She was tall and goddesslike in her black combat boots, with dark red hair that hung past the collar of her T-shirt. Sometimes when you tried talking to her she just shrugged or shook her head, but this, I'd learned, was to hide her stammer. She could get stuck in the middle of a sentence, at the beginning of a word, and instead of trying to finish, she'd just clamp her mouth shut and meet your gaze for a long, unnerving moment. When it happened, Curtis would sometimes step in, and he never looked embarrassed or uncomfortable. If he knew what she was talking about—for instance, the way to make a guitar sound like a motorcycle—he'd finish off what she was saying as though he'd been the one talking all along.

Sometimes, though, if it was just the four of us, he'd try to coax her to finish. He'd stroke her hair and say, "Come on, Lara. Don't rush yourself." Then she might start again, in a very low voice, and if she got stuck in the same place and gave a small panicked laugh that sounded like "huh," I could feel her frustration welling up in my own chest. I wanted to jump in and save her, finishing her sentences. But that was Curtis's job. He was always ready. Even when they were in different rooms, I knew he was still listening and monitoring her, so if she needed any help he'd be ready to jump in.

Joyce and I would see Lara walking around in Curtis's huge navy sweatshirt, smelling of his cologne, and it seemed like she carried his wide, warm protection wherever she went. I'd once noticed her sniffing the sleeves and I could almost feel the swoopiness in her stomach, the heat in her chest, and I wished that someday I might have something like that, too.

"Did you see the way he touched her face?" Joyce asked.

"He's getting her a ring. Pre-engagement."

"Do you think if I had a stutter . . ." she mused.

"Joyce," I warned. "Don't."

I knew exactly what she was thinking, and I didn't want to. Joyce was different around Curtis, especially when Lara wasn't there. She grabbed at his mirrored sunglasses, which nestled in his thick black hair, and I'd caught her staring at his calves when he sat on the ground in shorts. Curtis could be weird around Joyce, too. He teased her until she went crazy. And when Lara went home early, Curtis swung his arm around Joyce's neck.

The three of us ended up at the beach one day without Lara. Joyce and I had been playing a secret game of hyacinth girls when Curtis knocked on my door. We were trying to channel the thoughts of a murdered woman so we could stop her killer. But when Curtis mentioned the beach, Joyce said yes without even checking.

Now I watched Curtis scooping Joyce out of the water, his arms looping easily under her knees. And I watched Joyce let herself be carried by my cousin, her arm circling around his neck. We were the hyacinth girls together, but alone on my beach towel I felt like nothing, and this was complicated in my mind by a sudden prickle of desire. I wanted to be the one who Curtis was saving, his warm, wet skin under my fingers, and I also wanted to be the one cradling Joyce in my arms, defending her from assassins and killers. We were supposed to be closer than anyone, our minds linked forever, but that would all change if she liked Curtis more than me.

If we had ESP really, now would be the time to use it. I watched Joyce fling sand at my cousin as I sent her an SOS. *I need help—now! Come back to me this second.* And when this didn't work I stared out at the bright blue sea. If I walked out as far as I could, and let myself get swept away by the tide, would Joyce hear me then—would she swim out in time to save me? I pictured her sobbing over my body, carrying armfuls of flowers. She hadn't loved me enough—and now this hyacinth girl would be gone. I was thirteen years old. I thought my life might be over. But at just that moment, Joyce came running across the sand. She placed a cold wet hand on my neck, and it was such a relief. I was flooded with feeling: she was back and she was mine.

"Did you hear me?" I asked.

Joyce smiled as she nodded.

Dallas's dad was lighting tiki torches around the pool, and the music was getting louder, and then everyone started singing "Happy Graduation to You!" Shoes were discarded, and the girls became reckless, dancing loose-limbed beneath the spotlit trees. I watched Callie move fluently among different groups of girls, laughing and joking, and I told myself I didn't mind sitting by myself and listening on the periphery of conversations.

I tried smiling at parents I recognized, some whose teeth I'd worked on. They sported gleaming white smiles as they chattered away. I felt completely unsophisticated as they discussed ways of beating traffic to the Cape. Mandarin lessons. Golf tournaments. I heard a harsh bark of laughter, and when I turned I noticed the man, who stood alone by the grill, clutching a beer in one hand. He stared at the girls as they grasped at the air, chasing fireflies across the lawn. He wasn't anyone I'd seen before. I would've remembered. He wore tight black jeans, unlike the other fathers, and his attention was razor sharp, completely engrossed. I watched him stare for a little while, to make sure I wasn't just imagining, but from the way my skin crawled I knew it was real. In his eyes, these girls were vulnerable, but nobody seemed to notice. The other parents were rocking with laughter, unaware he was tracking their daughters. He raised the bottle to his mouth, eyes still focused, and I knew exactly what he was thinking and I had to act.

He craned his neck to see around me as I squared my shoulders. I wanted to block his view. Protect our girls. I narrowed my eyes as he smirked, but he was maddeningly unbothered. So I tapped him on the arm. "Whose dad are you?"

He didn't even meet my eyes. I was over thirty, unfuckable. Not like these young girls who were brand-new and soft. I would find out his name, humiliate him if I had to. Make sure that Callie never crossed his path again.

He shook his head. "I'm nobody's dad. I'm just here for Dougie."

Dallas's dad—Doug Price—was nowhere in sight. The man combed his hand through his wavy hair and didn't offer me his name. I wouldn't introduce myself either. I would just stand here blocking his way. I would follow him around if I had to, making sure he kept his hands to himself. I hated the fact that our girls were now so visible to men like this. That they had to be stared at, drooled over, and considered from all angles. At fourteen they were just coming to grips with themselves, trying to feel comfortable, but a man's gaze could change all that. It could shrivel and sap their power.

"How do you know Doug?" I demanded, as Dallas went galloping past. The man ignored my question, turning his head to watch Dallas. Then he stuck out his hand, swiping the air like he wanted to catch her.

"Excuse you!" I said, but my voice was lost beneath his.

"Oh, your pants are on fiiiiiiiiiire!"

Dallas twirled around and leaned forward, touching the fabric on her chest. And I imagined kicking him in the legs, shouting that he needed to leave right now. What I did instead was strictly impulsive, and easy to misinterpret. One of the people who saw it happen thought she saw us making out. Later, a mom would snarkily comment I'd looked cozy with the rock star, and I'd realize that the man I threatened was actually Doug's celebrity. But I didn't see any other options. Sometimes arrogance needs to be challenged.

I grabbed hold of his shoulder, pulling him down to my level, and then I pressed my mouth to his hair and whispered in his ear. "I know what you're thinking. Leave her alone." The man jerked his head away from me, and I saw that he was furious, the words of the hyacinth girls hissing in his brain. I watched him turn to leave the party and felt power rushing through me—like a thirteen-year-old girl who's just realized what she can do.

All My Interactions with Robyn Doblak, #3
For Rebecca/From Callie

From: R.Doblak@sparkon.com
To: C.Mckenzie@chronomail.com
Subject: You asleep?
Date: Thu, Dec 25 2008, 23:18:02

Heyyyyy Callie!

Guess what—I ordered my pit bull wristband. I was going to IM you but you're NEVER on. So I wanted to see if you had a merry sucky Christmas. My Xmas was sucky and not very merry. I didn't get a dog, everyone was fake jolly, and I was like I COULD KILL CHRISTMAS, I COULD BURN DOWN THE TREE!!!!! It just felt like everyone was pretending in case my dad was watching, like we had to be all sunshine and gumdrops, totally fake! But when I'm messed up I can't even hide it. I'm like how can we be happy when we're all just thinking about Dad?

My friends and stuff don't get it. They think I should be OVER it already, and because I'm not they think I'm doing it for more attention. Miss Baranski said it gets easier but I don't WANT it to get easier. I don't want to be happy and I'm SICK of being sad. Is it the same for you? You always seem happy. Hope your Xmas wasn't as bad as mine.
xoRobyn

From: C.Mckenzie@chronomail.com

To: R.Doblak@sparkon.com

SUBJECT: RE: You asleep?

DATE: Fri, Dec 26 2008, 8:42:47

Robyn sorry your Xmas was sucky—I kinda know what you mean. I used to feel the same way with everyone sitting there watching me. It was like they felt seriously sorry for me, thinking they knew EVERYTHING about me. As if they'd already decided my whole life story and they didn't care if they were wrong. So one year I kind of went crazy. I waited till everyone was opening presents. Then I went into the kitchen and got LOTS of ketchup. I put it all over my hair and face so it was dripping like blood and then I went running around the tree screaming about Satan. I wanted them to think I worshipped devils so I was chanting and singing. I told them my name was Evil McFrenzy and I drew a big pentagram right next to the tree!!!! They were just going bizonkers, so freaked out by what I was doing, and they forgot all about the past and I was like yesssssss! FINALLY!!!!

-C

4

One afternoon in mid-July when I was picking up Callie, I noticed that her hair was damp and there were wet bathing-suit marks on her T-shirt. "They finally got you in the water!" I exclaimed, patting her moist shoulder. I pictured her paddling around Ella's lake, joyfully overcoming her phobia.

"I wasn't swimming," Callie corrected me. "I just got splashed."

Every kid has her own quirks, and Callie's was to claim to hate water. Pools, the ocean, innocent babbling brooks. She swore she didn't know how to swim, even though I remembered when Joyce had taught her. I'd offered her lessons hundreds of times, but she was staunch in her refusals.

"Wouldn't it be cool if you took private lessons?" I asked, as we reversed out of Ella's driveway. "You could surprise your friends with your expert strokes."

"I'm not swimming." Callie snapped her gum. "Don't sign me up. I won't go."

"But you could just learn a few basics. For your own safety. What if you fell out of Ella's canoe? You can't always rely on your friends to save you."

Callie yanked her seat belt forcefully, like she might leap out of my car. "I don't go out in the canoe. I haven't done that in years."

"But I want you to be able to. I don't want you missing out."

"Why do you care so much? It's just—stupid."

She pressed her head against the passenger window, leaving a web of moisture, and I knew I should just drop it before this turned into a fight. We'd only recently made peace after the incident at Dallas's party. Apparently, I wasn't supposed to talk to the rock star—the kingly VIP. Callie had accused me of overreacting, and I'd tried to convince her I was justified, describing his nauseating leer in lengthy detail. But she still claimed I'd ruined the party—embarrassed her, embarrassed myself.

"Look, I'm not going to force you in the water," I said. "But for me, summer means swimming. All those days when your mom and I went to the beach, doing handstands in the sea."

"Well, that's disgusting," she said, "because you *knew* what was in that water."

I thought she meant the sewage—the regular overflows in Long Island Sound.

"That girl you thought was kidnapped," she continued. "What was her name?"

Autumn Sanger was the last person who the hyacinth girls tried to rescue. We were thirteen years old when Lara's friend disappeared.

"Is that why you're scared of the water?" I regretted having told her that story. Callie sometimes absorbed the wrong details, changing the message I'd meant to pass on.

"I'm not scared," she said. "But I know people die in the water." I could smell her peppermint gum as she worked it vigorously between her jaws.

"People die everywhere," I spoke carefully. "You can't avoid everywhere."

"Just because you loved swimming doesn't mean I have to. Your childhood wasn't so perfect. You forget all the bad stuff."

"Look, Miss Sass. I didn't forget anything. But even the bad stuff wasn't that bad. We were so carefree, anything seemed possible."

"So you accused some old guy of kidnapping and broke into his basement."

I slowed down the car, not bothering to brake smoothly. She really had a bee in her bonnet today. The joys of being fourteen.

"You're remembering that story wrong. I never went in any guy's basement. We were in his house for less than five minutes."

"Trespassing," she said. "You probably scared him to death."

"We were trying to do the right thing. We were only thirteen."

"You bothered him for no reason," she said harshly. "Because you were so carefree."

It had seemed like a good reason at the time. I remembered how Lara couldn't stop crying. Autumn was her friend. Our reasons seemed brave and irreproachable.

I didn't respond to Callie, letting her marinate in frosty silence. But after a few minutes, she tried resuming our conversation.

"Do you still remember her name?" Callie asked quietly. "Even though you didn't know her?"

"Yes," I said. "It was Autumn Sanger."

Lara came over crying that day. She didn't even notice what she'd interrupted. Curtis had been tugging Joyce's braid, stroking its soft tendrils, but he dropped her hair so fast, Joyce's head jerked to one side. I saw Joyce trying to hide a small frown as she smoothed her hair back. "Did you hear?" Lara's lips were trembling. "Autumn Sanger disappeared."

Curtis left the two of us on the couch, where he'd been wedged between us, and Joyce slid her hand across the cushion, still warm from his butt. They'd been flirting all morning, and I'd been trying to stop them. I'd blinked my thoughts steadily at Joyce, but she'd refused to hear a thing. "What do you mean? She ran away?" Curtis was slipping an arm around Lara, and I'd never even heard of Autumn Sanger, but my heart was starting to race. Something awful had happened—it electrified my blood.

"They think she got kidnapped." Lara spoke as though she'd run the whole way over. Little gasps in between, trying to catch her breath. The ceiling fan rotated slowly above us, as if life was continuing as normal, but Joyce's knees started bouncing up and down, like she was trying to run away.

"Girls, go to Rebecca's room," Curtis commanded.

"What? Why?"

When we didn't move, Curtis led Lara away so they could talk in private. But the doors in our house were so thin we were able to listen from the hallway. Curtis thought Autumn had run away. That's what he told Lara. He didn't think she'd been kidnapped at all—Autumn had talked about hitchhiking to California. But Lara said she'd know if she'd run away. And anyway, Autumn hadn't said good-bye.

Then she mentioned Mr. Hort and Curtis said no. No way.

Mr. Hort was an old guy who lived in our neighborhood. We'd all heard rumors about how he hired hookers and made them wear children's clothes. A girl from school once told me she'd seen them dancing in Mr. Hort's backyard. They were sucking on pacifiers, their hair in baby curls.

"He's too old and weak to do anything," Curtis said. Then I felt a tap on my shoulder. Aunt Bea was standing behind us, an amused look on her face. She was still wearing the T-shirt she slept in, which hung half-way down her bare thighs. I smelled smoke on her breath as she pressed her ear against the door.

"Don't tell me they're knocking boots already." She banged on Curtis's door. "Hey, you got Peeping Toms out here!"

Joyce's face went beet-red, and I tried to explain about Autumn. But instead of asking me for any details, my aunt told us to go to my room.

"We need to contact her," Joyce said, as we lay side by side on my bed. I'd already turned off the lights in hopes of encouraging ghosts and spirits. Joyce reached for my hand and squeezed it. "Do you think Mr. Hort took her?"

"Ask her," I said. "Let's call her right now."

"Autumn Sanger," we whispered again and again until the words melted together, and our voices became slow, and the backs of our throats ached.

Then I heard a small clear voice in my head. "Basement," it said.

All the hairs on my arms stood up. "Basement!" I announced to Joyce.

"Whose basement?"

I thought for a moment. "Mr. Hort's!"

Then I was there, in Autumn's place, locked in his basement. I was shivering in the darkness, rough cement beneath my back. It was cold. My throat burned. I heard footsteps creak above me. Then someone was knocking on my bedroom door.

Lara flipped on the lights and saw us lying there. "Rebecca, can I ask a favor? I need to borrow your sales club stuff."

Joyce and I had been selling greeting cards door-to-door through a mail-order sales club that summer. We lugged the heavy catalog around most afternoons, ringing doorbells and showing off samples. I jumped up to retrieve the catalog for Lara, anxious to help her. I thought she wanted to send Autumn's parents a card covered in candles or crosses, but Joyce was suspicious. Why did Lara want it?

Lara ignored her. "How do you guys usually do it? Just ring the doorbell and show them the brochure?"

"It's a catalog, not a brochure," Joyce said.

"We tell them we're from the Sunshine Sales Club," I explained. "We ask if they want any cards or gift wrap." Actually, it was Joyce who did all the talking; she had this whole very persuasive pitch.

"You can't take it unless we get to go with you," Joyce said.

"I'll bring it right back."

"You have to take us with you," Joyce insisted. And that's how we ended up in Mr. Hort's house.

Lara made us promise that we wouldn't tell Curtis, and that we'd let her do all the talking, and no matter what happened we wouldn't go inside. We walked down the street and around the corner, turned left at the intersection, and then crossed over to the neat white house with the blue mailbox in front. There was a freshly painted trellis in the side yard, and clipped hedges growing beneath the windows. The grass was trimmed, and pieces of shingle hadn't fallen off the roof. The three of us strode up to the door, like a miniature posse. Like hyacinth girls, ready to save one of our own.

Lara had started telling us about Autumn, feeding us facts as we'd walked over. Such as: Autumn liked to line her eyes with so much black it looked like she was peering out from deep inside a hole. The two of them had been friends for more than two years, trading tapes in the tank, which was the hallway at the high school where the metalheads hung out. Lara poked her eyes to stop herself from crying and I felt her distress sinking deep in my bones.

Then we were standing on his doorstep and Lara was ringing the bell. The door opened. Mr. Hort was standing there.

He was small and thin, and he spoke in a wet, fluty murmur. "Yes? Hell-o?" Eyes darting under heavy black brows. Lara was holding the catalog, and Joyce had taught her the entire sales pitch, but Lara didn't say a word. She just stared at him, unsmiling. I touched her arm, tried patting it. I didn't know what to do; I thought she'd been caught out by her stammer. Then Joyce was stepping forward. "Hello," she said warmly. "We're from the Sunshine Sales Club and we wondered if you—"

Lara gasped suddenly, like someone was choking her. Her wheezy rasp was terrifying, and for a second I thought she was dying.

"Water," she croaked, grabbing on to my shoulder. "Water." She bent over and I felt her nails going into my flesh.

Mr. Hort's eyes bulged with alarm, but as soon as he'd gone, Lara stopped choking. He had retreated to get her water, but it was all just a trick. "You stay here," she hissed at us, dumping the catalog in Joyce's arms. Then she opened the door and disappeared down the hallway, leaving us alone there on the step.

"She didn't tell us," Joyce said quietly. "What are we supposed to say to him?"

"I don't know. We'll just keep him talking."

But then neither of them came back. We were sure it was at least two minutes. Our hands had started sweating, and our faces were prickling hot. Joyce put her hand on the metal latch. "No. Don't," I said. But it was already too late: Joyce was opening the door.

The first thing I noticed was the smell. Medicinal, like cough syrup and antifungal spray. The smell of hookers, I thought, and when I looked around I expected a grown woman to appear, squeezed into the tiny shorts and rainbow shirt of a child. "Joyce," I hissed, as I followed behind her. "Joyce!"

It felt as though we were under a spell, being lured deeper and deeper inside, and soon it would be too late to escape. We were in the hallway and then the living room, where a dark blue curtain covered the window. Then I heard something rustling. Him. I felt faint.

"Where's the sick one? What are you doing?" he demanded, and the fluty notes in his voice had vanished. He held a cup in one hand and fixed his dark, scary eyes on us.

I looked around the room. There was a glass table lamp, a pointy-headed carved doll that reminded me of voodoo. I stretched my fingers. I could grab something and hit him. I would aim for his head, the side of his temple. Or his eyes.

We heard a door slam, and as Mr. Hort turned to look I took my opportunity. "Autumn! Autumn! Autumn!" I screamed, and then Joyce was joining in with me. And he watched us with horror or hatred or fear—I couldn't tell which.

Mr. Hort didn't chase us out the door, but eventually we turned and ran out on our own.

"Say cheese!" I lifted my camera and zoomed in on Callie. She stretched her arms lazily over her head and didn't smile as I snapped away. We were sitting in Mrs. Romero's garden in the late July sunshine—stalks of lavender thick with honeybees, a sparrow twittering in the bushes. I took seven or eight photos as Callie gazed quietly into the lens, and when I was done she didn't ask how she'd looked; instead, she wanted to talk about Autumn.

"Do you think she did it to get famous? Kind of wanting attention?"

Autumn had come up a few times now, ever since the day I thought

Callie went swimming. I guessed this might be a ploy to keep me from nagging her about lessons.

"I don't think so." I turned off my camera. "They said she was drunk and it was spur-of-the-moment."

"But she didn't leave any clues. She must have wanted people to look."

"There might have been clues. It's just nobody saw them at first."

Callie tickled her bare feet against the grass, swinging them slowly back and forth. "Not even her friends?"

"Autumn's friends thought she was kidnapped. She didn't tell them anything. That's why they had these big search parties in the woods and everywhere else."

"But Autumn could swim, right?"

I looked at Callie's summer freckles, her hair gleaming in the sun. The crease of concentration between her pale brows. I didn't want to feed her details she could use in arguments against me, but I started to nod. Autumn knew how to swim.

Besides these questions about Autumn, Callie talked about her new favorite topics that summer. Conservation. The threat of global warming. Three days a week she volunteered at the nature reserve, and every evening as she scraped mud off her boots, she briefed me about the box turtles and wood frogs she'd counted for their surveys. As July's heat wave blazed into August, she held forth on dying fish populations, algal blooms, the number of species at risk of extinction. I agreed to take three-minute showers, we started a compost bin, and Callie insisted she'd rather bike to her friends' than let me waste gasoline. I kept waiting for her to crack and start blasting the air-conditioning, but the temperatures didn't seem to affect her as she crouched in our yard, collecting leaves. I watched from the kitchen window as she methodically measured a tree trunk, and I was impressed but also boggled. How much longer could this go on?

She went to stay with my aunt Bea for the last week of vacation. She'd been looking forward to the visit all summer, and before she left she printed recipes off the Internet for things made with blueberries and beets and apples—foods that were supposed to be healthy for people with lung disease. My aunt had been diagnosed with emphysema years ago, and even though we weren't close or even moderately friendly, I felt obligated to support her relationship with Callie.

Bea kept no pictures of Curtis in the house, at least none that I'd seen on display, and she'd given the impression over the years that she wouldn't talk about her son. She'd thrown out all of his things, leaving only the small single bed under the window. The bed that Callie would be sleeping in, in Curtis's old room. Callie dumped her bags on the floor with a sigh—it didn't bother her. She wanted me to go home, to stop worrying so much. "I like worrying," I teased, but she was already waving. "Good-bye!" Callie yelled. "Byee!" she trilled. And I didn't want to leave her, but it was only for a week.

After Callie was gone, our house was too quiet. I turned on the radio, and then the TV, while whipping egg whites in a bowl. That month I was trying to learn macarons. The tiny delicate French confections. But despite my exertions, my work in the kitchen was not going well. I splashed my skin with the hot sugar syrup when I tried to whip and pour simultaneously. I sweated in the kitchen nights and afternoons, but each batch came out progressively worse. The shells were cracked or lumpy or flat. They looked like ugly brown rocks. And out of shame, I felt compelled to eat them, as if to cancel out all that waste. One afternoon, I broke a bowl out of carelessness; it was full of hardened sugar. And instead of picking up the pieces, I shoved another macaron into my mouth.

I needed to get out of the house, to get away from the smell of burnt sugar, so I ended up driving over to the green for some window-shopping on Main Street. I wandered in and out of boutiques and gift shops that burned expensive soy candles; I stopped in the modern art gallery on the corner to look at a sculpture made of red lights. The thing about living among the wealthy was that it sometimes rubbed off on you, the tastes and fashions, the desire for certain things. I wanted our walls to be that same shade of gray, and to buy one of those sculptures, and also the silk blouse in the window that cost more than my laptop. You'd wonder how these stores could stay in business with such extortionate price tags, but Dr. Rick was always reminding us that people had money here. Our schedules at the practice had been patchy since May, we were seeing fewer patients, and we'd been warned at a recent staff meeting that some of our hours might have to be cut. We were supposed to try to drum up business when we weren't with patients, making wheedling calls about six-month checkups. But it was always our wealthiest patients who started complaining about our prices, clucking their tongues, claiming to be "broke" due to home renovations. We didn't know exactly what Dr. Rick was planning, and wondered if all of us would bear the brunt, or if one of us, unlucky, would end up losing our job.

I had wandered to the far end of the green, where the French bakery flaunted its wares, and I contemplated the macarons with their spectacular pastel shells. A chubby man in brogues came out with a large white sack and a pleased expression. I touched the burn mark on my hand and smiled at him briefly. Gateway man? Macaron lover? He didn't give me a second glance as he shuffled past. Then I heard someone calling my name in a loud girlish voice.

Dallas carried a shopping bag in each hand and she grinned as she meandered over. Her tank top rode up on her stomach, and she'd clipped her hair into a twist. I hadn't seen Dallas much over the summer, not since Callie started riding her bike everywhere, and since our place was so small it never seemed worth inviting her over.

"Dallas, you look great!" I exclaimed. "What are you up to?"

She said she was back-to-school shopping; Ella was still trying on jeans in a store. She held up her bags and started describing the things she'd bought—necklace, sweater, pair of earrings—but then her smile faltered. "Is Callie okay?"

Dallas explained that she kept texting her, but Callie wasn't responding.

"She's visiting family this week," I said. "It could be her phone doesn't get great service."

I'd talked to Callie just a few hours earlier, and we hadn't had trouble with the reception, but it seemed like a plausible explanation and Dallas appeared relieved.

"I thought she might be ignoring me," she said with a smile, like the very thought of this was ridiculous. She looked down at her two bags, amused by herself. Dallas had a sturdier figure than Callie or Ella; she was strong and athletic, but when she dropped her chin you could see a smidge of baby fat.

"I'm sure she's not ignoring you. I'll tell her to call you."

"And tell her we miss her a lot," she said. "We can't wait for her to get back."

I asked Dallas about her weekend plans and she mentioned sailing around the Thimble Islands. "I would've invited Callie, but I know how she gets around water."

Dallas's eyes glistened with sympathy—I hoped it wasn't pity. All these priceless experiences, and Callie was missing out.

"She can swim." I felt exasperated. "She just refuses. I can't explain it."

"I think she's embarrassed," Dallas said. "With everything else she's practically perfect. But with swimming—" She bit her bottom lip. "Spectacular mess."

"She needs practice," I said. "But she won't take lessons."

"Me and Ella tried to teach her. It was like watching a cat tread water."

"You actually got her swimming?" I remembered the day of the wet bathing suit.

"Only once. Last month. She looked pretty bad. But we don't care how she looks; it's not like we're taking pictures."

"At least you got her in. That's better than I can say."

"We wouldn't let anything happen to her, but she doesn't want to trust us."

Dallas had this confident way of speaking that made you forget she was only fourteen. She exuded such poise, she could have been on TV.

"Callie trusts you," I assured her. "She knows you look out for her. You and Ella really helped her with that awful girl at school."

"Robyn." Dallas flicked one of her earrings. "*She* was a weird one."

"You haven't seen her since?"

"I'd probably run if I did."

"But you stood up to her when it mattered. That's the important thing."

"It wasn't hard." Dallas shook her head. "Nobody liked Robyn."

"Well, who would? A girl who does things like that."

"That's what I told Callie." Dallas wrinkled her nose prettily. "But she just doesn't get what can happen when somebody hates you."

"I suppose she's learning," I told Dallas gratefully. "She's learned now."

The next day I got a call at work from Aunt Bea. "I'm struggling," she said. "You need to come get her." I drove to the neighborhood where I'd grown up in Cansdown, and by the time I opened the front door of Bea's single-story prefab, I'd imagined the worst. Bea would be half dead, surrounded by EMTs, and Callie would be sobbing in the corner. But Bea was eating potato chips in her armchair, her oxygen tube fitted neatly into her nostrils, and Callie wasn't even there.

"She's out on the bike," Bea said offhandedly.

I'd made emergency arrangements to leave work after Bea called, thinking that something really serious must've happened. I'd forgotten that my aunt didn't understand what it was like to have a job with actual responsibilities.

"What happened?" I asked.

"I told you." Bea pouted. "I can't handle her. I'm on sixteen types of medication. You try handling a kid when you're on that much medication."

Bea's cheeks were hollowed out, and when she frowned, she looked both skeletal and childlike. Her hair hung unevenly to her shoulders in tufts, and although she was only in her fifties she looked closer to seventy. Despite her appearance, I no longer thought of my aunt as an adult. She was more like a miserable troll who couldn't be reasoned with. I tried to arrange my face as sympathetically as I could.

"Did you fight?" I asked.

"I told her she had to go and she didn't like it. You shouldn't have left her here so long."

"Yes," I said slowly. "But she was really looking forward to spending time with you."

"Well, it's not a good time," Bea said. "And I didn't ask for this."

I didn't point out that she *had* asked for this. I dialed Callie's cell phone, but she didn't pick up, and then Bea turned on the TV as if it had nothing to do with her. Bea and Curtis had lived with Mom and me until I was fourteen, and by the time she moved out, I'd realized how irresponsible and petty she could be. She'd moved here after she finally managed to hold down a job long enough to afford rent, but for the past six years she'd been too sick to work and had relied on my mom and welfare to keep her going.

"How long has she been gone?"

"I don't know," Bea said. "An hour?"

I made her promise to call me immediately if Callie got back before me, and then I jumped in my car, making an effort not to panic. I'd just cruise slowly around the neighborhood until I spotted her, and I wouldn't turn it into some big ordeal, dramatic tears, and accusations. She was fourteen years old—she could disappear for an hour in daylight, even if she didn't answer her phone, the one thing I always asked of her. Anyway, Cansdown was fairly safe, although not as safe as Pembury, but sometimes Callie's phone ran out of juice or she didn't hear it ringing. I drove along the curving suburban streets of the south side, and then I headed down the beach road, and when that produced no sightings I tightened my grip on the wheel.

Not far from Mr. Hort's house, I drove past a place I hardly recognized. There was a large new split-level on the spot that I remembered as a vacant lot. Twenty years earlier it was just weeds and broken glass, the place where Joyce and I caught up with Lara after running out of Mr. Hort's house.

"You dumbasses," Lara cried. "I thought I was going to have to go back there and get you." She collared us and then hugged us as we panted from our run. We were both exhilarated and pink-cheeked, thrilled by what we'd done. I leaned in to Lara, forgetting that Autumn was still missing. Forgetting that the three of us were supposed to be four. We scuffed our shoes together, ankles touching for reassurance, and then Lara lit up a cigarette, taking an urgent drag.

"I checked his basement and everything." She pushed her sweaty red hair behind her ear. "Autumn definitely wasn't there."

"He could've moved her," Joyce said.

He could've killed her, I thought. Then I looked at Lara. Had I just heard her thoughts?

I held the cigarette when she passed it to me, and took my first puff ever, feeling a mixture of pride and belonging; I was part of this awful tragedy. What an idiot I was, what idiots children can be. Longing for emotions that aren't theirs: desperation and sorrow. Believing a calamity will make them adults—like a puff of smoke, a sip of wine.

Fifteen minutes after I got back to Bea's house, we heard the front door. Bea was still watching TV, completely indifferent, while I chewed my cuticles, a nervous wreck. Callie's flip-flops slapped noisily against the floor, and then she stood in the doorway of the living room, staring at both of us with bright, clear eyes. Her cheeks were flushed and sweaty from the heat and the bike ride, and I took in all the familiar details that I'd missed over the past few days. The way the roots of her hair rose up from her forehead, almost spiky, before curving back down. The pale scar that cut across her knee from the time she'd fallen off the trampoline in the school gym. Her toenails, painted baby blue, and her wide freckled shoulders that always fit perfectly under my arm.

"Where the hell have you been? Where the hell?"

Callie crossed her arms and caught my eye. "I was just out on the bike."

"You're too much for me," Aunt Bea said unapologetically. "I'm not up to kids anymore."

Callie flinched, and then she turned her head, as if preparing for another blow. She pulled her hair across one cheek, and I glanced at Bea. She didn't even seem to notice. She rustled the bag of chips on her lap, and I willed her to shut up. "I missed you so much," I said, pulling Callie into a hug. "You can't just disappear like that." Her slender body was hot and rigid. She touched my back and then pulled away.

"You came to take me home?"

"Bea's not feeling well, so she called me," I explained. "I've been driving around looking for you. Why didn't you answer your phone?"

"I didn't hear it," she said. Then she looked at Bea with open frustration. My aunt put another chip in her mouth before Callie turned and skulked out of the room.

"You didn't tell her you were sending her home?" I asked, after hearing the bedroom door slam.

"I told her," Bea said.

"Well, she didn't seem to know." I felt a nastiness rising inside me. "How much money do you have left?" I'd given Bea an envelope of cash to pay for Callie that week, and if she was sending her home, she could just give it back.

"It's gone," she said sourly.

I left without saying good-bye. When Callie dragged herself outside, I put an arm around her.

"You okay, Callie?"

She didn't answer.

"I know this is hard, but you shouldn't take it personally." I mustered up as much charity as I could. "You know she's in pain and she's not a happy person."

Callie blinked at me in the sunshine and then shook her head as if it wasn't worth talking about.

All My Interactions with Robyn Doblak, #4
For Rebecca/From Callie

Rebecca, remember when I was five and I stopped sleeping for a while? I was staying with Grandma Susanna and Grandpa Pat, and at night I waited for Mom. I would listen for the sound of her key, then the bedroom door would open and I'd see her in the dark. Her jacket smelled like cold air, and she'd whisper, "You still awake?"

Sometimes she'd let me sit up in bed, and I'd show her how Grandpa Pat taught me to whistle through my teeth or I'd show her a scab I was growing on my hand. Other times, she'd tell me what it was like. She told me about the beetles and worms and the tunnels underground and it didn't scare me. I wanted her to know it didn't scare me. I waited every night and squinted into the darkness until I heard her key and then I could relax. I wanted to go with her.

Grandma and Grandpa heard me through the walls. They heard me talking and asked me what was going on. Then they said I was making it up and playing a joke. I screamed and they sent me to my room. I thought Mom wouldn't come anymore. But that night I waited and waited and finally she came. Then Grandma Susanna got sick and you came to stay.

Remember when you heard about Mom's visits, and you wanted to talk to me? You looked me right in the eyes and asked what Mom had said and how she looked. I could tell you were trying not to get too excited, and I decided I wouldn't tell you that Mom was just in her regular jacket. I said she wore a long sparkly dress with silver shoes and a veil. Then you asked if you could sleep in my room that night.

I remember you flossing my teeth and reading my favorite story about rabbits, then you lay down on the flip bed on the floor of my room. Sometimes when we lived in the old place and Mom was taking her classes at night, you would sit in my room if I had a bad dream. I could hear you breathing like then, and I started getting confused about where I was. I thought if I looked over one way there would be the blue bookshelf with stickers on it and if I looked next to that there would be the dresser with the painted yellow dog. But when I looked over, they weren't there and I remembered I was in a different room and even the window was in the wrong place. I wriggled around and heard someone turning over.

"Are you okay?"

I sat up. "Mom?"

"It's Rebecca."

I lay back down and the mattress creaked. I looked at the little cracks of light under the door and waited to hear her footsteps and the sound of her key. I knew you were waiting too.

"Sometimes she's late," I said.

"When you see her, is she happy?"

"Yeah. She goes 'hee hee hee.' "

"Sometimes I like to imagine, too," you said. Then you started telling me how if it was another year and you and my mom were still in high school you'd be in this same exact room listening to music. Mom would be where I was and you'd be on the flip bed, and when Mom fell asleep you'd look out the window at the same piece of sky.

"I miss her," you said.

"You have to listen for the sound of her key," I said.

"Okay."

I remember looking at the window and starting to feel sticky. I pulled on the neck of my pajamas and then my blanket slipped to the floor. Mom still hadn't come. I knew how much you wanted to see her and I could feel how hard you were trying. You were the one who believed me, and when you asked me those questions about Mom it seemed like you believed I was older and smarter than anyone you'd ever met. I'd felt how important my answers were, but now Mom wasn't here and I had the same feeling I always got when I'd lied or was trying to trick someone. Sticky icky. I wanted to shove you out of my room like it was your fault Mom wasn't here. I reached for the light switch, and the lampshade rattled.

"What's wrong?" You were blinking.

"She's not coming."

"Oh, sweetheart." You breathed in and out for a long time. When you spoke, your voice was clammy. "Maybe if we go to sleep, she'll visit us in our dreams. In the morning, we can tell each other everything she said to us."

I think it was then, when I was five years old, that I realized I couldn't do what you wanted. You wanted us to lie and you wanted to pretend. That was when I understood that what I'd felt before had been a trick—a trick I was playing on myself. Mom couldn't come now because she hadn't come before. Dead was dead and dead was gone. That was what everyone kept saying. I didn't turn the light off for a long time and you didn't tell me that I had to. I decided I'd never fool myself again or anybody else.

But then I changed my mind last Christmas, after I got this message from Robyn:

From: R.Doblak@sparkon.com
To: C.Mckenzie@chronomail.com
Subject: RE: RE: You asleep?
Date: Sun, Dec 28 2008, 23:18:02

So I've been lying here in bed for about the last eighteen hours, and my mom's like, WHAT ARE YOU DOING, HAVING A STARING CONTEST WITH THE CEILING? And I'm like, I GIVE UP!!!! I CAN'T FACE THE WORLD!!! Then I remembered about you and the ketchup and I felt the littlest bit better. It's like people look at us and they think they know all our secrets, even before meeting us or anything they've got this whole idea. Blargh. *She vomits* Pooor Robyn. I'd rather be Evil like you were, or maybe a Pit Bull. Anything's better than feeling so pathetic.

I told my mom if we got a dog I wouldn't feel so shitty, and she was like, "Robyn, don't you know? Your dad was just joking." And I did, but still. My dad had this whole plan. When he was really sick, he decided he'd find a way to come back. He was going to reincarnate as a dog, or haunt one, whatever. He said we'd have to pick him out in a pet store and call him Papa. Feed him lots of steaks, put on the Mets when they were playing. He'd lie around the house all day, protecting the family, and I knew it was a joke, but I swore I was going to do it.

xoRobyn

5

On the ninth anniversary of Joyce's death, a Saturday this year, I packed the rosebush, the hyacinth bulbs, and a small shovel in the car. Then I went inside to make French toast.

French toast was an old favorite, and I fried it in butter the way Joyce had taught me. It smelled of cinnamon and lazy Sunday mornings, Joyce standing next to the stove in a sweatshirt, cutting the cooked bread into pieces that Callie could pick up with her fingers. I still preferred the flat, sweet taste of the cheaper artificial maple syrup, and I squeezed the plastic bottle so that a heavy brown stream covered my slice. But I wasn't really hungry and I managed to swallow only a few small bites.

When I knocked on Callie's door around eight, she was still asleep, nestled deep under the covers. I turned on the light and hesitated in her doorway while she blinked at me with unfocused morning eyes.

"Hey, hon. I made French toast."

She groaned. "I can't move."

"You exhausted?"

"I think I'm sick."

I crossed into her room and lay my hand on her forehead. Her skin was cool and slightly grainy, as if a handful of sand had been rubbed just below the surface.

"What hurts?" I asked.

"Everything. My stomach. I can't get up."

She bunched up her face and closed her eyes as if she were doing an impression of someone dying from a terrible, agonizing disease. The plague, or maybe smallpox. When Callie was younger, she'd sometimes faked illnesses to get attention. It was her toe, her ear, her elbow. Once, she'd complained that her hair hurt. Joyce always stroked her head and made a fuss, feeding her pieces of candy that she pretended were medicine.

"Gosh," I said. "Are you in a lot of pain?"

"Mmmm-hmmm."

"Show me where your stomach hurts."

Callie waved her hand vaguely over the covers.

"Is it on the lower right-hand side? That could be appendicitis."

"Nuh."

"I'll get the thermometer," I said, rushing out as though every second counted.

While Callie held the thermometer under her tongue, I looked around her room. The shelves above her desk were filled with pinecones, seed pods, and bits of twigs and bark. On the top shelf there was an open canister of banded feathers and then smaller, unidentifiable lumps she'd collected at the nature reserve. Something like honeycomb, something else spiny and gray. She labeled everything, and I knew that each new specimen had been carefully selected and positioned, organized by some complex scientific order that I couldn't understand.

The thermometer beeped and Callie's temperature was normal. "Let me take your pulse," I said, consolingly.

I held her limp wrist in my hand and counted as I looked at my watch. It was normal.

"Hmmm. A little fast," I said. "Does it feel fast?"

"Yeah."

"Just try to relax for a minute. I'll get you a cup of tea to settle your stomach."

I put together a tray for her with a plate of warm French toast, two Tylenol, and a cup of ginger tea. I wondered whether she'd smile if I brought in some of those white and pink licorice candies that Joyce used to pretend were medicine, but I didn't have any, so I just stirred extra sugar into her drink. I was still hoping that we could be on the road to Cansdown before ten if I gave her enough sympathy.

Callie sat up in bed as I passed her the tray. She was wearing the same wrinkled T-shirt she'd worn the day before. There was a picture on the front of Jimi Hendrix riding a snowboard. She'd bought it used, for three dollars, but then she wouldn't let me wash it. She was in her second week of high school, and was trying to look enigmatic. Too cool or cynical or jaded to wear school colors to her first pep rally. "It's meaningless," she had told me when I'd mentioned school spirit. "The color I'm wearing won't make any difference."

Now she glanced down at my French toast and frowned. "I can't eat this."

"Oh. Then just leave it. Do you think I should call the doctor?"

She shrugged, brought the tea to her lips, slurped.

"How is it?"

"Okay."

"Did you eat anything strange yesterday? Could you have food poisoning?"

"It's probably a cold," she said. "I just need sleep."

"Well, I won't go today if you're sick. If you're too sick to go, then I'll stay home with you."

"I can stay on my own. I'm fourteen. I stay home all the time."

"But what if you got worse? I'd need to be around to get you to the doctor . . . or the hospital," I said, hamming it up.

"It's not *that* bad, Rebecca."

"But I know you wouldn't miss today unless you were sick. We'll just reschedule and bring the flowers another day."

"Let me see how I feel after the tea," Callie said.

"Okay. But we won't go if you still feel horrible. I'm sure that missing it this once won't be the end of the world. Right?"

Twenty minutes later, I heard the shower running, and I knew that she was coming. We left for Cansdown just before ten, and although Callie was wearing the same dirty T-shirt, I didn't say a word.

*

My mom didn't approve of our twice-a-year visits to the cemetery. She thought it was the equivalent of watching a weepy movie or staring at pictures of starving orphans: it was unnecessarily morbid, it would end badly. She didn't realize that thinking about Joyce was something we did already, every day. It wasn't a choice, and it wasn't always sad. It was just a way of remembering and coping and keeping her in the air.

Callie's old grief counselor was the one who'd first suggested we write the letters to Joyce. The McKenzies had kept Callie away from the funeral because they thought she was too young to understand, but by the time I became her guardian, a year later, it was clear that hiding the truth hadn't made it hurt any less. The counselor explained that writing letters would help Callie to finally grieve, as well as to negotiate a new kind of relationship with Joyce. When we wrote to her, she lived in our words. When we thought or spoke about her, she wasn't gone. There was an absence but also an opening: we could find ways to keep her alive.

Together, we'd placed a stone in the shape of a heart on Joyce's grave, and left our first letters anchored underneath. By that point, fewer things were cluttering her plot, and it made me feel calm to see it.

In the early months after Joyce's funeral, I'd become upset when I noticed the mementos that had been left on her grave. There were cheap gas-station bouquets, dirty yellow candles, a Santa Claus ornament with a mean silver hook rising out of his cap. Someone had left a Beanie Baby that was now rain-soaked, and a bag of orange circus peanuts—a thing I'd never seen her eat in her entire life. It didn't make sense, and anyone who wandered past would've got the wrong idea completely. They would've imagined that Joyce was some kind of sentimental dimwit. But I knew that she would roll her eyes at the pile of soggy junk and die laughing at all those cheap flowers.

There'd been a couple of articles in the local newspaper after her death, and the only explanation I could come up with was that some well-meaning strangers had read about her and decided to drop off this meaningless trash. Anyone who'd really known Joyce wouldn't have tried to insult her this way. One day, I collected all the dirty trinkets and carried them to the garbage can at the edge of the parking lot. Then I went back and picked off the plastic flowers, the photos of babies I didn't know. Those went in the garbage, too. When her grave was clear, it felt more like her again.

By the time Callie and I laid the heart-shaped stone on her grave, the frayed pink ribbons and stuffed toys didn't upset me as much. I knew that I could clear them off like ordinary trash. Over the years, these things slowed to a trickle and then finally stopped. But we still came here regularly to leave our letters for Joyce.

After the exit for Cansdown, I drove along the route I always used to get to the cemetery. I passed a dilapidated motel with a single truck parked out front, low industrial buildings, wholesalers, and empty parking lots strewn with garbage. Cansdown was no worse than it had been when I was a kid, but my years of living in Pembury had made it seem even shoddier. The endless auto shops, the scrubby weeds sprouting from the asphalt, the dismal places where you could cash a check. The recession wasn't helping, but I knew that the blue tarpaulin used to patch the fence outside the used-car lot had been hanging there for years.

The cemetery gates were open, and as I drove up to the parking lot, Callie began to stir. She'd been dozing for most of the drive, and there was a bright red mark on her cheek from where it had pressed against the door. She tilted her head back as she shook out her hair. Then she shimmied her shoulders, stretched her long legs. Sometimes it took my breath away, how at certain angles, with a shrug or a yawn, she was her mother exactly. I was glad she'd come today; I was relieved I wasn't alone.

"Okay, Cal, let's give your mom those roses."

In the trunk of the car, the rosebush had wilted. White petals had fallen to the floor. Callie had chosen it the day before. I'd told her she could buy whatever she wanted, and after she disappeared inside the garden center, I'd filled a bag with hyacinth bulbs. Afterward, I'd wandered the aisles and finally found her squatting beside a row of rosebushes.

"Roses are a great idea," I'd said.

It was only then that I noticed the color of the blooms she'd chosen.

They were a deep purplish brown, almost black. They were hideous, actually. Ugly and dead-looking.

"Do you think your mom would want black roses?" I asked carefully.

Callie pursed her lips. "I don't think she cares."

Then her mouth twitched, like she was about to smile, and I realized she was making fun of me. Or of Joyce. Either way, it was disrespectful. But then she seemed to realize and she tried to make up for it. She had walked over to the white rosebush, glancing up at me for approval, and it wasn't until now, as I cradled the root ball in my arms, that I realized the cemetery might not even let us plant something so big.

Callie let the shovel bang against her leg as we made our way over. The cemetery was the largest in Cansdown, and it mixed rich and poor, northsiders and southsiders. Joyce's mother had died of a stroke and was buried here less than a year after her daughter. And Autumn Sanger was here, too; I'd visited her grave once. As we passed Autumn's row, I remembered hearing the news. She'd been missing for several days, and Joyce and I kept trying to summon her. We whispered her name into the grass, listened for her voice in the whir of sprinklers. If only she'd tell us *whose* basement, we could break in and save her. Then Aunt Bea found us in the yard. She crossed her arms and told us, "They found her. She drowned. She washed up under the docks this morning."

Callie had got ahead of me and I hurried along to catch up. I placed the bush at the foot of Joyce's grave, and in the sun, the stones seemed to waver, sharp, then blurred. I blinked as Callie stuck the shovel into the ground, beginning the hole to the right of Joyce's headstone. She didn't check with me first—she just started digging. I took out my pile of letters, and watched as Callie lifted out the soil. Her hair was matted against her neck in sweaty clumps and she looked uncomfortable in her oversized shirt.

"Let me do some," I said, but she didn't stop. The earth came up quickly, and I knelt on the ground, holding the letters we'd written for Joyce. Then I lifted up the heart-shaped stone. Opened the plastic folder underneath. And in that moment, I saw the red ink.

What the hell?

"What's wrong?"

On pink-lined paper, the red words slanted:

> *Your daughter hurts people. She threw the paint and sent the picture. Callie deserves to die like you.*

If I'd expected it, I might've hidden it, but my mind wasn't ready. I hadn't thought of Robyn Doblak in weeks, maybe longer.

Callie had stopped digging when she heard me gasp.

The red handwriting looked evil, tipping backward on the page. I dropped it on the ground like it was powdered with anthrax, but when Callie reached for it, I tried to grab it back.

"Cal!" I said. But she already had it.

In the bright sunlight, she stood as still as a statue. Her face was pale, as if a fine film of dust had settled on the surface. I snatched the paper out of her hands as she wobbled and then started to sink. She didn't cry out, she simply collapsed to the ground. Then she arranged her legs in front of her, dangling wrists over knees.

"Put your head between your legs," I coached, thinking of my old dizzy spells.

She dropped her head and I rubbed small circles on her back. "I'll go to the police," I told her. "I won't let her get away with this. Just try to breathe. Breathe slow, honey."

She spoke from between her legs.

"I told you I was sick. I shouldn't even be here."

I touched her hair, stroked it. It was slippery under my fingers, and

I watched her back rise and fall with every breath. It was a shock, of course, finding out somebody hated you. Hated you enough to threaten you, to find your mother's grave.

"I'm sorry," I said. "I don't understand what's going on."

"She wouldn't have wanted me to come if I was sick!"

"Callie," I said. "Has Robyn done anything like this before?"

With her face against her knees, she looked like a very small child playing hide-and-seek, waiting to count to one hundred so that I could hide.

She shook her head, still hiding her face.

"She hasn't contacted you until now?"

"Nuh."

"I'm gonna get you home," I said. "Are you okay to stand up?"

"What about the roses?" Callie murmured between her legs.

"Forget it." I glanced at the bush.

"No," she said faintly. "It isn't right."

I slipped the note into my pocket and picked up the shovel. As it clinked against earth, I pictured Robyn here at the grave. She marched back and forth, spitting on Joyce's stone. I chucked out more dirt. What kind of child did a thing like this? If she so much as laid a finger on Callie, I'd really *do* something. I started digging faster, and then I tried to fit the bush in, but the hole wasn't deep enough. I had to keep going. I was starting to sweat, and Callie kept her face hidden, and if Joyce could see us now, I knew what she'd say. JUST GO HOME. I didn't think she even liked roses. My hands burned as I lifted the soil, and when I tried the bush again it finally fit. But after I'd refilled the hole, I saw that the creamy blossoms looked dirty and the branches seemed too shabby and thin. *Just yank it up,* I thought. But I couldn't do that in front of Callie. I needed to get her home and there was no time for the hyacinths.

All My Interactions with Robyn Doblak, #5
For Rebecca/From Callie

IM Dec 29 2008 12:45:52

12:36:21

LithoCALpus: Robyn? Are you alive?

12:36:40

robynroarxo: #underthecovers4life

12:37:10

LithoCALpus: Ok what are you doing?!!!!! Growing dreads and becoming a hermit?

12:38:09

robynroarxo: I feel 😵 blaaargh

12:38:33

LithoCALpus: Blarggh? WHY?

12:38:54

robynroarxo: my whole body is screaming noooooooooooooooooooooooooooo!

12:39:16

LithoCALpus: Can you get up for 5 minutes? Might make u feel better.

12:40:12

LithoCALpus: Eat some cereal & watch cartoons. Think up new ways to kill Xmas! 😈

12:40:33

robynroarxo: Xmas isn't the problem

12:41:06

robynroarxo: I just want everything to be over.

12:41:29

LithoCALpus: Robyn did you do something?

12:41:35

robynroarxo: ?????

12:41:45

LithoCALpus: ((hurt yourself))

12:41:51

robynroarxo: do you even care?

12:41:58

LithoCALpus: Obviously! Yes!!!

12:42:09

robynroarxo: No . . . nothing.

12:42:15

LithoCALpus: You better not!!!

12:42:27

robynroarxo: OK. Just forget it.

12:42:40

LithoCALpus: OMG!!! Forget it?!!!!!!

12:42:50

robynroarxo: I won't do anything.

12:43:07

LithoCALpus: How do I know you're not lying?

12:43:53

robynroarxo: I swear on my life.

12:44:18

LithoCALpus: Swear on Miss Baranski's.

12:44:32

robynroarxo: I swear on Miss Baranski.

12:44:40

LithoCALpus: Now you have to get out of bed.

12:44:45

robynroarxo: I will soon.

12:45:22

LithoCALpus: NOW ROBYN I MEAN IT.

12:45:36

robynroarxo: What difference does it make?

12:45:43

LithoCALpus: RIGHT THIS SECOND

12:45:52

LithoCALpus: Don't make me come over there!!!!

12:46:13

robynroarxo: 😃 😃 😃

12:46:45

LithoCALpus: Don't make me get a haunted dog to come bite you on the butt. 😈

12:47:10

robynroarxo: 🤫 Hey don't tell anyone—about my dad haunting a dog.

12:47:24

LithoCALpus: I know. I won't.

12:47:35

LithoCALpus: AS LONG AS YOU GET OUT OF BED!!!!

12:47:53

robynroarxo: Ok fine I'm up.

12:48:26

LithoCALpus: Really? Prove it.

12:48:55

robynroarxo: I'm putting on my socks.

12:49:11

LithoCALpus: See it's not hard. Just stop thinking so much.

12:49:19

robynroarxo: Is that what you do?

12:49:38

LithoCALpus: Yeah I don't think about anything at all!

6

"Do you have any texts, e-mails, or phone messages from her?" Detective Serrano asked, as he lifted the edge of the note with his pen.

He sighed when I shook my head. Took halfhearted notes as I described the paint incident in middle school. "It's a direct threat," I insisted. "It had to come from Robyn."

"What about the picture she says yours sent?"

"What?"

"She threw the paint and sent the picture," he read.

"She's a fantasist—God knows what else she's making up. She knows Callie didn't do this, but she can't admit her own guilt. She's desperate to push the blame onto anyone else."

"Well, you won't get a restraining order without any proof. What you've gotta do is keep track of everything. Make a note of any contact she makes. Ninety-nine percent of the time these kids are just trying to scare each other."

I tried convincing myself he was right as I drove home from the station. Robyn was just fooling around, making idle threats. Teenagers and their contradictions. Their desire for drama, their grandiose self-importance, their belief that nothing they do will have any impact on others. Joyce and I were exactly the same on the day of Autumn's funeral.

We weren't allowed to attend, but we watched Curtis getting ready. He wore a navy blazer and left the house early, smelling of soap. He seemed older to me now, shoulders squared, chin jutting, like he was going on a journey to a place I'd never know. I imagined grief like a big white room, filled with gauzy billowing curtains, where men gritted their teeth at the ceiling, straining against their own pain.

Joyce hadn't seen the new picture of Autumn, so I ran to get the newspaper. Autumn's eyes were narrowed at the camera, and it looked like she was about to burst out laughing. Her mouth was set in a dramatic pout, and her bangs were curled up in a flip.

"She's pretty," Joyce said. "I like how she's done her eyes."

"Maybe we could try," she continued. "To see what it would be like."

In the bathroom, I found an eye pencil in Aunt Bea's green makeup bag. Joyce sat on the toilet seat as I rubbed the kohl pencil beneath her pale lashes. I rested one hand on her temple. I could see the pores on her forehead and the soft faint hair along her jaw. I moved the pencil gently back and forth, darkening her skin, and when I looked into her eyes, I noticed all the different colors. Flecks of yellow and hazel inside the liquid gray and blue.

"Your eyes look like pools in Africa," I said. Water, earth, sun, and stones.

Joyce laughed. "What does that even mean?"

"I dunno." I giggled and looked away.

She took the pencil from me and began to work on my face. When she was finished, we leaned against the sink so that we could examine ourselves in the mirror, close-up. The effect was alarming, but we didn't wince or turn away. Our eyes were glassy. Next to the dark lines our skin had become pale. We played with our new faces, pouting and squinting at ourselves, and we seemed like different people. We could have been Autumn's friends, crying in a room full of curtains. We might've got lost and disappeared like her.

Since nobody was home, we didn't have to be careful. We could go out in the yard and gather daisies for Autumn. Joyce and I moved with exaggerated slowness, heads drooping sadly, eager to feel her tragedy, hungry for more feelings. Joyce dropped to her knees in the shade, and I stopped beside her, then she spoke to me in a strange voice. "What if she was in love?"

I gazed across the yard to the chain-link fence, which glinted in the sunlight. The only sounds were from cars and cicadas, the drone of a lawn mower in the distance.

"If she was in love with Curtis and she knew she couldn't have him, she might've done it then. Walked into the sea."

I looked at Joyce and shivered although the sun still beat down on us. Her eyes were different. "I'll be her and you be Lara," she said.

She got up and began to walk through the grass as if she were wading through water, then she wobbled and tripped, fighting the strong current. Joyce turned and waved at me, and the throb of regret hit me all at once.

"Wait, don't go," I yelled, and I could hear the waves roaring, and the night sky was so black and empty, and I clutched at my throat.

"Love ya," she called behind her, before throwing her arms back and forth in the air, getting tossed around in the waves, kicking the ocean violently. I was still holding the flowers as I watched her begin to sink.

"No," I called out, but she was already dying. I ran to her and started to shake her, scattering flowers everywhere, pulling her head up to my chest, rocking her there. "Autumn! Autumn! Please wake up!"

It felt real, and I was beginning to sob. She was dead and I was alone.

I kissed her face, stroked her hair, picked up my flowers and placed them on her chest. I didn't make a decision to start stuttering, but I was so swept up in the moment, and I felt Lara's faltering voice catching in my throat. "H-h-h-ow could you?" I hiccupped miserably. "I-I-I w-wanted t-to save you." She didn't open her eyes, but then she was crying, too. She was dead. It was all over. A fifteen-year-old girl. We wept contagiously, powerfully, and I held my throat like a real hyacinth girl, my voice lost forever, unable to speak.

We didn't know anyone was watching. They were supposed to be at the funeral. But then I heard a noise, and I turned and saw them standing shoulder-to-shoulder.

"Assholes," Lara roared. And Joyce sat up beside me, wiping her hands through her dripping makeup, while Lara yelled at us to get off the ground.

My hiccups had stopped, and I felt myself shriveling, as if I could dry up and blow away, a dandelion seed.

"It's not a game," Curtis scolded us. "Get up now!"

He'd been holding on to Lara, as if he would stop her from coming after us, but now he let her go, and she opened her mouth. "Animals," she spat. And on this day her voice didn't fail her. It was quick and vicious. Then she turned and stalked away. There was no time to explain ourselves, to tell her how true our feelings had seemed. To say that we'd never make fun of her—we'd just wanted to be in her place. We watched her disappear across the lawn, her hair bright against her T-shirt, and it was already too late. The loss we'd imagined was turning real.

Curtis watched us for a moment, and when he looked at Joyce his eyes softened. "You should take that makeup off," he said. "It's not right on you."

I still hadn't got up off the ground. My joints felt hot and achy. Like I was made of shame, which weighed more than lead or gold. I held on to Joyce. This was our last game of hyacinth girls. The last time that I thought of myself as someone who was mostly good.

* * *

"You were definitely right today," I told Callie. "I'm sorry I took you when you were sick."

Callie lay propped up in bed, drinking ginger ale. Her curtains were pulled shut against the sun, but the sounds of Saturday afternoon came in through her window. A dog barked. Silverware jangled and glasses clinked in someone's kitchen. I was pretty certain that Callie wasn't sick, but she deserved some TLC.

"Sometimes I get stuff like that wrong, but you just have to remind me, okay?"

She put the glass down on the bedside table. "You don't listen."

"If I'm not listening, then just say, 'Wake up! Earth to Rebecca!' and I'll listen. Okay?"

"I'm not going to say that."

"We could have a secret password—like banana—and any time I'm not listening, you could just be like, 'banana!'"

She rolled her eyes, and her summer blanket rustled as she shifted in bed. I just wanted to cheer her up—show her we didn't have to worry—so I started doing an impression of Detective Serrano. I stuck out my bottom lip, all gruff authority. I made my voice deep and manly, pretended to polish my imaginary badge.

"Oh, and he asked me about the picture. You know how the note said, 'You sent the picture'?"

"I didn't send her anything," Callie said, serious again.

"Or maybe did you send a picture of her?"

"No. No way. Banana, Rebecca, banana."

"I knew you hadn't," I reassured her. "Is there anyone else who could've written that note?"

"I don't know." She rubbed her finger over her lip.

"Well, look, here's what I think happened. Robyn's still trying to convince us that she's the victim. Maybe she's even convinced herself that it all happened like she said. She wants to be blameless, so she's trying to blame you, but it's really important that you don't feel guilty."

Callie nodded gently in her bed, a pale princess.

"Now, I don't want to sound mean," I continued, "but I'm going to be honest. You know how those kids bothered Robyn at your school. It could be they sensed that she wasn't quite right. Like she gave off a bad vibe, a creepy weird vibe, and they sensed she was the kind of person who could do something like this."

"It's like someone's born," Callie said, "and they think they're normal but they're only normal to themselves, not anyone else."

"It can be tough for some people," I said, noticing the furrow in her brow. "But that doesn't give them the right to come after you."

I couldn't sleep that night. Every time I closed my eyes they snapped back open, and although I was learning to make fritters that month, I had no interest in going to the kitchen. By three a.m., I was thinking about the highway. It would be empty and cold at this hour, the sky still black, the road disappearing into the distance until I saw the red-and-white smokestack before the exit for Cansdown. I wanted to look in the plastic folder again. I thought I might've missed something. And I was worried about all the old letters we'd left for Joyce. Robyn could steal them. She could read Callie's private words to her mother. God knew what she might do with information like that, probably post it on the Internet.

When I pulled up to the cemetery it was just after six. The gates were locked, so I parked on the side of the road and started walking along the low stone wall that surrounded the cemetery. I walked until I found a spot where the wall had crumbled, and then I stepped over the rubble and crossed the lawn to Joyce's plot. I could see the scraggly rosebush as I approached and I wondered if Cerise Doblak might be involved as well. How else would Robyn get here?

Then I was crouching down on Joyce's grave, slipping my fingers under the flat edge of the message stone. Joyce's name was printed in my handwriting on a few aging envelopes, and "Mom" was written on all the others. I told myself I wasn't stealing Joyce's letters. I was just protecting her daughter. And Joyce would understand. I wouldn't need to explain.

I knelt on the ground, wishing we could hang out for just a minute. "Let's get out of here," I'd say.

"Is Delrio's still open?"

It was, so we'd go get pancakes together like this was no big deal. It wouldn't even need to be a huge catch-up session. Joyce would slide into the booth and tap her fingers along the side of the plastic menu, and we'd immediately start talking about something silly . . . best pancake toppings ever. Toasted almonds? Strawberries? Not bananas! Whipped cream? I knew exactly what she'd order: buttermilk pancakes—a short stack, with orange juice. We could skip over her mother's stroke, her father's depression, his subsequent decision to pass guardianship to me. When our plates arrived, Joyce would reach for the maple syrup and I'd just watch her for a moment. Joyce with her little brown birthmark, bringing a forkful to her mouth.

I didn't even realize that the gates had opened. It was only when the green truck pulled to a stop at the side of the grassy track that I realized

I wasn't alone anymore. A man got out and stood there, watching, as I brushed the grass from my knees. Then he started jogging down the row toward me and I knew I shouldn't be there. I wouldn't get very far if I tried to run. I clenched my keys between my knuckles and prepared to jab him. I'd have to fight because I couldn't let it happen here. When he was about six feet away, he halted suddenly and I saw he wasn't big. If I could bring up my knee exactly right, I might get away.

"You okay?" His voice was husky and I took in his details quickly. Medium build, blue baseball cap, late twenties. Not very tall, maybe five-seven, zippered sweatshirt, sandy stubble, light brown hair.

"Ye-es."

I saw him noticing the keys in my hand and he took a step back. I looked at the truck again and realized instantly what should've been obvious. He worked here and I was trespassing. I was stealing from Joyce's grave. I was still clutching all her old letters in my left hand.

"I was just leaving these for my friend," I said quickly. "I'm absolutely fine."

He looked at the letters, which were obviously old, and I saw one corner of his mouth lifting. The squinty creases around his eyes deepened like he was going to laugh at me. I squatted down and lifted the message stone, cheeks burning, as I replaced her letters.

"Hey, no worries." He turned and started walking to his truck. I watched as he drove past the parking lot, into the wooded area at the back. Then I retrieved Joyce's letters and shoved them into my purse. I should've just told him the truth: we were being harassed. Maybe he could've helped us, keeping an eye out for Robyn. I started walking in the direction of the path he'd taken, suddenly needing to explain our situation. After a short hike through the trees, I saw a stone building. The truck was parked in front of a large garage, and I pressed the buzzer at the entrance. After a moment, the door opened.

The man stood in front of me. His gray eyes were sleepy and he leaned easily against the door. "Hey."

"Hi."

He waited for me to say more, but when I opened my mouth nothing came out. I didn't know where to begin. There were stolen letters in my purse. "I—I want to explain."

I bit my lip and stared at my feet. The right words would make everything clear, but my mind stuttered and then stopped. I had the worst kind of stage fright, and I wanted to run back to my car.

"You want a cup of coffee?"

I followed him into a small office where there was an old metal desk and a matching filing cabinet. He offered me a squeaky swivel chair, and I sat there, watching, as he moved nimbly around the room, filling the Hot Shot with water, looking for a spoon, putting instant coffee in two mugs. Something about him reminded me of the guys who played Hacky Sack in college. There was a concentrated energy to his movements, as if he was the type of guy you'd ask to build your tent in the woods, or start a campfire from scratch. He wasn't fazed by a tongue-tied woman who stole letters off a grave.

I tried to relax. If I pretended this was just a small problem and even flirted a little, he might be more sympathetic. I crossed my legs awkwardly and leaned back in the chair.

He poured the hot water and began to talk as if nothing was wrong.

"I always drink two coffees in the morning—three on a Sunday. One before I leave and one when I get here. Sugar, a little cream. We've got half-and-half, okay?" He held up a single-serve creamer tub. "My six-year-old loves drinking these things. She thinks they're better than milk. Whenever she sees me making coffee, she's always like, 'Can I cremate it for you?' Uh, okay. Cremate my coffee. She doesn't know why I'm laughing when she says it. Tell her when she's older. What can you do?"

He stirred the coffees and looked at me over his shoulder. I managed a small smile as he handed me the mug. Then I pressed the warm ceramic between my fingers and took a breath.

"My best friend is out there." I stared into the brown liquid. "And you'll think this is crazy, but someone's been bothering us—me and her daughter—and I was worried that they might come back here and steal our letters."

He didn't sip his coffee. He just listened, hands folded. He didn't wear a wedding ring; his eyes were on mine.

"I couldn't sleep last night because I found something on her grave."

I began to describe Robyn's note and I could feel him watching me. He had a patient, steady gaze, and he didn't try to hurry me along. It had been a long time since I'd really unburdened myself and I started oversharing about Joyce, explaining how we visited her all the time and how important this was. When I mentioned that Callie had collapsed, he pressed his lips together. Then he shook his head like he couldn't believe the crap that people did.

"She lost both her parents, so she's already been through a lot. But imagine getting a note telling you to die like your mother."

He asked me how Joyce had died and I told him the truth, even though I'd lied to Callie for years, saying she was hit accidentally. I don't know why I told him. I didn't even know his name yet. It was like being in some kind of Neverland, weightless and dreamy, where I could drink coffee with strangers and say words like *murdered*.

"Oh, shit," he said. "The father, too?"

"No." I reached for my hair. "Curtis killed himself."

All My Interactions with Robyn Doblak, #6
For Rebecca/From Callie

Rebecca, remember last January when I told you I had to do a report on Sojourner Truth? And then I went to the library carrying a big bag full of scarves? I'd bought Robyn a little present. We didn't tell anyone we were meeting. And since nobody ever went in the library basement it was definitely the smartest place. Down there it smelled like radiator dust, old books, and baloney sandwiches. I had my Latin lessons in that basement, so I knew it would be safe. But I still had the jiggles walking in, like something bad was about to happen, even though meeting was my idea. I wanted to cheer her up.

Robyn was sitting at a table in the back, still wearing her coat and hat. I tried sneaking up behind her, but she heard my footsteps and fast breathing. "Boo," I said, swinging my bag carefully onto the table. Robyn's eyes flicked behind me like I wasn't the one she was waiting for. Or like I'd brought someone else along and was hiding them in the stacks.

"I didn't know if you were coming," she said.

"Why wouldn't I come? I told *you* to meet me."

Robyn looked down at the table, holding her head with a thumb and two fingers, like a sleepy bear who wanted to crawl back into her cave.

"So."

"Yeah."

"Cold out."

"Serious."

"I'm still shivering all over."

"Me too."

I sat down at the table, but I kept my coat on. I thought we might leave in four seconds, forget we'd done this, never talk again. She felt eerily like a stranger, but it was worse than just a stranger, because we'd shared a lot of stuff but it was so awkward, face-to-face.

Robyn pointed at my bag. "Is that my present?"

You know the saddest thing I ever heard? That story about Robyn's dad. Not how he got leukemia and died, but how he planned to be reincarnated. Imagine if he did it. He comes back to be with Robyn. Only some other weirdo gets him because she's not allowed to have a dog. I was still thinking about it at the mall, when I went there with Dallas and Ella. How Robyn's dad wanted to stay with his daughter, and how my own dad was kind of different. I ended up walking into the mall's pet store and looking at all the puppies, even though I didn't have enough cash and I knew I couldn't do it. But when I turned to leave, I saw the tank full of moving shells.

Robyn stood up beside me while I unwrapped the plastic carrying case. I'd used as many scarves as I could to keep him from getting cold. But then my stomach was clenching up because how was I supposed to tell her? I should've messaged her beforehand, pretended it was just a joke. *Here's a hermit crab, lol. Guess what? It's Papa!* It was too stupid to say in person. I looked down into his case. "Uh, yeah. For you."

I watched Robyn's eyelashes dance up and down like shiny spiders. She tapped on the plastic and he pulled in his legs.

"I thought you could call him Papa." I swallowed. "You know, instead of a dog."

The radiator clanged. She seemed to be thinking. Then she smiled and opened her hand. I lifted his chalky white shell.

"Papa," she repeated.

"Yeah, if you want to."

I pushed back her fingers so her palm was flat, and then I put him in her hand, showing her how to hold him. She giggled when his legs poked out—they were kind of crooked. Then he moved his two black antennae, like he was considering who she was. We both sat down on the floor, and Robyn let him crawl across the rug. Then she lay down on her stomach after taking off her coat. And all the weirdness got wiped away when we started to build an obstacle course. We set up books all over the floor and Papa crawled around them, and we were being sports commentators, describing his every move. "Can he do it? Can he? He's over the top!"

"Woo-hoo! Papa! The gold goes to Papa."

We were getting hyper-amused and Robyn took her boots off, then I was doing Papa's voice. I made him sound like Santa. "Robyn, have you been a good girl?"

"Oh, yes, Papa."

"You don't pee in the bathtub?"

"No, never!"

We started laughing like e-tards and eventually Papa got tired, so we put him back in his case and started sprinting up and down the aisles. Up above us people checked out books, tapped on computers, and picked out novels, but down below we were doing cartwheels, climbing chairs, and up on tables. Robyn put her hands on her hips like she was surveying her kingdom, and I could smell the scent of her scalp because she'd just pushed her hat over my head. Then I was climbing up beside her and somebody shushed us, but it was just a nobody and Robyn's head went down on my shoulder. She burrowed against me, like a dog with a pillow, except my shoulder wasn't that soft. "Ow, bony!" Then something was racing through us, and we needed to keep it going, to keep this up, as long as we could. She put my boots on her feet. I tied my scarf around her waist. We were laughing and snorting because we would never leave this basement. We'd make clothes out of paper, lick the glue off the bindings, we'd live off the crusts of sandwiches people threw under the shelves. Who needed sunlight or snow when you were queens of the basement? Robyn's eyes were sparkly and excited, and then she swooped down to check on Papa.

"You okay?"

She picked him up and let him crawl toward her wrist.

"Robyn," I said in his voice. "You don't have to miss me anymore."

She didn't look at me, and then I wished I hadn't said it. I didn't mean to make her cry. I put my hand on her arm.

"Don't you miss yours?" she asked, and I had to shake my head. Then I tried telling her something I'd almost forgotten.

"On my bus, when I was little, we drove past a graveyard every day, and all the kids would hold their breath so that the dead people couldn't come get them. If you sneezed and no one said 'bless you,' a ghost would steal your soul. And I used to dare myself to do it because I wanted to meet my dad. I did these tiny baby sneezes at first, so nobody heard me. And then I got louder and louder, but nobody came."

I shoved my hair out of my face. "Lucky it didn't work. I didn't know him at all."

Robyn was watching me sadly, her eyes like melting chocolate, and I wished we could run around again, stop being so intense. I tried being silly, pretending Papa had farted. Then I wondered out loud how it felt to live in a shell. I was just joking around, but Robyn took me seriously. She didn't say a word as she scooted behind me. Then she wrapped her arms around me, putting her chin on my shoulder. Her face was right next to mine, and I didn't try to push her off. "It feels like this," she said, and then she squeezed me tighter.

7

"I was dreaming about Autumn," Callie said, when I got home from the cemetery. She was still curled up in bed, her voice childish and sleepy.

"What?"

"I saw them kill her."

I pressed my hand against her forehead—warm but not hot—and noted the dried rheum sticking to her lashes.

"They met her at the beach. Then after they held her under, they made it look like suicide. Or an accident. Whatever. They were the ones who cleared up her stuff."

Are you asleep? I wondered. *Who are you talking about?* The events of the previous day were still fresh in my mind.

"Are you worried that Robyn's going to hurt you?"

She shook her head, mouth pinched: *this isn't about that!* But her renewed interest in a crime from the past seemed deliberately timed.

"I don't want you to worry about people hurting you," I said. "Is there anything you need to tell me?"

"I think she was being bullied and her bullies killed her."

I pictured a girl covered in paint. "Bullets!" they chanted. "Bullets!"

"You're talking about—"

"Autumn." Then she slapped her wall, exasperated. "I'm trying to remember."

Her hand hadn't left a mark, but I stared at the wall, curious. An outburst like that *wasn't* Callie.

"Hon, this isn't healthy. I don't want you worrying about Autumn. Are you bringing her up because you think *Robyn* might be dangerous?"

An extravagant eye roll, perfectly executed.

"Everyone's dangerous. Or everyone could be. You can't tell just by looking at them. People are the same as pit bulls."

I started questioning her more deeply, but I made no progress. *Why do you think she went to your mom's grave?* No clue. *How did she know where your mom's buried?* Don't know! *Did you speak to her much at school?* Almost never.

"Dallas said she was in love with you; do you think that's true?"

Callie squirmed, as always, at the mention of love.

"She just wanted to impress me, I guess."

She sounded weary of guessing and explaining Robyn's motives. I was grilling her like I didn't trust her, falling right into Robyn's trap. I realized that Robyn was smart. Sneaky and bold enough to trick a school principal, and if she'd wanted me to second-guess Callie, her note was a good way to start. Whether Robyn was dangerous or not, I had to be cautious. Callie was obviously becoming anxious, dreaming about murders and missing girls. I told her that I'd met the cemetery caretaker and he'd promised to check on Joyce's grave. Then I mentioned that I'd removed all our letters from her mother's plot.

"Why? Those are private!" She bolted up in bed.

"I know. That's why I took them, so she couldn't come back and read them."

She was shaking her head and I realized I'd made a mistake. I shouldn't have told her. She wanted her letters to stay with her mom.

"What are you going to do with them? Throw them out?"

"No, honey, they're in the glove compartment of my car."

"I just feel sick," she said, and then she slumped back down.

I let her stay home from school on Monday. I didn't think she was really sick, but I figured she'd been through a lot. If she felt safer at home, let her stay home. Baby her for a while until she perked up. I called my mother and she was repulsed when I told her about Robyn's note. "That's awful," Mom said. "She sounds insane."

I mentioned how I'd upset Callie, taking her letters off Joyce's grave, and my mom's high, scratchy voice immediately deepened with suspicion. "What's she hiding? I would read those if I were you."

It wasn't unusual for my mother to be paranoid about everything. She was always searching for hidden motives in ordinary behavior. Flowers meant he cheated; a lost wallet meant a gambling problem. But Callie had a right to privacy when writing to her mother. I imagined her letters were heartbreakingly honest, raw, and sad. I wouldn't want people reading the things I wrote to Joyce, either.

"I used to read your diaries," Mom said coolly.

"No, you didn't."

"Oh, yes, I did. How else would I know about all your little crushes?"

She said this with such gleeful pride that I almost put the phone down. She seemed to find the memory hilarious: spying on me, the love-struck teen.

"And I knew this lady," Mom was saying, "who had a sixteen-year-old daughter, straight-A student, never gave her any problems. So one day she sees this e-mail, she'd left it open on the computer, and it turns out the girl was secretly working as a prostitute."

"That was a TV show, Mom," I said, disgusted. "This is exactly why I don't tell you anything."

"That's why I had to read your diary," she said. "You never tell me anything."

I offered to make Callie's favorite for dinner that night—macaroni and cheese—and when it was ready, she came into the kitchen and began plucking the dying blooms off the bunch of chrysanthemums I'd put in a pottery jug. We sat down to eat and she started goofing around. She got cheese on the sleeve of her bathrobe and sucked it off: "Yummy!" Then when I went to get some paper towels, she started sucking the ends of her hair. "Cheese hair," she said. She took the paper towel, dabbed her sleeve, and then, without taking her eyes off of me, licked the paper towel. "Mmm. Good cheese." She looked at me and started to giggle, and maybe I should've been irritated, but her giggles were contagious. I watched as she picked up her water, tried to take a sip, and nearly spit it all out on the table. I put down my fork as tears seeped out of my eyes; it was the first time we'd laughed since we'd read Robyn's note. She was feeling well enough to fool around, and every time our giggles diminished into sighs, she caught my eye and made soft, encouraging puffs through her nose.

"You weren't really sick, were you?" I asked.

An hour later, she threw up in the bathroom.

I made an appointment to take her to the doctor after work on Tuesday. I knew it was probably just a stomach bug, but I was starting to worry. "I think it's just the flu," she said, drooping. "I just need rest." I needed rest, too, but my mind circled endlessly. I thought about Cerise and Robyn Doblak. Then about Autumn and Lara and Joyce. I wasn't sure if I'd done the right thing, explaining Joyce's death to the man at the cemetery. He'd shaken my hand before I left, giving my fingers a fast squeeze, and I'd felt his calluses against my palm as he told me his name. Danny, he'd said. I blushed, giving him my phone number. He said he'd call me with an update, and I'd been waiting to hear his voice. He was no gateway man, of course. Unless your gate led to a cemetery. Or a place smaller than ours that probably smelled of sloppy joes. Okay, that was snobby. Who knew what foods Danny liked? I bet he'd enjoy my fritters—I'd been working on them all September. I was just starting to get the batter right, and the potato ones had been amazing: fluffy and crisp, not falling apart at all.

Now the idea gripped me. I would bring fritters to Danny's office. I could say I was just checking in on Joyce, and that I'd wanted to thank him. Not sweet fritters, though. Something savory. Forget pineapple and orange; he'd enjoy something with spice. I started whipping up the batter as I imagined finding him in the cemetery, following him to the stone building, slowly unzipping my jacket. I knew I couldn't have a boyfriend; I needed to focus on Callie. But my fantasy continued, and I began to feed him fritters. His lips opened. His eyes were sleepy and serious. And then he chewed and swallowed, his teeth brushing against my hands.

My phone rang while I was waiting in the doctor's office the next day. Callie had gone in to see Dr. Bishop alone, and I was nervously tugging my arm hair. She never usually saw her doctor without me, but now she'd decided that she was old enough. Fourteen years old, she could handle this herself. I felt like a cook who's been banned from her own kitchen, imagining pots boiling over, and it took all my strength not to burst through the door. Of course Callie would be fine, but she might not tell him everything. He might ask the wrong questions. I might've had something to add. It took willpower to remain seated calmly, but my help wasn't needed. Then my phone was ringing and I heard a man's voice.

"Is this Rebecca?"

I actually smiled. I felt unexpectedly buoyant. Children were playing on the floor, clacking beads on an old-fashioned toy.

"It's Danny, from the cemetery," he said, as if I wouldn't remember. "I don't want to freak you out."

"No," I said, encouragingly. I don't know what I thought—that he'd actually ask me on a date? That he just wanted to say hello?

"I found something," he said. "You're not going to like this."

I brought latex gloves and Ziploc bags to the cemetery. I'd dropped Callie home first. I ended my call with Danny just as she came out of Dr. Bishop's office. She was smiling and laughing at something the doctor had said. "I'm okay," she mouthed to me. Then Dr. Bishop explained about the viral gastroenteritis. She hadn't thrown up that day, so she could return to school tomorrow. I told her I had to run a quick errand and then I sped over to Cansdown.

Danny met me at the cemetery. He'd found the note under Joyce's stone when he checked that afternoon. Robyn must've pushed down with her red pen, almost ripping holes through the page.

> Nobody cares or understands me on this fucked-up planet and what if I wasn't meant to be here and everyone saw I was a mistake? Every day I walk around listening to them laugh and laugh and all of us know that I should be dead. I was a shitty mistake and I'm ready to be erased. I want to look up and the sky will be DIRT!

Danny cocked his head to one side, so he could see me under the brim of his cap. There were sweat stains under his arms, and his body radiated heat. Blood rose to my cheeks like a trigger had been pulled.

"They told me she was in love with Callie."

"I didn't even see her here."

"She must be getting desperate, trying to get our attention."

Danny shuffled his boots against the grass and leaned close to my shoulder, looking at the note.

"It sounds—real."

"I know. She must want it to."

"You don't think it's a cry for help?"

"I think she wants Callie to feel guilty, like it's her fault. This girl is manipulative. Who knows how she's really feeling."

Danny took a step back, moving away from my shoulder. Nice. I sounded like an asshole, discrediting a suicidal child.

"You gotta take something like this seriously, though, just in case. Kids end up doing stuff, spur of the moment."

I wondered if Robyn knew anything about Callie's father. If she did, this was even crueler. She wanted to disturb her in a way that hit home.

"I'll call her mother," I said, placing one hand on Danny's arm. "I'll let her know we're worried. But I just get the feeling she's playing with us, like this is all part of some game."

All My Interactions with Robyn Doblak, #7
For Rebecca/From Callie

The only way I can really explain it is like with symbiosis, like how in science we learned about the microbes that live on our bodies. There's like 100 trillion of them—on our eyelashes and skin and in our mouths and stomachs—and it's like having all these secret lives growing inside us. They need us to survive and we need them, but we can't ever see them, nobody else knows they're there. That's how I think it was with Robyn and me. When we went back to school in January we didn't start hanging out. We didn't sit together in the cafeteria or wait for each other outside our classes. Robyn stayed with her group and I stayed with mine, but sometimes we caught each other's eye and smiled for a second.

We still talked every night, telling each other stuff nobody else knew. Her dad. My mom. The lives we wanted to have. I would become an ecologist and Robyn would be a famous blogger and we would share an apartment and adopt lots of dogs. Then when we were old we'd move to a nursing home and sit together on rocking chairs, until we both died on the very same day.

IM Jan 22 2009 15:16:21

15:06:41

robynroarxo: Can't stop thinking about you today

15:06:55

LithoCALpus: How many times?

15:07:28

robynroarxo: Probably over 1000 . . . when my alarm clock went off, when I opened my blinds, when I saw the sky, when I brushed my teeth . . . calliecalliecallie

15:08:31

LithoCALpus: 🙂 I thought about you too

15:08:40

robynroarxo: ?

15:09:24

LithoCALpus: You were kind of in my dream last night. We were sleeping under a tree, and you were holding my hand, and when I woke up my hand was open like you'd just let go.

15:13:18

robynroarxo: ♥ ♥ ♥ I wouldn't let go.

15:13:40

LithoCALpus: ((Squeeze))

15:14:00

robynroarxo: Not. Letting. Go.

15:14:25

robynroarxo: I wish you were here right now.

15:14:30

LithoCALpus: I wish that too.

15:14:49

robynroarxo: If you put your hand on my heart you wouldn't believe how fast it's running.

15:14:59

LithoCALpus: I believe it. I can hear it.

15:15:12

robynroarxo: It's saying I ♥ u.

15:15:45

robynroarxo: I really feel it Callie.

15:15:58

LithoCALpus: I know. Me too.

8

"Is this a joke?" Cerise Doblak said, after I'd read her the note over the phone that night. "That doesn't sound like Robyn at all."

"It was written in *red ink*," I said. "Choppy writing on a pink-lined paper."

"So?"

"It's not the first note she's left for Callie."

Then I had to tell her about the threat we'd found over the weekend.

"Oh, give me a break. You're accusing her of threatening *Callie* now?"

"Who else would still be blaming her for the red paint in class?"

"And how would Robyn even get there? How'd she find the cemetery that you guys go to?"

"Maybe someone told her," I said. "But the point is she needs help. I wouldn't have called you unless I was worried. I know we're not friends, but I'm sincerely concerned."

"Sure, like you cared so much before. When I called *you* up about what Callie had done, you *really* seemed to care."

"If it was me, I'd want someone to tell me if Callie was in Robyn's situation. I'd be grateful to have a chance to get her some help."

"Yeah, I'm really grateful," Cerise sniped. "Very grateful. Thanks so much!"

"Not everyone gets a warning," I said. "Not everyone finds out in time—and if Robyn's depressed, this could be a cry for help."

"There's no way Robyn would leave a cry for help with you."

After we hung up, I wondered if she was right. Maybe Robyn wasn't suicidal. Maybe Cerise knew her daughter so well that she was right to blow off my warning. But it seemed negligent and hardheaded for her to ignore even a sliver of possibility. If she was wrong, God forbid, imagine how she'd feel.

"Rebecca!" Callie said. "Where'd you go?"

She hadn't knocked, and she stood in the doorway of my room, her hair dripping shower water onto her shoulders. She looked at the plastic bag in my hand. The pink lines and red ink were visible. I slipped it behind my back, but she'd already seen.

"Did she come back?"

"Has Robyn been in touch with you?"

"No—is that?" She took a step forward, but I wasn't going to let her read it.

"The good news is she hasn't threatened you," I said, opening a drawer and shutting the note away. "Robyn's just depressed. That's all she wrote about."

"Depressed? Like how?" Callie gaped at me, curious.

"I don't know if she really means it. She might just want attention. But either way, I let her mom know."

Callie's eyes lit on mine. "What did her mom say?"

"I think she was confused. Hopefully she'll talk to Robyn tonight."

Callie squeezed the water out of her hair and watched it trickling down her arm. "What if she can't be helped?"

"I think—" I paused. "I think everyone can be helped."

"Maybe her life's hopeless and she knows it can't be good."

I wondered if Callie was thinking of her father. We'd never fully explained his death to her. All the counselors advised us to say that Curtis had been "sad." It wasn't a lie, exactly, it just omitted nearly everything. And in retrospect is seemed a little reckless, telling *that* to a child. Like being sad was actually dangerous, a precursor to death.

"Lots of people *feel* hopeless, but none of them are truly hopeless," I told her. "And when people give you a warning it's because they want help."

"Maybe she'll drown herself."

I looked at her, standing there in her shortie pajamas. Her knees were bare. Her mouth was flat. "Why would you say that?"

"Like Autumn." Callie looked at me and I was sorry I'd told her. She was getting sucked into tragedies that had nothing to do with her. She hardly knew Robyn, and neither of us knew Autumn, but both girls' stories had a powerful pull. I sat Callie down on my bed and told her that life was never as bad as people imagined. But when someone was depressed things seemed worse than they were. "It's like wearing goggles that made everything look crappy," I said, and then Callie told me about a movie where the bad guy was depressed. It didn't occur to me until later that she'd changed her opinion on Autumn. She'd stopped wondering if she was murdered, and now accepted that it was suicide.

Some said that Autumn Sanger killed herself after breaking up with her boyfriend. Others whispered she'd had an abortion and did it out of guilt. As for me, I sometimes wondered whether she'd been playing at sorrow like we had, acting out the dramatic scenes that had popped into her head.

In my mind, Autumn's death would be forever linked to Lara. To a kind of nostalgic yearning I felt when I saw her with my cousin. I was a yearner, I wanted to go back, to excavate our old friendship. But Lara was resolute; she wouldn't trust me again. She'd become distant and clipped as if I were the dreariest kind of stranger. And when I tried to apologize she stared right through me. I was a rat, a flea. Something she didn't have time for. Yet it seemed impossible to me that our connection could have vaporized, leaving no visible mark on our bodies, no trace of feelings once shared.

"You've still got me," Joyce said. "Why do you care about Lara?"

Joyce had remained my best friend and my biggest influence. More than my mother, or my aunt, or even my cousin. The best way I can explain it is to describe a game we used to play as children. Aged twelve, we sat face-to-face, moving in tandem, anticipating each other's next move. When Joyce pushed her hair back with her left hand, I did the same with my right, her own mirror image. Together we scrunched our eyebrows, stuck out our tongues, wiggled our fingers, and pressed the soles of our feet together until we could sense the tiniest twitch coming, the moment before it happened, like we were each other's truer selves. Even in high school we changed in sync, becoming less silly and impulsive. We turned practical-minded together, studying for the SATs. We planned out careers, wrote college essays, applied to the same universities. Me following her and her following me. Occasionally, when I watched Joyce wrapping her arms around some boy's waist, or leaning her chin against his shoulder, there was a moment when I felt a little lost. Then she would catch my eye and raise one eyebrow, like this was just another game we were both playing, and I'd loosen up and turn to the boy I was with. I might touch his arm for a moment, or laugh a little at whatever he was saying, feeling safe that I was keeping up with her. Joyce wouldn't leave me behind.

By the time I left for college, Curtis was engaged to Lara, and when I came home after my freshman year, their wedding was only six months away. I believed my hyacinth-girl days were long past, all those childish heroics, but then I started picturing scenarios where Lara and I would reunite. She would lose her engagement ring and I would find it. She'd break down on the highway and I'd give her a ride. Or I'd be held up at gunpoint and Lara would call the police, standing by the door as they came rushing in. Afterward our eyes would meet, victim and savior, everything forgiven, our connection sparking back to life.

It was nothing so sensational in the end. I had gone to their apartment to visit Curtis. My cousin was still in the dark uniform that made him look like a cop: black acrylic pants, serious-looking belt, short-sleeved shirt with a badge sewn over the pocket. He'd been a courthouse security guard for three years since graduating high school, and he was telling me a story about a man who'd tried to bring a weapon into court. "It was a custody case," he said. "And this big dude sets off the detector coming in. He was old—probably thirties—going a little bald on top." Curtis smiled, swiping his hand over his own undiminished hair. "So I'm standing there, about to ask if he's got anything in his pockets, when he reaches his hand in like this." Curtis mimed a quick little grab into his pocket. "And pulls out—I shit you not—a five-inch metal shank."

"He's holding it out like he's thinking what to do next—like maybe it would be a good idea to stick it right in my chest—and I'm all FUCK, because my boy Andre's in the bathroom, it's just me, got one hand on my baton, ready to go whoosh BAM, smack it right out of his hand, but at the same time I'm acting all laid-back, like I don't even realize something's wrong, and I go, 'Sir, would you please put your weapon in the tray?'"

Lara had come in as he told this story. She was drinking a glass of iced tea.

"And this dude," Curtis continued, "he drops it right away. He just drops the thing in the rubber tray, like it's a set of frickin' keys or something."

Curtis shook his head. "It's a custody case and you're gonna bring a shank to court? What you gonna do, stab *me* to get your kids back?"

"He didn't get custody, right?" I asked breathlessly, and Curtis reassured me he hadn't.

Maybe I'd struck just the right note. Of concern and sincerity. Or enough time had passed that old wounds had started to heal. Lara asked if I wanted an iced tea. And then she gave me a coaster. A week later, unprompted, she started telling me about their wedding. I peppered her with questions, tentative and excited, and she told me about the Christmas theme and the white fur stole she'd wear around her shoulders.

"You're as giddy as a schoolgirl," Joyce said when I told her. "I don't know what you're hoping for."

She thought Lara was using me to get in better with my family. But my aunt already liked Lara more than me, so I knew that Joyce was wrong. I tried explaining why Lara's friendship meant so much to me, but then I started talking about Autumn, and my ideas got all mixed up. If Autumn hadn't killed herself, and she'd really been kidnapped, we wouldn't have acted out those scenes, and I wouldn't have hurt Lara. There would be no funeral to come home from, and Lara wouldn't see me stuttering. I wouldn't have discovered that I was cruel, and all five of us would've stayed friends. Joyce, Lara, Curtis, me, and Autumn, too, maybe.

"That's pretty far-fetched," Joyce said.

"Don't you regret what happened?"

"The only thing I regret is that she's marrying your cousin."

Joyce's crush on Curtis had become a joke. When we'd run into him at the seawall in July, Joyce pretended she was going to get arrested so she could visit him in court. She started calling him Officer Meathead, Officer Friendly, and Curtis laughed and narrowed his eyes like he was trying to see something almost invisible. But then he said he had to get going. Lara was waiting at home.

I thought it was still a joke. That's why I didn't believe her when she showed up at the convenience store where I was working an afternoon shift.

"Something big," Joyce said, leaning on her elbows across the counter. "Me and Curtis."

The coffeepot gurgled, and I could hear cars and trucks rushing by on the highway outside.

"Hooked up."

I stared at the small brown birthmark below her eyelashes.

"No, you didn't."

Joyce cocked an eyebrow and said she'd called him up. They'd gone for a drive in his car. Then he'd put a blanket in the backseat.

I did a little karate chop on her arm. "Bullshit."

The bell above the door jangled, and Joyce picked up a Twinkie, moving to one side while I printed out lottery tickets for a customer. She had to be lying. It was the same as if she'd walked in and claimed she'd smoked crack and it was so amazing. The person I'd known as Joyce would not have done this thing. It had to be another joke, a test to see how I'd react.

She said they'd done it in the backseat. Twice. Lara thought he was out with friends.

"Oh, really," I said.

"Afterwards, he took me up to the roof of the snack bar—at the beach. He pulled me up so we could see the stars."

The pain in my legs was sudden, almost thrilling. It shot up into my thighs, a needling prickly heat, making me want to stamp my feet against the linoleum floor. Joyce dropped the Twinkie back onto the plastic rack, and I realized she'd been telling the truth. I scuffled my hot feet back and forth, and forced myself to look at her. Then I wanted to slap her.

"You're so selfish," I said.

Joyce did a little double take, like maybe she'd just heard me wrong. She looked like a girl I'd never met before, with a very pink face. I wondered how much redder her skin would become after I'd smacked it.

"I thought you'd be happy for me."

"It's wrong, Joyce!"

I picked up the Windex spray I'd left on the counter and began to squirt it in cool little bursts. I'd been with Lara the night before. She was showing me flower arrangements. White roses and holly berries: very wintery and elegant. I'd been dreading the moment when she stuttered, nervous about how we'd both react to it, as if the memory of my performance six years ago would come rushing back. Lara was talking about juniper boughs when she suddenly clamped her mouth shut. I recognized the signs, but I didn't hesitate or act uncomfortable. Instead I jumped in calmly to complete her thought. *It'll be so festive with all the red ribbons.* And Lara nodded like I'd just read her mind.

"What about Lara?" I hissed at Joyce. "Did you ever think about her?"

"Come on. Be serious. She's not your real friend."

I shuddered and then started to shiver. The air-conditioning was suddenly freezing on my hot skin, and I considered sitting down behind the counter, peeling off my sneakers and boiling socks, waiting for her to leave. When I was with Lara I felt redeemed. I was flattered that she wanted to confide in me. She was so adult and yet still vulnerable, and I wished I'd explained this to Joyce. I was sure if she'd just understood, she wouldn't have done this. I started to rub the counter fiercely, ripping off paper towels. Why did she have to tell me? Why involve me? Because she knew I'd choose her over Lara—I'd have to join in her betrayal. But if Joyce and Curtis were falling in love, where would that leave me? I'd be alone, trailing behind, never able to catch up. I'd lose all three of them; they were already miles away.

Suddenly I was scared to look at Joyce. I knew her blond hair was escaping from her ponytail in the humidity, and without looking I could've traced her profile, the tilt of her nose, the roundness of her lips, using my finger on the Formica counter. If I lost her—if I was losing her—it was worse than I imagined. More painful than wasp stings and lonelier than being buried alive. I couldn't live. I'd stop breathing. I'd lose everything without her. If she and Curtis were in love, I'd die. I'd die.

Joyce's voice rose. "Are you jealous or something?"

I clamped my teeth down to keep them from chattering, and when I opened my mouth again I told her to get out of the store.

We didn't talk for four weeks. I missed her every second, and there was never a question in my mind about what I had to do. As much as I cared about Lara, Joyce was a part of me. I decided that I wouldn't lie to Lara, but I couldn't tell her the truth, either. I'd just have to avoid her, ending our friendship. I never wrote Lara a note or gave her any explanation. I simply slipped away, making myself absent, and when she came looking for me, I was already long gone. It hurt more than I'd expected, like throwing a part of myself in the ocean. A part I'd only just recovered, and had wanted to keep safe. I didn't know if Lara was sad, furious, or merely indifferent. I never said good-bye to her. In that way, I was just like Autumn.

* * *

"Do you think I should call the police?"

"Yeah, maybe," Danny said. "I don't know. Sounds extreme."

I called Danny after talking to Robyn's mother. I wanted to let him know that I was taking this seriously. He'd been right to be concerned, it was the mark of a sympathetic person, and I wanted him to think that I was sympathetic, too.

"I bet Cerise would be horrified if the police showed up at her house."

"Mmm. Not cool."

"But maybe she just doesn't get it," I said. "She doesn't remember how it feels. At that age, when you get lost, it's like the end of the world."

We talked for a while about my responsibility. I said if my neighbor's house was on fire I'd call the fire department, even if my neighbor had told me she had it under control. I'd need to make sure that the fire didn't spread, and I wouldn't feel safe until all the flames were out. But Danny thought it was different, not like a fire at all. He said if I saw a kid playing with matches, I'd let their parents know. But it would be way too early to call 911. He thought I should give Cerise a chance to deal with the problem. Then he said if Robyn was his daughter, he'd be questioning her right now. And I realized I was interrupting bedtime—I'd forgotten he had kids.

"They live with my ex," he said. Then he started telling me what happened. He came home from work one day last spring and all their things were gone. His life had been ripped apart. His girlfriend left him without a word, and she moved his son and daughter more than a hundred miles away. He saw them twice a month, which really wasn't enough. I pictured him sitting at a dreary table, empty chairs on either side of him. "I try talking to them on the phone, but they're only little," he said gloomily. "They want to hang up on me after only two seconds."

"Well, I don't want to hang up," I said, and then we talked for almost an hour.

The next morning, Callie got up for school on time without me having to bang on her door. I could hear the shower running, then her hair dryer, and when she came into the kitchen she looked exactly the way she used to. She wore makeup and her stretchy red jeans; her shirt was one of the new ones we'd picked out at the mall over the summer. She ate a bowl of cereal without complaining that she felt sick, and then rinsed it out before leaving for school. Every detail confirmed that she was back to normal— and if I felt any concerns about Robyn, I pushed them away.

But as I worked through my morning hygiene appointments, I started wondering about Cerise Doblak. When she called me last April, she said that Robyn came home crying every day. She had *known* Robyn was unhappy. She'd pulled her out of school because of it. Robyn had confided in her mother about what was going on. The bullying, the names, the comments about her chest. If Robyn was depressed, wouldn't her mother know? Wouldn't she make an effort to get her some kind of help? I couldn't figure it out, and I became snappish as the day went on. Then a little girl with severe tooth decay was sitting in my office.

The girl was four years old, wearing a Dora the Explorer T-shirt. Her mom looked up from her phone, exclaiming, "Oops, just baby teeth!" And I started trying to explain how it could affect her permanent teeth. The decay could spread; it could cause an abscess. The mom glazed over like she couldn't care less and I thought of Cerise Doblak, and suddenly I was irate.

"You need to supervise her when she brushes!"

"I do! I supervise!"

"Nobody else can do this! She's your responsibility!"

Splotches of red appeared on her neck. Her daughter's mouth was a tiny *o,* and I could picture this girl at fourteen: teeth crooked, gums inflamed. Tongue thick with bacteria and her mother still shrugging. "Oops! Oops!" I didn't mean to be so judgmental. But there were parents out there who really *couldn't* guide their children. Joyce, Danny. What would they give to be there each evening, ushering their kids into the bathroom and reminding them to brush? Looking back, I could've been calmer, more understanding of the mom in my office. I might gently ask her about juice before bed, suggest a reduction of sugary snacks. But she seemed so unconcerned and I blazed with self-righteous anger. I couldn't yet see that in many ways we were just the same.

Dr. Rick must've heard me ranting. He swept in like a jolly old uncle. "Rebecca?" he said. "Everything okay?"

Dr. Rick was in his late fifties, sported a year-round Bermuda tan, and snapped off his gloves with a sharp pop at the end of each examination. He always exclaimed at how beautiful our female patients were and sometimes offered up his cheek for a kiss; with the men, he was jocular and familiar—even if it was a patient's first appointment. In a bad economy, he did what he could.

"Rebecca been treating you nice?" Dr. Rick asked, rubbing the little girl's curls.

I was excused from the remainder of the appointment. The incident would be recorded in my personnel file. And as I left, I started mumbling a dozen apologies. *Sorrysorrysorry*, like I was the oblivious parent. *Sorrysorrysorry*, like I understood how these things could happen. *Sorrysorrysorry*, like I'd be sorrying that afternoon, when I got the call from Callie's school and heard about the chocolate.

Callie was being suspended for two days. I locked myself in the staff bathroom and listened to Callie's principal describe how Callie had sworn at her social studies teacher before running out of class. "She used the F-word," Mr. Wattis said. "She told Miss Laing to 'Eff off.'" Callie had run out of the building, and attempted to leave school grounds before getting stopped by a gym teacher. And before any of this happened, she'd smeared a bar of chocolate across her desk.

"Chocolate?"

"Yes," Mr. Wattis said. "It was very messy."

He told me that the outburst was unprovoked, as if she went around swearing like this regularly. As if she was one of those kids who threw eggs at the neighbors. I didn't argue this time around. I didn't ask if he had the right Callie. I didn't bring up her science awards, or her time on the honor roll. I wanted every fact and detail. I needed to understand what was happening. If someone was really framing her, I needed evidence first.

All My Interactions with Robyn Doblak, #8
For Rebecca/From Callie

One day in art class, Robyn wiggled her eyebrows and held out her wrist. She was wearing a pit-bull-awareness wristband, the same as mine. Another time she was passing out watercolors and she said my name when she got to my table. Then she held out my paper and looked in my eyes like she was waiting. Online I could do it. I was weightless and floaty. I could leap over clouds and skip over mountains. But with Ella sitting next to me, I knew it was impossible. I felt like I'd die if I moved an inch. I stared down at my hands and then Robyn dropped my paper and Ella was like, "Total dicksplash."

IM Jan 28 2009 19:40:28

19:34:02

robynroarxo: It's because of your friends right?

19:35:12

LithoCALpus: It's not just them. I don't want everything to be different.

19:36:16

robynroarxo: But it IS different so it's stupid pretending we don't know each other. I want us to be real. I want to be WITH you at school.

19:36:31

LithoCALpus: i think it was better before

19:37:39

robynroarxo: Before we knew each other!

19:37:58

LithoCALpus: That's not what I mean . . .

19:38:13

robynroarxo: What then?

19:38:54

LithoCALpus: 🙂 I just want to keep talking to you like this.

19:39:19

robynroarxo: But you're somebody else at school. You won't even say hi.

19:39:24

LithoCALpus: I can't. OK?

19:39:49

robynroarxo: If ppl have a problem they're not your real friends. You're not like them anyway. You should be who you are.

19:40:28

LithoCALpus: 🤐 Let me think about it. Don't pressure me.

Then, I think it was in February. I don't know what happened. It was like one day she just decided that everything had to change. Robyn was standing in the cafeteria breakfast line when I came in with my friends. We'd been doing our morning rounds, passing our phones back and forth, smudging lipstick on each other's shoulders. We skipped and hollered, smacking each other's butts, and the last thing I expected was that Robyn would wave.

"Callie," she called. "I've got Papa with me."

She wore a purple nylon bag around her wrist, and it swung tipsily as she waved at me. She pointed at the bag. "Papa," she said.

Dallas gave me a little shove. "Is she talking to you? Did she just say Papa?"

Ella lifted her head from Dallas's arm. "Isn't her dad dead?"

Robyn slowly dropped her hand when she realized I wasn't coming over.

9

That evening, as she went over her story, Callie picked at the edge of a throw pillow. We were sitting in the living room, and I'd set out a plate of banana fritters that neither of us wanted to touch. She was lying to me. She was slumped across the sofa while I sat in an armchair, watching the teal fibers of my pillow unravel in her hands.

"I had to go to the bathroom. So I just ran out." Her voice was dry, coagulated.

"But you ran out of the school. You didn't run to the bathroom."

"I got lost."

"How could you confuse an exit with the bathroom?"

Callie closed her eyes and wiggled a finger inside the pillow. Something heavy, like black weather, seemed to enclose her and at the same time block me out.

"Did Miss Laing say something to upset you?"

"No."

She dipped her head, refused to meet my eyes. I'd already asked if someone had put her up to it. I'd even wondered aloud if she was getting her period. Callie pulled a small tuft of white filling out of the pillow.

"Tell me again about the chocolate," I prompted.

Callie stared at the white fibers in her hand. "The chocolate was already there when I came in."

"Well, do you think one of Robyn's friends could've left it? That girl Lucinda?"

She gave a small puff of exasperation. "No, Rebecca."

"Well, how do you know for sure—if you don't know who?"

She didn't answer and I had the sudden urge to shake her. I wasn't handling this well. Everything she said made me feel more hopeless. It was like we were trapped in a maze of hedges and she was leading me farther and farther from the exit, choosing wrong turns on purpose, pretending to be as disoriented as me.

"You needed to go to the bathroom—fine," I said. "Maybe you weren't feeling well. But why on earth would that make you swear at your teacher?"

Callie started scratching her thin arms. I watched as her nails left chalky tracks across her skin.

"I don't know." She stared at the lines on her arms. "It just popped out."

"Nothing just pops out. Callie, you know how to control yourself. And you're allowed to make mistakes, but this isn't like you."

The pillow fell off her lap as she suddenly leaned forward. "Stop pressing that."

I looked down at my right hand. It rested just below my clavicle. My tattoo was hidden under my shirt, but she knew it was there. A purple hyacinth, in honor of her mother. "You're always doing that," she exploded. "It's like I'm giving you a heart attack. But I know what you're thinking."

I dropped my hand to my lap and held it there. Her lips drew back with disgust, and then she jumped up and stomped into the kitchen. "I'm not like my mom! Maybe I'm more like *him*!"

I followed her into the kitchen and watched as she turned on the faucet. She stood in front of the sink with her arms crossed over her stomach. We didn't usually talk about Curtis—she hadn't brought him up in years. She flinched oddly when I touched her on the shoulder.

"What's going on?"

Callie jabbed her fingers under the water, and it spattered against the sink. "I smashed the chocolate because I wanted to. Not everyone does things for a reason. Sometimes we just DON'T have a conscience."

"You have a conscience," I murmured. "Your dad did, too."

She wrenched the water off, and I could see her hand wobble. "You never leave me alone," she said. "I just want to be left alone."

She ran to her bedroom and I followed her there. She jumped into bed with her shoes on and pulled up the blankets so I couldn't see her face. I steadied myself.

"What made you say you don't have a conscience?"

She didn't answer.

"If you heard something about your dad, you should tell me, because it might not be true."

The mass of blankets didn't move and I felt so desperate. To connect to her again. To insist she had it wrong. She was all I had in the world, and I'd sworn I'd do anything for her, but where was I supposed to begin when she wanted only to be left alone?

The next day, Callie's principal held his office door open for us and wore a careful fixed expression that seemed to discourage friendly chitchat. His hair was thinning and he shook my hand before motioning for us to sit. The last time I'd seen Mr. Wattis was during a prospective parents' evening when he'd given a speech about the extraordinary number of graduating students who went on to top-tier colleges. I'd leaned over to squeeze

Callie's arm that night, thinking about the future, when she'd open her acceptance letters and we'd drive through the college gates, marveling at the immaculate stone buildings, the trailing vines of ivy. I'd never anticipated that we would be sitting here like a pair of troublemakers, absorbing Mr. Wattis's stern gaze.

He asked Callie to explain what happened in class, and she kept her eyes on her lap as she began to speak in a low, unconvincing voice. She repeated the same story she'd told me, only now she claimed she'd dropped the chocolate. She said it had fallen on her desk and she'd smeared it accidentally. It wasn't a prank, just an accident. Her chin drooped toward her chest, and her shoulders slumped. Without meaning to, I began to imitate her posture, and when I realized, I straightened my neck and pushed my shoulders back. I could feel Mr. Wattis watching me, and I wondered how often kids lied to his face.

I realized I was going to have to tell Joyce's dad. He'd agreed to pass guardianship to me when he was at his lowest point, eight years earlier. He'd lost his wife and daughter, he was overwhelmed, and there I was, acting like an expert. I'd been helping Joyce to raise Callie for two years at that point, and I swept in to help him like I was some kind of authority on raising children. *This* is how you get her dressed in the morning—*this* is what you do when she won't eat her breakfast. He didn't understand that I was only just practicing the things that Joyce had taught me. He'd thought that when it came to Callie, I was instinctive and naturally skilled, and I let him think this, even though I knew it wasn't true.

"I got lost," Callie said. "I was trying to find the bathroom, but I ran outside instead."

Mr. Wattis glanced at me sharply.

"I was about to go back in when I saw where I was," Callie said. "But then that guy grabbed me and brought me in here."

She looked so hopeless and bewildered. I thought of how other parents in Pembury defended their children. They weren't shy about challenging authorities on their kids' behalf.

"She's never had problems like this before," I interrupted. "But there's a few things you should know."

They both looked at me as I felt the burden of what I had to do.

"Her mother passed away." I looked Mr. Wattis in the eye. "And we just marked the ninth anniversary this weekend. We've both been upset, and I don't mean this as an excuse, but I think it's a factor."

Callie was leaning forward, and I noticed that her jaw was stiff. "You forgot my dad," she said. "My dad's dead, too." There was a taunting lilt to her voice, like this was a challenge, and then she sat back in her chair, crossed her arms, and glared at the wall.

Mr. Wattis cleared his throat, and I heard myself trying to explain.

"Both of Callie's parents passed away. Her father was my cousin. I'm her guardian."

The principal fixed his mouth in a sympathetic shape and I realized that he already knew. All this stuff was in Callie's school records. She glowered at the wall, and Mr. Wattis began to explain about a behavior contract, and I felt dazed as I realized that I shouldn't have mentioned Joyce. Her death wasn't a lucky charm to be flashed in times of trouble. It wasn't something I could whip out to show off to strangers. It wouldn't win us sympathy, and Callie's punishment was going to stand. Two days of "in-school" suspension. A written apology for Miss Laing.

Afterward, in the car, I didn't say a word to her. I just fastened my seat belt and wished that I was alone. I wanted to forget about everything and think about my future kitchen, which would have stained oak floorboards and Japanese knives on a sleek magnetic strip. There would be pots of herbs on the windowsill: basil, parsley, cilantro. And every wall would be shiny white, covered in subway tile. Callie had shoved her fingers into the air vent. Her voice demanded attention.

"You love telling everyone about Mom, but never Dad. Was he so evil?"

I'd keep a whole shelf of artisan honey, tiny pots of jam.

"Rebecca!"

"Of course not."

"Is it because he killed himself?"

I shook my head. Glass cake stands.

"Did he kill her?" She chewed her lip angrily, and I tasted blood, too. The spotless kitchen vanished. "Did he kill my mom?"

After Joyce's confession, I avoided Curtis as well as Lara. But in the last week of August, Curtis walked into the convenience store, where I was finishing my shift. My cousin's adolescent strut had turned into something more solid and purposeful, and I noticed how droplets of rain had stained the shoulders of his T-shirt. It had been pouring outside for hours, and beads of water stood out on his stubbled cheeks. As he stood before me, his skin looked green in the artificial light.

His voice cracked. "You know about Joyce—"

I nodded and looked at the sleek black hair plastered to his forehead.

"I need to talk to you."

I followed him out to his car the way I imagined a hostage might follow her deranged kidnapper. The sodium lights in the parking lot lit up the diagonals of rain, and we sat there with the windshield wipers going, even though we weren't driving anywhere. There was a cool dampness in the car, the smell of wet hair and leather shoes, and I dared myself to look in the backseat. But the wipers were like magic wands, bewitching me, sweeping away the rain so I could watch the line of red brake lights on the raised highway.

"I gotta know," Curtis murmured. "Is Joyce sleeping with anyone else?"

I combed my fingers through my dripping hair, twisting it around my fingers. The wipers waved at me, pausing and then rising smoothly. It was strange, just the two of us again, sharing secrets. I could feel Curtis waiting for me to speak and I knew how Lara must feel, testing tongue behind teeth, sorting out breath and sound while he watched so alertly.

"Do you love her?"

"Joyce?" He sounded surprised. "No, man, no. I just fucked up."

Curtis's knee began to judder and I looked down to see the place where his bones met.

"It was a mistake. I never cheated on Lara before 'cause she'd kill me. That's what her dad did to her mom and it's the worst thing I could ever do to her. I love her. You know I wouldn't do that, but it was just a mistake. One time."

I felt an awful relief hearing that he didn't love Joyce.

"So you know what Joyce's saying," he continued. "I don't know if she's making this up—to get back at me or what—but she's saying I got her pregnant."

I opened the car door and the rain started coming through. I could hear the rush of traffic, the nice fresh wetness of getting away. I needed to get out of there, but Curtis was leaning over my lap, pulling the door closed. He wrapped his fingers around my sleeve like he was on a tilting boat, and I looked at the backseat. It was empty and cramped. I couldn't imagine Joyce lying there naked. But I knew she wouldn't make up a pregnancy. "Rebecca?" His voice was still tense.

Joyce hadn't slept with anyone else, not since February.

"Joyce hasn't slept with anyone else," I said. "She wouldn't make it up."

Curtis dropped his head against the steering wheel, letting go of my sleeve. He moaned in a theatrical way, and I thought about jumping out of the car. I could throw up and then run to my own car, try to drive away. The soft humps of his shoulder blades contracted as he made harsh little noises into the steering wheel. My cousin was almost twenty-one— too old for this, I thought, especially since he was supposed to be getting married in December. As he shook and moaned, I decided I couldn't feel sorry for him. Suddenly I wanted to be cruel.

"Curtis," I interrupted. "Are you going to tell Lara?"

He raised his head slowly. "You gotta help me fix this."

Four months after Curtis's wedding, I drove back from college and parked in the concrete parking garage of St. Luke's Hospital. I'd pictured myself as a central part of the action: standing at Joyce's bedside, bringing her drinks or ice chips, clutching her hand. As it turned out, Mrs. McKenzie didn't call me until after the baby was born. A small part of me still wondered if Curtis would show up at the hospital. I'd left a message with Aunt Bea, and as I walked through the corridors, I was looking for his dense matt of hair, the smooth shape of his shoulders. The last time I'd seen him, he was wearing his rented wedding tux, and he'd seemed so stiff after I hugged him that I reached for his jacket and pretended to brush away an invisible hair, just to steal an extra second. I hadn't done what he'd asked. I'd never even mentioned an abortion to Joyce.

Curtis didn't visit Joyce in the hospital. He didn't see Callie when she was a newborn, when she had her first teeth, or when she began to crawl. Very occasionally, I heard he sent a little cash to Joyce, but it was never very much—he was worried that Lara would find out. He'd confessed to

Lara a month before their wedding, and by the time he leaned over to kiss the bride, the bruises on his face had completely healed. The story was that Lara had kicked him for a good half-hour on the bathroom floor, cussing him out, while he just lay there, taking it. He promised he'd never see Joyce again and he wouldn't have anything to do with the baby. He also wouldn't have anything to do with me; Lara was sure I'd been helping them cheat. During the ceremony, I sat beside my mother in the pews, admiring the white fur curling around Lara's shoulders, the shining corkscrew curls that spilled out from her silver tiara. I'd promised to avoid her at the reception. She hadn't wanted me there at all.

I hardly saw Curtis after his wedding. Our visits didn't overlap at Christmas and we didn't share a Thanksgiving meal. There were no birthday cards exchanged, no friendly calls. He moved out of Cansdown with Lara, and I thought he must be very pleased to be starting fresh. But when I held Callie or popped my pinkie finger into her mouth to soothe her, I understood things in a way I never had before. My cousin had done something unforgiveable, not just to me and Joyce, but also to his daughter. He had walked away as though a child meant nothing, and gradually I was starting to see how a child could mean everything.

As I watched Callie cruise around the McKenzies' living room on her hands and knees, I started to think about my own father and how he must've been a monster to leave a two-year-old without a second thought. I'd never been angry about the way I was abandoned, but now, suddenly, I was. My father had carelessly and selfishly walked away as though my life meant nothing. He'd treated me like I was irrelevant, and now Curtis was showing me exactly what kind of person my dad must've been.

To Joyce, I condemned him. I thought she would appreciate my loyalty, but when I said that Curtis was beyond redemption, she seemed embarrassed. I imagined cursing him, reducing him to tears, forcing him to explain—but I could never think up a good enough explanation.

Then, the winter before Callie turned two, Lara had her first miscarriage. A few weeks later, Mom called me at college, all worked up.

"Did you give Curtis pictures of the baby?"

"No."

"He told Lara it was you. If she calls up, you should say it was you."

"What are you talking about?"

"Lara found pictures he was hiding from her—of Callie. He said you sent them to him at work. You think he's seeing Joyce again?"

Joyce denied it when I asked. She said she hadn't seen him, and she hadn't sent any pictures.

After I graduated, I moved back to Cansdown, found a job in a clinic, and saved up to rent an apartment with Joyce and Callie. Joyce brought a lucky bamboo plant that grew out of a glass, and placed it on our kitchen shelf in honor of our jungle theme. Then our new life was beginning, and I was so pleased to be helping, bringing home a paycheck, braiding Callie's hair as she grew heavy on my lap. I held her small gummy hand as we crossed the street in a three-person chain, and whenever I wanted to talk to my best friend she was right there, sitting across from me at the kitchen table, encouraging her daughter to eat another green bean.

To me, the arrangement seemed normal—no different from what Mom and Aunt Bea had done when they were raising me and Curtis. But it was Mom who started giving me a hard time about it. "What happens when you or Joyce wants a boyfriend?" I told her we were both too busy for boyfriends at the moment, and she said, "Oh, so it's *that* kind of arrangement."

It wasn't what she thought, but I didn't miss having a boyfriend. I had a family now.

Lara had her third miscarriage when Callie was four. By then, Joyce had started taking evening classes at the community college to become a paralegal. I was putting Callie to bed one night when the phone rang.

There was a long silence. I almost hung up, thinking it was a sales call, but I could hear breathing.

"Hello?"

"Is Curtis there?"

It was Lara. I'd barely spoken to her in years. When she came to my grandmother's funeral, she'd mumbled she was sorry for my loss, but she wouldn't meet my eyes. She remembered what I'd done.

"Lara?" I asked. "Are you okay?"

"Yee—" She stopped. There was a long pause.

"I haven't seen him," I said. "But I was sorry to hear your news."

She made a noise like someone had just poked her in the stomach. It reminded me of the panicked huhs and hmmphs she made when she couldn't speak. I was trying to think of something sympathetic to say when she erupted.

"*She* did it to me." The phone sizzled in my hand. "WHORE!"

Lara's calls started to become a regular thing. She called at night, usually at least once a week. Anytime Curtis went out, she called our apartment. If Joyce answered, Lara cursed her out until Joyce slammed the phone down. When I answered, Lara wanted to know where Joyce was. I guessed that Curtis might be cheating on her, but I wanted her to know that it had nothing to do with us. Sometimes I tried to convince her that Joyce wasn't involved. I'd say, "She's sitting right here with me," or, "She's at school." If Joyce was there she'd roll her eyes at me and mouth "nutcase," but I was starting to feel sorry for Lara. Mom told me that her last miscarriage had started at work, and afterward, Lara hadn't been able to face going back. I remembered how I'd abandoned her after she'd given me a second chance, and I decided to stay on the line, to try and make her calm.

Maybe I was lonely, too. Things were changing between me and Joyce. Our talks weren't quite the same: we spoke mainly about Callie.

We no longer goofed around at night, joking and sharing secrets, and if I asked her too many personal questions, Joyce would suddenly turn cold. I didn't understand why, but she was erecting new boundaries. Then I started noticing little things—like Joyce smelled different. She came home late, smelling like men's cologne, and when I asked her where she'd been, she claimed her class ran late. Or traffic was bad. Or she had to do some extra research and forgot to call. One night Joyce collapsed on the sofa and said she'd been out for pizza, but she had a rumpled glow that made my skin itch. It was one thing if she wanted to date, but why wouldn't she tell me? How could she rely on me so much and then lie about where she'd been?

"It's nothing," Joyce said. "Don't be paranoid."

I wondered if Curtis said the same things after he'd disappeared for hours. Lara had called me earlier that night and I wondered if I should mention it. I could just drop in her name and then watch for Joyce's reaction. But Joyce wasn't in the mood for questions; she was going to bed. As she brushed past me I caught a whiff of something musky. It was the same cologne I'd noticed before. Sweet like lettuce, ocean breezy. Manly, protective. I sniffed as Joyce walked past and inhaled Curtis.

✳ ✳ ✳

In the parking lot behind Pembury High, I lied to Callie. I lied to her in the same way that I'd been lied to myself. I told myself I was protecting her and that she couldn't understand. She must've thought the same things when she lied to me.

"So why'd he do it?" she asked. "Why'd he kill himself?"

I thought of the ringing phone. The sound of Lara's breath in my ear.

"Even if I could read your dad's mind, I wouldn't know why," I said. "When people do things like that, sometimes even *they* don't understand why. And if someone tells you a person must've done *this* because *that* happened first, it's just a guess. People put together lots of facts and still miss the truth."

"So he slit his wrists," Callie said softly.

I rested one hand on her shoulder. I didn't know where she'd got wrists from.

"No, sweetheart. It was pills. He overdosed on pills."

All My Interactions with Robyn Doblak, #9
For Rebecca/From Callie

I think my life would be completely different now if I'd waved back to Robyn in the cafeteria. I could've gone over and played with Papa, without caring what anyone thought. But Robyn dropped her hand when she realized I wasn't coming over. Then Ella started giggling. "Does she keep her papa in that bag?"

"His ashes. No, his bones," Dallas cackled.

"A bag of daddy bones! Callie, where are you going?"

I was headed for the lobby because I needed to get away, but my friends were on my heels. Dallas was laughing.

"Is that your new bestie? Did you guys start a club?"

"I don't know that girl. She was talking to someone else."

"Oh, sad face! Did you join the Dead Dad Club? The Dead Daddies Club. The Club of Dead Dads." Dallas chewed each word, testing it out, and then Ella joined in. They said it together. "The Dead Daddies Club!"

This was fun, funny—OMG hilarity! I wouldn't lose my jelly over a dead-dad joke. I smiled, sort of, as sweat trickled down my neck, and then I reminded myself that this was all Robyn's fault.

"She thinks her dad lives in an imaginary dog," I said. "She's such a freak."

I didn't know I was going to say that until it came out of my mouth. Then it was too late. Ella and Dallas were laughing.

"Did you see that shirt she was wearing?" Ella gasped. "Über-ganky."

"She must've forgot her bra," Dallas said. "You could see those skinny nipples."

"They're like bullets," I agreed. "So gross."

"You know what you need?" Danny said. "You need to go eat some cake."

I was curled up in bed, holding the cell phone in one hand. I'd called him again, but he didn't seem to mind.

"That's what I do when I feel like crap," he said. "You know that place Elaine's? If you tell them it's your birthday, all the waiters and waitresses have to come over to your table and sing 'Happy Birthday' to you. They all smile at you and clap at you and they give you free dessert. Like, 'Happy birthday, dear Rebecca, happy birthday to you.'"

"I don't think cake will help," I said.

"You won't know until you try."

I imagined getting in my car, driving to Cansdown, meeting him in a diner. I remembered the firm grip of his callused hands and pictured the creamers on the table, the little pink packets of sugar. I was already starting to bargain with myself. Maybe we could just be good friends. By the time Callie was eighteen, I'd be thirty-eight, and maybe he'd still be single. We could start slowly. We'd meet up in diners and cafés and drink bad coffee.

"I wish I could, but I can't leave Callie."

He was quiet for a moment. "I used to get in some trouble in school," he said. "I got suspended plenty of times for fighting and messing around. I was like this volcano, somebody would poke me and I'd explode. I was all, 'You gotta problem with me? I'll give you a problem.' Half the time I was lashing out at the wrong people—some kid would get at me and next thing you know I'm chucking stuff at the teacher."

I imagined Danny as a curly-haired runt, waving his fists in the air. His motives were comically simple—unlike Callie's.

"I don't know if it's the same for her," I said. "She's not fighting, and this is all new to her—the lashing out. She's been asking me about her dad. I think part of this is grief."

"How long has it been? Nine years?"

"It's difficult for most people to imagine," I said. "Nine years isn't that long."

"Did she tell you what her teacher said before she started swearing?"

"She claims she wouldn't let her go to the bathroom."

"Some of the things that go on in high school could make anyone start acting crazy. You wouldn't believe some of it—it still makes my blood boil. And if you're on the wrong side of it, forget it—you're done for," he said.

"I mean, I grew up in Cansdown. I know it can be like that, but where we live . . ."

"And kids are secretive—they don't always want you to know—especially if she's getting into it with friends."

I couldn't help it. I felt judged. He could tell how bad I was at this—how unmotherly—so he was trying to impart some of his natural parental wisdom, but it felt like he was reading to me from a parenting brochure. I'd read those pamphlets: how to protect your child from bullying, from drugs, from low self-esteem. They were full of perfectly useful information, but in this case they had nothing to do with Callie.

"Her friends are her biggest defenders," I told him. "They were the ones who protected her from Robyn."

Danny was quiet, waiting for me to come up with some other explanation, and I remembered the way I'd felt in his office, and I decided to tell him.

"You know, she was there when her mother was killed. Callie was five years old when it happened, and they told us she couldn't have seen anything because she was asleep in the back of Joyce's car. But now I'm starting to wonder. I'm thinking she might've had some kind of flashback. Because wouldn't the noises have woken her up—the lights and sirens? Everything happened only a few yards from where she slept. And maybe Robyn's note triggered her memory, telling her to die like her mother."

Danny exhaled softly. "Why don't you ask her?"

But he didn't understand how impossible that would be.

*

"Where's Mommy?" Callie used to ask when Joyce was at her evening classes.

"She's studying at the college," I told her.

"With the man?"

"What man?" I asked, squatting down to her level.

Callie made an adorable giggling face, shrugging, unable to tell me. And when I pressed her further she named her favorite cartoons. When I mentioned this to Joyce, I noticed how she turned her face away, pretending to be busy brushing crumbs off the table.

"She's got a great imagination," Joyce said.

"Also, Lara called again."

"Why don't you just screen her calls? Don't encourage her so much."

I watched Joyce dump the crumbs in the garbage, before wiping the sweat off her upper lip. She wasn't wearing any makeup, but her cheeks were pink.

"If something was going on, you'd tell me, right?"

"Jeez, Rebecca," she said. "Nothing's going on."

Then one day I saw Curtis in Cansdown. He was putting gas in his car. Broad shoulders. Brisk movements. Serious-looking belt. I started crossing the forecourt, unsure of my intentions. Would I hug him or punch him? Start berating him over Callie? I hadn't seen him in so long. I didn't know if we hated each other.

"Hey, you," I said.

Curtis seemed surprised, but he didn't snub me. His voice wasn't chilly; he even smiled a little bit. His face was puffier than before, and he'd shaved off his sideburns. We started talking about his mother; Aunt Bea was having problems with her lungs. "They told her to quit," Curtis said. "But you know my mom." He started mimicking the way she chain-smoked, bringing two fingers quickly to his mouth, and he seemed so much like the man I remembered, the boy I'd grown up with, that I looked into his dark unblinking eyes and wondered how he could do it.

I fiddled with the keys in my pocket. "Did you know that Lara calls us?"

"Yeah, I heard that," he said, giving the gas pump one last squeeze.

He seemed so unconcerned that I had to push him further.

"She knows something's going on. You should be careful."

"Sure." He glanced at the meter. "But it's only once in a while."

"Nothing's going on," Joyce swore. "They're just visits with Callie." Curtis had thought I knew. Why wouldn't my best friend tell me?

"I didn't know how you'd take it," she claimed. "You act like you hate him. Plus, you were talking to Lara. I didn't want you to have to lie."

She didn't say she thought I'd be jealous. She didn't need to.

How often? Where did they meet? How did they arrange it?

Every four weeks they'd get an ice cream and walk on the beach. Joyce had his number at the courthouse; they called each other at work. "Rebecca, I'm sorry," she said. "I didn't think you *wanted* to know."

And what about those times she'd come home late after her classes? I remembered her rumpled glow as she threw herself down on the couch.

Joyce suddenly bristled. "You don't own me. I can date."

⋆ ⋆ ⋆

I picked up a strudel after work on Friday. It was raspberry, Callie's favorite, and I pictured us polishing off the crumbs as we talked over cups of tea. She'd finished the second day of her in-school suspension, and I'd decided I needed to push her further. I wouldn't ask her about the past, I'd just focus on her problem at school. I imagined our heads tipping together, beams of light across the kitchen table, a golden-haired girl embracing her kindly guardian. She'd finally explain about the chocolate, and I'd consider reducing her two-week grounding. And if she brought up any memories from the past I'd tell her that none of it was her fault.

When I got inside, Callie was sitting cross-legged on the sofa, eating raw baby carrots out of the bag. She was watching a reality show about models, apparently absorbed, without a phone or computer screen dividing her attention. "Robyn left something for us," she said, without lifting her eyes from the screen.

The sheet of paper was on top of the mail, on the sideboard by the front door. The pink-lined page had been folded in half.

SUNDAY NIGHT, 1 A.M., BRIDGE OVER FLINT STREET, JUMPING.

"Where was this? Did you see her?"

"No. It was just in the mailbox when I got home."

She said there wasn't an envelope. Robyn must've come here. My legs started to tremble. She knew where we lived.

"She must know she's got our attention," I said, switching off the TV and putting down the strudel. "She knows I called her mom before. But why would she come here? How does she know where you live?"

Callie began opening the strudel, working the white string off the edges. "Maybe someone told her. Who knows?"

"Well, it's harassment," I said. "Even if it is a hoax. She wants to scare you into thinking she's going to jump off this bridge. Otherwise why else? Why now?"

With a final yank, Callie opened the box and looked at the strudel.

"Revenge," Callie said evenly. "To teach me a lesson."

Teach her a lesson, I thought. What wonderful lessons! Robyn squirts paint on her shirt and blames it on Callie. She goes to Joyce's grave and leaves a note saying Callie should die. Now she threatens to kill herself by jumping off a bridge. What kind of lessons were these? Lessons in psychopathy? Lessons about what happens when you don't love a maniac back?

"She has nothing to teach you," I snapped. "Nothing at all."

Callie dipped a finger into the crust of the strudel and then looked at me guiltily, as if waiting to be told to get a plate and a knife. "If she's going to jump, someone has to go there," she said tentatively. "To the bridge on Sunday. You'll stop her, right?"

"No," I said. "I'll call up her mother and end this right now."

Callie watched me as I got out my cell phone and found Cerise's number. It went straight through to voice mail, so I left a message asking her to call me back. Then I called a second time and told her about Robyn's intentions. "Sunday night," I said. "Don't let her out of your sight."

Callie was picking at the strudel. She pulled off a chunk with her fingers. I looked at her sticky red hands as she popped the pastry into her mouth.

"'Don't let her out of your sight'?" she repeated, once I'd ended the call.

"What's wrong with that?"

"You sound crazed. I bet her mom won't listen to you."

"What do you want me to say?" I asked. "I'll call back and leave another message."

"Oh, great," she muttered. "Why don't you just use your ESP?"

I felt myself flushing. I hated personal sarcasm. But I counted silently to ten; the note had obviously provoked her.

"Look, I don't want Robyn to get hurt. But right now, you're more important. I don't want *you* to be upset by this. I'm not going to let her do that."

"But you're not going to stop her."

"I just called her mother."

"Nobody really cares about her," Callie said darkly. "Her mother won't help her. She sent *us* this note and now we know what she's going to do."

"You just said she was doing this for revenge on you. We don't know if this is real—or if Robyn even wrote it."

"Who else?" Callie said, pulling a coil of hair across her eyes. I could smell her shampoo—lemons in the sun.

"You don't know for sure. You didn't see her."

"I know because." She pulled more hair over her face. "Because of what I did."

I stared at her for a long moment. Maybe I was dumb, gullible. I never saw it coming with the people I loved best. Callie appeared the same as always, the light falling on her in patches; she looked just like Joyce. Just like her mother.

"What did you do, sweetheart?"

"I'm not a sweetheart," she said.

I opened the glove compartment of my car and started pulling out her letters. I opened each aging envelope that she'd addressed to Mom. She didn't come running out of the house to stop me, screaming like a banshee. Or rip herself in two like Rumpelstiltskin. Maybe she didn't even guess what I was doing in my car. Or she might not have cared what I thought of her anymore.

Hi Mom, What's new? Oh yeah nothing. I guess I'm supposed to imagine you hanging out with all the dead celebrities. There'd be this giant screen and you'd gather around like it was Super Bowl Sunday, and you'd watch everything I did with all your celebrity friends. But then they'd start yelling "Nooooooo! Cooooome onnnnnnn! What's this chick's problem?" And you'd go, "That's not my daughter! Somebody change the channel!" Then you'd regret someone like me ever came out of your perfect body.

I rolled down the car window. Callie had written this last May—she'd used a colorful font on her ink-jet printer. We were visiting Joyce for Mother's Day, about a month after Robyn left school. About a month after Callie was accused of being a bully. I laid the page on the seat beside me, needing a break, just for a second. Then I looked through her older letters, addressed to Mommy. I read about a paper owl she'd made in third grade, getting her nails done with Dallas. These were better, innocent, but I could pretend for only so long.

> *I know you were perfect—Rebecca talks about you ALL the time.*
> *It's like she knows I can't remember so she's trying to push you*
> *into my brain.*

I reached impulsively for another old letter and examined a Christmas tree she'd crayoned, each branch topped with gold star stickers. Callie had written about going to the zoo, seeing the penguins. I remembered how we'd stood by the railing, watching them waddle around their enclosure. She blew them good-bye kisses and I'd promised we'd go back soon. Why hadn't we ever gone back? Where had the time gone? I picked up her letter from four months ago.

> *And if you're really the way she says I wouldn't even like you,*
> *and you wouldn't like me either so I guess we're both lucky you're*
> *dead.*

All My Interactions with Robyn Doblak, #10
For Rebecca/From Callie

After Dallas spread it around, everyone started calling Robyn Bullets, and when I tried to IM her at night, she wouldn't answer back. I couldn't apologize because I couldn't get through to her, and I couldn't catch her eye in class because she wouldn't look at anyone.

Rebecca, you always said you were proud of me and you thought I was a good person, and I know I didn't deserve it, but I thought one day I'd change. I'd stop making the worst decisions and do something amazing and then I could finally be proud of myself. I'd be as good as everyone hoped.

I knew what a good person would do when they started barking at Robyn. When they stuck pencils under their shirts and rubbed the tips, yelling, "Bullets! Bullets!" A good person wouldn't sit there, with a sick smile on her face—she would stand up and start shouting. She would smash someone in the head. I knew if I really cared, I would go over there and change things. I would help protect Robyn and become her shell. But I didn't do anything, I just sat there, a mess of feelings. I didn't want anything to do with her and I still missed her all the time. I left notes in her locker. I tried texting. I watched her hurrying through the halls, hunched up in her puffy coat. On the outside I was this mega-bitch, but on the inside my heart was pounding, and I wondered what would happen if I suddenly reversed.

It happened in art class last April. Robyn wasn't wearing her coat.

"Bullets," Ella called. "Ooh, your bullets are so hard!"

Miss Dimmock was out in the hall, yelling at Adam Liebowitz, and she'd closed the door behind her, leaving Robyn unprotected. We were painting masks that day. We each had a papier-mâché face to work on, and Miss Dimmock had opened all the windows because the fumes were so strong. When Ella called out to her, Robyn pretended she couldn't hear. Robyn's hair covered up her face and she drooped over her mask. "Bullets," I heard again, and my paintbrush wobbled. "Bullets," Ella said, and my lips pulled back.

"Why are you such a bitch?"

Ella stiffened. "Excuse me?"

I pushed back my chair and my legs suddenly shook. Could I really leave Ella? She'd been my best friend for so long, but my heart was pounding furiously and it told me to stand up.

"Fuck you," Ella said, as I took the first step.

I started stumbling forward, eyes on Robyn, as I moved across the room, unsure of what I was doing. My pulse was cranking because I knew there was no going back. If I sat down with Robyn, everyone would know. I would lose Dallas and Ella and all my friends and all my secrets. I'd be a fish caught on a hook that I'd swallowed myself. I didn't care. I took another step closer.

Robyn was still painting, head low down. She wore a white shirt and she curled her arm around like a fence. She hadn't even noticed me with all the commotion. I stopped in front of her table while everyone watched.

"Robyn," I said softly. She didn't look up. She'd been painting black whiskers and she held her paintbrush still.

Two guys shouted something and I glared back at them. I needed to get a chair. I would need someplace to sit. But Robyn still hadn't seen me. Maybe she didn't know. "Robyn," I said louder, and then the hairs on my arms stood up.

Her eyes were cold and wet, and her mouth was sort of open. I could see some of her teeth as her lips moved. Then my face was burning and my insides were exploding and I felt the bullet hit me and start tearing me apart. Total odium. I saw it on her face. She would love me never again. It couldn't hurt any worse. I'd left my friends for nothing, and how could I go back? I was a million miles from earth, cold and dead and empty. I was dropping out of a plane and there was nowhere to go but down. My hand was floating up and then I saw what it was holding. A bottle of paint. I'd been using it on my mask.

"Bullets!" I said. It was a bright blood red.

11

We didn't have much time. It was already beginning. In just over forty-eight hours a girl would try to take her own life. She had been ridiculed by her classmates, oppressed by grief and loss, and as I walked up the stairs to our house, she had already made her decision. Her story wouldn't end like Autumn Sanger's, with a funeral packed with tearstained mourners. And the point she was trying to make would quickly become warped by the press. I couldn't yet imagine the vengeful plans of this heartbroken teenager, but if I'd had even the tiniest glimpse, I would have run up the stairs three at a time.

Callie was lying in bed, one arm thrown over her face. And more than anger or guilt, I felt waves of pity. You think you know someone. You take this for granted. You can't imagine that the things you've said will cause them pain or insecurity. I'd told her stories about Joyce: how she saved me, her courage and goodness. True stories, but there was another side to them, too. How could Callie ever live up to the glorified heroics of her dead mother? She couldn't, she'd suffered, and the image I'd projected wasn't even true.

Callie lifted her arm from her face, and I showed her her own letter. Then I told her what I'd done, reading her messages in the car. She didn't start screaming or trashing her room, swearing about breaches of privacy. She lay silent and still, like an escaped convict in a field of corn.

"Is this how you see yourself? Did you really think we regret you?"

Her face crumpled. Tears filled her eyes.

"I will never regret you; that could never happen. But your mother wasn't perfect, and I don't expect you to be."

I was handing her tissues, and Callie was sniffling and rubbing her eyes, wiping her face against her arms, swaying slightly. "I need to hear you say it. Did you throw the paint on Robyn?"

She nodded, yes, and I remembered what Cerise had told me: *Callie humiliates her every day.* This was about more than just paint. This was about a girl who'd been bullied, branded a weird liar, accused of throwing paint on herself, and forced out of school. Callie had made her feel worthless, and I had enabled her. *Bully,* Mrs. Jameson said, but what had caused it? How could you pinpoint a definite reason and be absolutely certain? Our town, my parenting, her peers, the loss of her parents? Society? Or something else that existed deep inside her? A compulsion that lay in all of us, none of us innocent, everyone capable of hurting, even destroying, someone else.

"If that had been you, how do you think you'd feel?"

"I'd feel hopeless," Callie said slowly. "Like my whole life was ruined." Then she continued, unprompted, with an impressive stream of empathy. "I'd feel like everyone hated me and nothing was ever good." She was blinking and crumpling up tissues, and I let her for a while. I thought she needed to understand the anguish Robyn must've felt. "I'd feel humiliated. I'd want to die," she snorted.

"Would you deserve it?"

"No." Callie sucked the tears off her lips and her regret struck me as genuine. She'd lied and fooled me before, but this felt honest-to-God real. Motherly or not, my instincts were right. Her distress was sincere and I'm glad I didn't doubt her. At that moment, I wanted to hug her, reassure her that she wasn't a bully. Promise this was just one mistake and we were going to fix it. But was that even true? Could it be undone so easily? And what about the witnesses? Had Callie forced them all to lie?

"That wasn't me," she said. "My friends asked them."

We were both responsible now. I remembered Callie's tearstained face on the day Mrs. Jameson called me. I'd been so relieved she wasn't a bully. I accepted every word out of her mouth. I'd repeated her friends' stories willingly to anyone who would listen. I argued with Mrs. Jameson. I focused on the ink and the paint. My stomach lurched as I remembered someone else. The student witness: Lucinda Berry. She'd changed her story the day after Callie guessed it was her. I was about to press Callie further, prying out every last misdeed. But Callie was tipping her pink face upward, and then she told me that they had been friends.

"Me and Robyn."

I stared at her, slack-jawed.

"Nobody knew," she whispered. "We used to IM, but then she blocked me."

"You wrote messages to *Robyn*?"

She said that she had. I waited to see if she'd blush or hesitate, stumbling over her story—giving away the lie. But what if it was true? Robyn had known where Joyce's grave was. She'd come to our home to leave this message for Callie. What if Robyn had been leaving these notes because there really was something between them? A ripped-up friendship. A reason to care.

"I'm going to need to see those messages," I said. "Everything you guys wrote. And I want to hear the whole story, good and bad."

"It's all mixed up in my head," Callie said. "I don't think I can say it out loud."

"So write it down for me. Start from the beginning."

————————

All that weekend, I tried to reach Cerise. The messages that I left must've sounded more and more desperate. "I just want to help. I'm sorry that Callie contributed to this. We both want to make sure that Robyn's okay." It would be a disaster if Robyn hurt herself. I knew it would be absolutely devastating: a girl's future obliterated without thought or cause. A family destroyed, a life wasted. All because of a betrayal between two friends. It wasn't that I couldn't understand it. It was a thousand times worse when a friend hurt you, when the person who claimed to love you suddenly lied and treated you like garbage. Without her, you lost your bearings. You lost your trust in everything. It was all shadows and departures, final moments, final breaths. I wanted to grab hold of Robyn and explain how this wouldn't go on forever. She'd make new friends, her pain would lessen, and she'd find herself again. I left rambling messages for Cerise, but she didn't call me back.

Robyn's safety was one thing, but I was also concerned about Callie. If Robyn succeeded, Callie would be burdened with a crushing guilt. The things you did in childhood weren't supposed to affect you for the rest of your life. A few thoughtless moments of cruelty weren't meant to permanently change who you were. Robyn had been Callie's friend, and Callie had hurt her, but she couldn't have imagined that things would end up like this. With Robyn's life on the line, and her own future at risk.

On Saturday, Callie hung around the house in a coconut-scented fog, eating cereal out of the box, printing out her messages from Robyn. She seemed chastened and newly aware of what was at stake. Her head drooped slightly as she handed me the first two pages. I looked at the title, "All My Interactions with Robyn Doblak." Then I read about how Callie had met Robyn while waiting to see the school social worker. Robyn had started crying, and Callie had wiped her tears. For just a second, my bullshit detector went off. Would Callie really wipe a stranger's tears? It sounded a lot like the stories I'd told her about Joyce. But after reading their first set of IMs, my doubts started lifting. Here were two kids in the same boat. They'd both lost a parent. And Callie couldn't have faked IMs from last December.

Callie's orange flip-flops slapped across the floor as she moved from her bedroom to the kitchen. No music came out of her room. She didn't ask to turn on the TV. "I'm still putting them all in order," she said. "Has her mom answered yet?"

I shook my head. I could only hope that Cerise was taking my warnings seriously. Either she was driving Robyn to the hospital right now or she was deleting all of my messages.

"Maybe we should go over there," Callie said.

"That's probably not a good idea."

"But I have to tell her I'm sorry. I want to see her before it's too late."

We drove through the historic district of Pembury, past the old Victorian homes where there were candlelit tours every December around Christmas. The roads were narrow and winding as we headed out past the red farmhouses that had been given million-dollar renovations, past the singular herd of cows that grazed in the field. I slowed as we crossed the small bridge over Flint Street.

Robyn's house was a white ranch on the outskirts of town. Yellow leaves had fallen across the yard. We walked up to the front step and I pressed the doorbell. Callie chewed her thumbnail and stuck close to my side, bumping into my hip, shuffling her feet anxiously. We waited for the door to open, but it remained firmly shut. The Doblaks' curtains were closed. I couldn't hear anyone moving around inside.

"They're not home." Callie frowned and pulled a handful of hair across her mouth.

I banged on the door with my knuckle. "Cerise?" I called. "Robyn?"

I dialed her number again as we stood on the step. "Cerise," I said when her voice message clicked on. "Callie wants to apologize to Robyn. She's admitted what happened. We want to make sure Robyn's okay."

Callie hugged herself as I spoke, then she shivered like she was cold.

"Have you called the police?" Danny asked. I could hear cars in the background. He'd answered his phone while he was working outside at the cemetery.

"They said they'd send a patrol to her house, but I know she's not home. We were just over there. I don't think they took me seriously."

"Well, I checked your friend's grave. She hasn't been back here."

I started telling Danny about Callie and Robyn's friendship. I'd read their first five interactions, and had watched nervously as their bond grew. But Callie had lied to Robyn. She'd made up a story that never happened, claiming Joyce's nickname as her own: Evil McFrenzy. Callie said she was tired of being pitied so she had covered herself in ketchup, ran around our Christmas tree, worshipping the devil. The whole point of the story was changed. Callie wasn't saving anyone. She'd rewritten the entire thing just to make herself sound wild. But then, maybe I didn't get it. I supposed she was helping herself. And Robyn, too; she was empathizing with her. Robyn believed her, of course. Why wouldn't she? She wished she was Evil, too, and their kinship had grown from that. I knew how girls wanted to be the same, to relate over similar feelings. To bitch about the way that nobody understood them. Was it good they could come together in this imaginary online world, creating versions of themselves as they wished they could be? It seemed to help Robyn—at least at first. She'd been depressed over Christmas and Callie's story had cheered her. Then when she started talking about suicide, Callie turned into her counselor. She'd told Robyn to watch some cartoons and get out of bed. I was proud when her encouragement worked, but then I remembered what must've come later. Callie had helped her and then hurt her. She'd attacked her friend. We needed to do something. What could I do?

Danny cleared his throat. "Do you want me to come to the bridge with you?"

I had thought he would never ask.

How could you stop a fourteen-year-old girl from jumping off a bridge? On Sunday night, Danny met me in a restaurant parking lot not far from the bridge over Flint Street. He'd brought flashlights and a Thermos of coffee. He was wearing a short jacket and the sleeves were frayed. Callie had asked if she could come, but I'd decided against it. I didn't want her seeing anything traumatic.

Danny followed me in his truck to the bridge, parking behind me on the side of the road. We arrived after midnight, and the air was cool as we walked up to the bridge. There was a paved walkway on one side, and I followed close behind him. A single car drove past, slapping us with wind, throwing up grit. It didn't stop. Danny's baseball cap was gone and his messy brown curls smelled like smoke. He leaned close, handing me the Thermos. In the center of the bridge, we stopped and looked down. We were at least thirty feet up. There were no real barriers that would stop a kid from jumping. Down below, cars periodically rushed past in both directions. Their headlights bleached out the dark, but we couldn't see everything, and I worried for a moment that Robyn was already in the road. She could've changed her plans or lied in her message. She might intend to run into traffic while we watched from above.

"How are we going to stop her?"

"You go on one side, and I'll take the other," Danny said.

"And if we see her, what, shout to the other?"

"Yeah. And try and keep her calm."

"I don't know how big she is. I'm not sure if I'll be able to grab her."

"Just call me and I'll come running."

I took a swig of the hot, bitter coffee. Then Danny did the same, wiping his mouth with one hand. He must've felt me staring because he suddenly leaned closer. The sky was starless, and his breath came out in a small white cloud. "You feel responsible?" he asked.

"Yeah. Callie hurt her."

"No matter what happens, you shouldn't blame yourself."

He swooped down suddenly, and then his lips were on mine. Just for a second. It was over that fast. I hadn't been kissed in years—mouths were something I viewed clinically. Teeth, gums, biofilm. But Danny's mouth was hot—a little acidic. His nose touched mine, his lips tickled. Then he pulled away and turned to walk to the far side of the bridge.

Danny flashed his light to signal to me that things were okay on his end, and I signaled back, still touching my lips with one hand. I felt a strange calm come over me as I moved my flashlight along my side of the bridge, illuminating a moving shadow, a whistling branch. It felt like time was emptying out, or maybe it stood still for just a moment. The moving silver arm of the clock paused and then started ticking again. *Do you know where your children are? Do you know who they are? Do you know what they're capable of? Is there still time to save them?* I rubbed my arms and kept alert, waiting for Robyn to appear. I realized I hadn't even considered what I wanted to say. I'd never met Robyn, and she wouldn't know who I was. I would have to explain quickly. I was Callie's guardian. I had come to apologize. I was apologizing for Callie. I was apologizing for the paint. Then I would tell her that I understood. I knew how it felt to be alone and desperate—to feel betrayed by a friend. It could make you a little crazy.

At dinner that night, Callie and I had discussed Robyn's motives. Callie had promised she'd finish writing everything by the time I came home. I still didn't know exactly what happened with the paint—I'd read only as far as last Christmas.

"I think she wants revenge," Callie said. "If she blames us, we'll be murderers. And we won't ever be able to forget. She'll be a part of us forever."

"Like Autumn Sanger," she added, and for a moment I shivered. I remembered how she'd brought up Autumn after we'd found Robyn's first note. She'd said that Autumn was bullied and her bullies killed her.

"Well, I won't let her jump," I told Callie. "So nobody's going to be a murderer."

As I waited for Robyn, I chewed the side of my knuckle. Then I glanced down at the road, fearful of spotting her body. It could happen that quickly. You wouldn't always see it coming. Sometimes you lost everything before you realized what was at stake. Then I couldn't help it. I was thinking about Joyce. I'd lost a friend, too, and I'd betrayed her first.

On the night Joyce died, Lara called me.

"Rebecca?" Lara sounded confused. "Did Curtis call you?"

"Oh, Lara, hey." I hadn't planned what I'd say if she called. Joyce and Callie had gone out to meet Curtis about twenty minutes earlier. It was the first time they'd done it openly, the visits no longer a secret from me. Joyce had hurried Callie to put on her shoes, giving commands on an imaginary walkie-talkie. "Agent Callie, do you read me?" She made the sound of static using her mouth, and I tried not to feel resentful about being left behind.

"Did my husband call you?" Lara was insistent.

"No. Why?"

"I just hit redial on our phone and now I'm talking to you."

"Okay, but I haven't talked to Curtis in ages. It must be a mistake."

"Is Joyce there?"

"Sure," I said, and then regretted this immediately. I should've just said she was out getting milk.

"Can I speak to her?"

"She's busy."

"She's busy? What's she doing?"

I panicked. I froze. Then I hung up the phone.

I had never hung up on Lara before. The phone started ringing. It rang, then stopped. It rang and rang again. I realized this would be proof to her. Another betrayal. I cursed my own stupidity as I lay on the sofa. Eventually the phone stopped ringing. I thought it was over. But then fifteen minutes later the banging began.

Lara stood in front of our apartment door, holding her stomach. She grimaced at me unhappily, her eyes red from crying. But her voice was strong. Bitter as coffee.

"You were lying, weren't you? She's out screwing Curtis."

Lara doubled over suddenly, like she was about to vomit on our doorstep. But instead of puking, a painful howl came out. I looked around our well-lit hallway, expecting neighbors' doors to start opening, complaints about the noise, but nobody came out. Lara's howl tapered to a moan, and I made as if to touch her, but her hair was unwashed and she looked like she hadn't slept.

"Lara, no. Just listen."

She lifted her eyes to my face. "What did I ever do to you?"

Here was the cool, beautiful girl who I'd once admired, hunkering down like she'd been shot, coming to me for help.

"It's not what you think," I said, trying to block the doorway with my body.

"You never liked me," she said. "It's the same as last time. You act like you're my friend so they can keep cheating."

Lara's hands went to her pockets and I recognized this gesture. She pulled out a pack of cigarettes and tried tapping one out. Her fingers were clumsy. There was a small hole in the seam of her T-shirt. She started flicking her lighter and then took a deep drag.

"You're wrong," I said more steadily. "She's just out getting milk."

"What store?" Lara asked.

"I don't know. You're not supposed to smoke here."

"Guess I'll just have to wait until she gets home."

Lara glowered and kept smoking. I wondered what she'd do when Joyce came back. How would she react to seeing Callie here in the flesh? On the one hand, I could empathize. I'd been suspicious of Joyce until recently. My mind had buzzed with betrayals that were so much worse than reality. I knew how Lara felt, and I could so easily fix it. But I'd promised Joyce that I would keep her secret.

"I think this is a misunderstanding." I cleared my throat. "Do you want to come inside for a second?"

Lara followed me into the apartment, ashing her cigarette on the floor, stumbling over our rug, moving like a caged animal. She looked at our stained brown couch. Callie's rain boots next to the door. I could hear her hiccup as she brought her cigarette to her lips.

"They're not cheating," I told her. "Callie's out with her. If she was fooling around with Curtis, do you think she'd bring her daughter along?"

We were standing in front of the couch. Lara didn't move to sit down. She narrowed her eyes at me, as if this was a trick.

"Callie's not here?"

I shook my head, waved at the empty bedroom.

"He's still cheating." Lara sank down on our couch, and then she said the most miserable thing. Later, I'd wonder if she meant it at all. She knew me well enough to choose words that would instantly move me. She remembered my old hyacinth-girl days, and was aware of my weakness.

"I'm going to kill myself," she said. Then she started describing the rope she'd been saving. "I want him to find me hanging next to our bed."

Lara's threat was melodramatic, but I immediately believed that she meant it. That she would leave our apartment and go home and do it. Wrap a rope around her neck, climb up on a chair. For just a second my mind went to Autumn, recalling how desperate I'd been to help her— when her private despair had leaked like gas into my life. My heart was pounding, and maybe Lara knew exactly what she was doing: hooking her misery into my skin, giving me one last chance to fix it. Did she think that I could save her? That I could save anyone? That I could untie the piece of rope she'd just looped around both of us?

Robyn was late or her mother had stopped her. It was already one-fifteen and she hadn't arrived. The clock had jumped forward as I ran my flashlight over the bushes, and I wondered if she was watching us, waiting for us to leave. We couldn't stay here all night, but I told myself to be patient because how would Callie feel if Robyn jumped? I still hadn't forgiven myself for what happened to Joyce. "Your husband isn't cheating," I told Lara. "He's visiting Callie. They get ice cream at the beach, that's all it is."

After Lara left that night, I opened all the windows, as if this would clear the anguish that still lingered in the air. She'd believed me. She'd cried. She stopped talking about killing herself. I agreed that they should've just told her instead of sneaking around. Lara drank the tea I gave her. She said she'd go home and rest. She said this sincerely, and then I watched her turn to leave.

It was a balmy September night, and apparently the beach parking lot was busy. Music drifting from car windows, people inhaling the salty air. Curtis and Joyce didn't even notice the blue Chevy that was idling nearby. They were engaged in a delicate maneuver: getting Callie into the car. She had fallen asleep after a boisterous hour in the playground, streaks of ice cream crusting her face. Curtis kissed his sleeping child, bending to place her in the car seat, while Lara watched, feeling as though her heart might burst. Here was her husband with the child she couldn't give him, with the woman who'd had his daughter. He cradled his own flesh and blood with a tenderness Lara craved. She would never have this. She couldn't share it. It was worse than cheating. She squeezed her own neck with both hands. She would do it and he'd find her hanging. That's how she would end it. But instead of driving home, Lara put her foot down on the gas.

I held my cell phone in my hand. It was one-thirty. I had a sudden profound urge to hear Callie's voice. I would tell her to get some sleep. Robyn wasn't coming. She had to be waiting anxiously, hoping her friend was okay. Our home phone rang and she didn't pick up, so I dialed a second time. Then I tried her cell, keeping an eye on the approach to the bridge. No answer. I texted. No response. When our answering machine picked up for the fourth time, my heart started racing. What if Robyn had lured me here? What if she knew that Callie would be alone? I started flashing my light at Danny. S-O-S. S-O-S.

"I need to go home," I yelled. "Callie's not picking up."

"You want me to come with you?"

"No. You stay here."

Everything flipped in a single instant. I ran to my car, still dialing Callie. When Lara hit them, Callie was safe in the car, asleep already. And we didn't want her to know—to imagine how it must've happened. Her father flying through the air, her mother bleeding on the asphalt. Callie safe in the car, dreaming of ice cream, fairies. We couldn't allow her to feel guilt. We couldn't add to the nightmare. Curtis in the ICU, and Joyce, how could I say it?

I tried to remember how Joyce had looked when she'd said good-bye to me. Was there anything special? A wink, a smile? Did she raise her hand as she said my name, tossing her golden hair over one shoulder? I couldn't remember her exact words, the look on her face. I thought of the way we'd rehearsed this moment in my backyard years ago, and I was trapped in an ant hole. Circling gray doom.

I visited my cousin only once. I was afraid to see him. I felt I was pulling apart at the seams; I had given them all away. I looked at my cousin, my old protector, bandaged and bruised, and I couldn't admit to him what I had done. I'd thought that I knew Lara, but I hadn't seen that she was dangerous. And she'd known me better; she'd tricked me into this. Curtis looked frail, despondent, and I never told him. Perhaps if I had, he could've blamed me instead of himself. I stood by the plastic rail at the end of the bed and described Joyce's funeral. I asked if he was in pain. I told him that Callie was with the McKenzies. I said I'd come back and see him, but I never got the chance. After Curtis got out of the hospital, he went to Bea's house to recover. But he quickly went downhill as he struggled with the facts. His wife had tried to kill him. She was going to prison. He'd put his daughter's life in danger. And Joyce was dead. One day Curtis went into the bathroom and opened a bottle of painkillers, then he swallowed them until he was gone.

I ran up our staircase and opened our front door. It was quiet, and I could smell the chrysanthemums in the kitchen as I called out her name, rushed through the rooms. Callie's door was open, and I pulled back her covers, already aware that her bed was empty. Her sheet was on the floor, but she wasn't here. Then I was running from room to room, a hollow wail cracking my nerves.

"Callie! Callie! Oh my God!"

She wasn't here. She wasn't home. She was gone. Taken. I was trapped again, and each second was sucking me deeper.

I almost didn't notice her phone on the floor. It was just lying there in the hallway, on the floor outside my room. I bent down and the noise was brutal, like bones crushed inside my throat.

Beneath her phone was a single sheet of paper.

Red ink, pink lines.

Sorry Rebecca. It was me. C

CALLIE

If you called my name underwater, it might sound like anything.

A frog belching. A fish singing. Green leaves flapping on a tree.

It could even sound familiar, like a nickname they called me when I was a baby that I'd forgotten long ago. Or just a second ago, because names disappear underwater.

I might hear you, but I'd still sink. I can't swim.

In the lake behind Ella's house, the mud swallows everything—leaves and bugs and fungus and fish bones and bird bones and mold and dust. Last July, I stood in the shallows and let it swallow my feet while Dallas and Ella raced. I blew the silver whistle and then watched them chop the water with their arms. Ella was winning because she always won. She'd been captain of our middle-school swim team and had a row of trophies that made a hollow ting when you tapped them. When she kicked, the brown water turned white, and when she reached the floating Styrofoam ball that was the finish line, she treaded water and waited for Dallas.

They never swam right back to me. They both wore goggles, and I could see them ducking under the surface to flutter their arms like hula girls and blow giant silver bubbles at the sky. My toes sank past soft, squishy animal brains and I waited to turn to stone. The skin on my feet would become syrup and my bones would turn into fossils, sinking lower and lower into the watery waste.

"You've got to at least learn to float," Ella said, when they finally came back to where I stood.

She squinched her little fox's nose at me, and because I'd known her forever I followed her into waist-deep water. At school, Ella practiced her signature "I don't give a shit" runway walk—shoulders rising, feet crossing fast to the beat of a playlist only she could hear—but in the lake she glided smoothly in front of me.

I lay back when she told me to. Cold water pressed me down; poking fingers held me up. The sky spread out to the edges of the universe and a fat gush filled my ears.

I thought I heard laughter, then words. "Top Russian mops."

I struggled for a moment and water trickled out.

"What?"

"Stop tensing up."

I dropped my head back. Ella kept her hands underneath, holding me up as she floated me deeper. I turned enormous and weightless at the same time: an iceberg, an ark, the algae drifting in the sun. Dissolving, my fingers dragged the surface while a thousand living things passed through. Sky reflected lake, lake reflected sky. Ella smiled down at me. I billowed out with the ripples and was half asleep when she pulled her hands away.

I flapped, kicked toward the bottom, sank. Gulped a dirty mouthful, sank. Ella was already miles away.

"You have to swim to us," Dallas called.

My head tilted, choked. Brain sizzled. Arms slapped up and down. Words washed back down my throat like mud while panic stole my legs, dragging me under. Pulling, swallowing, deep, deeper, deepest.

They were still laughing when I started to kick. I thrashed and pushed and then my foot hit something. The bottom. I drooled scummy water and walked the rest of the way back.

Ella and Dallas didn't look sorry.

"Ella," I shouted. She turned her back to me, shaking with silent laughter.

I hiccupped, burped wetly. Dallas glared with slitty snake eyes. "You swim like a baby shits."

"Baby shits," Ella gasped, laughing harder. Dallas puckered up and squeezed her eyes shut like she was trying to push one out.

I didn't know the name would stick. Babyshits. That's what they called me. That's who I became.

I didn't go home that afternoon. Instead, I lay down with the dandelions, the ants, and the pimpled dirt while they went to get three Bacardi Breezers from the fridge in the basement. The sweet liquid fizzed in our stomachs, and when the world started spinning we held the grass tight in our fists so we wouldn't fly off past the sky and clouds to the black frozen galaxies beyond. I kicked my feet in the air and Ella caught one, looked at my small white toes. "You have fetus feet," she said, and smiled.

I felt okay for a minute, and then Dallas pointed at my half-finished drink. "Do you like milk better, Babyshits?"

I tipped the bottle to my mouth. Dallas was good at making names stick. Pubic Monster, Double Dick with Cheese, Tit Rash. Bullets. She'd smile and say it to your face until it caught. Her dad had a show on the radio and when she was little, he recorded her talking about the red piss cherries we'd thrown at Alex Penders, who lived next door. She called Alex "Piggy Kibble" because he ate dog food, and after her dad broadcast it on the radio he got so many calls about how funny Dallas was, he decided to talk about her each week. Even though nobody we knew listened to the radio, Dallas said her dad had more than a million listeners, plus people who downloaded the podcasts, so when Dallas told him something millions of her fans might hear about it.

Like in seventh grade, when there was this girl Josie Dixon who had these wiry black hairs sprouting out of her chin.

"She got the five-o'clock shadow," Ella said. "And it's not even ten."

"That bearded lady needs a razor."

"Hobo Joe," Dallas said, and the name was so perfect it stuck, and then it went viral.

Every time Hobo Joe walked into a classroom, there was a paper cup waiting on her chair. We filled it with nickels and pennies—whatever we had. Dallas once left a dollar with a message on it. "Pluck it. Wax it. Get those chin pubes OUT!" Hobo Joe finally waxed off all the ganky hairs, but it was already too late. We started leaving razors, and then a bottle of Nair.

Josie told one teacher that Dallas had started it, but Dallas knew exactly how to play it. Blue eyes wet with tears, breathy and innocent, lower lip puffy and trembling. She didn't even get a detention, and afterward she went up to Josie. "You should listen to my dad's show," she told her. "You might get a shout-out soon."

When we heard that Hobo Joe was transferring to another school, Dallas raised her hand to me for a high five.

"Credit," I said, slapping her hand.

"Full-frontal credit!" Ella said, shaking her hips. And I knew we weren't supposed to feel bad at all.

We called ourselves DH, which stood for Double Hockeysticks. Like hell, we each carried a sharp pair of sticks in our name: daLLas, eLLa, caLLie. You didn't cross us. When Ella leaked period on the back of her pants, no one tried calling her Spot. When I served at volleyball and it flew backward instead of up and over the net, no one started laughing—they just passed the ball back to me for another try. Together we were DH and when the three of us walked down the hall, it was like all the sweatballs shrank even smaller, wishing they were us, but also scared of what we might do. We could do anything. Everyone knew, and if you didn't know, you soon learned. Ask the kids in our grade, ask teachers. Ask the school secretary—she found out.

On the last day of eighth grade, Ella lost her school yearbook. Like me and Dallas, she'd spent the morning handing it to the A-listers and even some of the blah-blahs, telling them, "Sign it," and then checking to see if they'd written anything juicy. The teachers were playing DVDs that nobody bothered to watch, so we wandered in and out of classrooms, practicing our autographs, posing for pictures, and eating candy. Then at some point that afternoon, Ella noticed her yearbook was missing. When it wasn't where she thought it would be, we realized it was stolen.

Dallas set up a blockade in the hall, and we marched up to people, telling them to open their books. We scanned the front page for Ella's name and slammed it shut when it wasn't there. Some kids held their books open before we even said so, but one little mouse cheese stuffed his away in his bag and wouldn't take it out for me. Dallas stormed over, total odium. "What's wrong with you? Are you a thief?"

He stared at her and then handed it over. When I looked inside, I saw no one had even signed it. It was just his own name. I banged it shut and passed it back at him.

"Maybe it's in lost and found," Ella said. We went to the office, where Mrs. Lutz, the school secretary, was talking on the phone.

"Did you have a yearbook handed in today?" Dallas called out.

Mrs. Lutz raised a finger for us to wait, and Dallas gave her flea eyes. The secretary had no idea who she was dealing with; she was still on the phone.

"Um, she lost her yearbook, so it's kind of important."

Mrs. Lutz put one hand over the phone. She was triple ganky: her skin was picked at, and her plastic glasses made her look like a frog. "You need to wait," she said.

"You need to check lost and found."

Mrs. Lutz turned her back to us and kept talking. "So annoying," Dallas said loudly. Ella looked at the ceiling and bounced her shoulders back and forth like she didn't mind waiting; she was dancing.

Forever later, Mrs. Lutz got off the phone and came over to the window. "What did you girls want?"

"She lost her yearbook, so you need to check lost and found."

Mrs. Lutz looked at us straight. I remembered how she'd bought cupcakes at our class bake sale and gave everyone a big hulky smile, but she wasn't smiling now. "Nobody's turned in a yearbook. Why don't you check your locker?"

"Well, we did. That's why we're here. But you won't even check the box," Dallas said. "Someone might've slipped it in there when you were on the phone."

"I don't like your tone."

"Please, will you check, Mrs. Lutz?" Ella begged.

If Mrs. Lutz had laser eyes she would've burned Dallas right there on the spot. She had no idea who we were. How could she? She was stuck in the office all day, a complete disconnect. She finally turned around and stuck her hands inside the big cardboard box marked *Lost and Found*.

When she looked back at us, her cheeks were red and Ella giggled. "I told you it's not there," Mrs. Lutz huffed. "Why don't you get back to where you belong now?"

We might have gone somewhere else—wandering around, checking other kids' yearbooks—but just then Dallas sucked in her breath and pointed. There was a stack of brand-new yearbooks on a chair in the corner of the office.

"Whose are those?"

"Those all belong to someone," Mrs. Lutz said. "They haven't been picked up yet."

"Can I have a look?"

"I'm going to have to ask you to return to class now."

"How do you know they're not ours? I just want a look."

We could see that Mrs. Lutz was about to go bizonkers. "I DON'T want to have to call the VICE PRINCIPAL on the last day of school."

Dallas started laughing. Ella joined in. Me, too. Mrs. Lutz came up to the window.

"You're being very rude right now. I'll need to get your names."

Ella turned her back, she was shaking so hard. Dallas snorted and started to walk away.

"You have to guess our names, Irene Lutz!"

Ella and I followed Dallas, falling into one another, sick with it. When we were partway down the hall, Dallas screamed out in a high-Lutzy voice, "I don't want to call the VICE PRINCIPAL on the last da-ay!"

"I need to get your naaaaaaaaaaaaaaaaaaaaaaames!" Ella shrieked.

We ran and screamed. We were DH. The opposite of Lutz. We were ultra-people, sharp as sticks, while ganky Lutz-Butz was probably crying and shaking and waiting to go home so she could pick all the skin off her face.

On the day they named me Babyshits, I remembered Mrs. Lutz. I remembered Alex and Josie and all the rest. They were like blobs of mud I'd swallowed. They bubbled inside me, oozed out through my pores, and I wondered what I'd done to become someone like them.

From: C.Mckenzie@chronomail.com
To: R.Doblak@sparkon.com
Subject: (no subject)
Date: Thu, Jul 16 2009, 21:56:14

Robyn

There's something I need to tell you even if it makes you hate
me. Even if it makes you want to cut off my head and stick it up
on a rusty post.

It was my fault about your name. I was the one who first said
Bullets. And if it makes you feel any better I've got a name
now, too. They've started calling me Babyshits, but I bet that
won't make any difference. You'll say what goes around comes
around and you'll be happy I almost drowned.

Sometimes I wish we could both be Evil McFrenzy, getting
revenge on all those liars, but then I'd need to get revenge
on myself too, because of how I lied to you. That whole story
about Christmas, it wasn't even true. I never put ketchup on
myself and ran around the tree screaming. I only told you I did
because I wished it was true. C

* * *

Maybe they were just bored that summer, but after they tried to drown
me, DH still texted me to meet at the mall. They'd changed their phones
so when I texted, my name came up as BABYSHITS on their screens.

They wanted me to see, and they held their phones out while their mouths collapsed into laughter.

"Epic," I said, laughless.

"Babyshits, your shirt's really cute," Ella cooed. I was wearing a green Abercrombie tee I'd worn a thousand times before.

"'Course it looks good on her. It's the color of babyshits!"

"Credit!"

Ella rolled onto Dallas's lap, gooey with laughter, and they watched me with hungry eyes to see what I would do next. I stuck my hand in my pocket and squeezed the twig I'd started carrying.

"I don't give a shit what color it is," I said.

Dallas's tongue hung loose from her mouth as she lisped, "I don't give a shit."

I pressed the sharp end of the twig against my thumb and waited for them to stop laughing.

When I got home, I went behind the shed in the backyard where some trees were growing. This was my place. I pressed my hand against the trunk of the biggest tree and waited to feel something. Not a heartbeat, but a hum. The cool calm that grew up from its deepest roots to its tallest boughs. I pressed hard against the bark, and when I pulled my hand away there were ridges on my skin. Bugs clicked in the air and I waited for the air to become my lungs, the earth to become my body. Trees sucked mud and rain and air—turned them into bark and branches and leaves. Then they were mud again. I wished no one could see me. I walked over to the smallest tree and wrapped my hand around the cold trunk—it was the size of Dallas's wrist. I squeezed. I picked up a yellow-and-brown leaf from the grass and slipped it into my pocket.

Every time DH invited me along I carried a leaf and a twig in my pocket. When their mouths flew open, slobbering with laughter, I slid one finger in my pocket and touched the soft leaf-skin, the biting twig.

I could be as silent and blind as a tree. With no eyes to see, it would just be the sun on my limbs, leaves twisting in the breeze, my roots deep and moist in the ground. If two girls came up to me with a sharp blade and cut a name into my bark I would hardly feel it. Someday I might even forget it was there.

In the food court of the mall, Dallas pressed her fingers into the fattest part of her chin. As she jabbered, I wondered if the small potted tree near the escalators would be planted outside when it grew too big. Dallas said she wanted liposuction.

"You look amazing, but the surgery would probably make you even better," Ella said. Ella started pushing up the tip of her fox nose to show how she'd look after she turned sixteen and got a nose job. Then they turned to me, to see what I'd change.

Everything, but I didn't know how to say it. There would be an operating room, and a doctor with a metal cart full of scraps. He would sew bark over my hands and face, then plant seedlings into my shaved scalp. When the surgery was done, I would head for the woods and never return.

"I think her cheeks are weird," Ella said.

Dallas looked at me with flea eyes. "They're crooked. And a little too flat."

"Cheek implants for Babyshits!"

I stood up and walked toward the escalator near the potted tree. Dallas called after me, "You know your problem, Babyshits? You think you're too fucking perfect."

The leaves were damp from rain that day. When I stood behind the shed and reached up to touch one, it felt like Robyn's cheek. Another was her hand, and I held it for a second. I thought of the way the shower curtain sometimes billowed out, touching my back so lightly it could be somebody's warm fingers. But no one would touch me now. I was Babyshits.

When I went inside, Rebecca was home. She was wiping the counters with bleach and there was a salad on the table. She smiled at me. Rebecca was my always-cheerful, turtleneck-wearing, cupcake-loving, raspberry-tea-drinking, germ-obsessed, possibly-lesbo guardian. Even though she was thirty-four and younger than most people's parents, she didn't act young. She never went out and she liked torturing me with random rules and bad music, like jazz from the 1930s. When my principal called her about Robyn, she almost died. She couldn't believe I'd do anything wrong. She thought my friends were wonderful—she'd once said Dallas reminded her of Mom. She didn't mean it in a bad way, but she was a complete disconnect when it came to what they were really like. If I'd told her, I knew that first she wouldn't believe me, and then she'd probably dissolve into a puddle. Best friends meant everything to her.

She took a grapefruit out of the refrigerator and cut it in half as she asked me how they were. For the last month I'd kept her away from them, saying I was riding my bike to help the environment. But half the time I just rode around instead of going to their houses.

"You know, hon, I was thinking. If you'd rather spend the last week of summer with your friends, I'm sure we could shorten the time you're supposed to stay with Bea."

"No. That's okay."

"I just know how it is when you're fourteen. You want to spend all your time with your friends." She pressed two fingers against her chest and I knew she was thinking about Mom. She had a tattoo of a spiky purple flower under her collarbone that she didn't like anyone to know about. She always touched it when she was thinking about Mom, who had been her best friend.

"I told Grandma I'd help her. So I definitely want to go."

"I just wonder what you'll do all day."

Rebecca had total odium for Grandma, even though it was her own aunt. Whenever I visited, she barely came inside, and later when she picked me up, she'd sniff my hair and say it was fine if Bea wanted to kill herself quicker with a million cigarettes, but she had no right to risk my life too. Grandma didn't like Rebecca either. She made faces behind her back and called her The Enforcer.

"I hear The Enforcer's got you working for free this summer," Grandma said the last time we talked on the phone. I'd been volunteering at the nature reserve since July, and the truth was I actually liked dissecting owl pellets and counting amphibians, but I'd never admit it to Grandma. She wanted us to be on the same team, and for my upcoming visit, she'd Tivo'ed a whole season of the vampire show Rebecca said was too gruesome for me to watch. Grandma and I both had a sweet tooth, and I knew we'd spend most of the week eating strawberry shortcake and chocolate cherries, maybe sipping some of her beers while watching TV in her living room and forgetting about my life. I couldn't wait.

"I'm going to help Grandma go to her doctors' appointments," I told Rebecca. "And I'll cook food for her, too."

"Well, it's good of you to want to help," she said. "But if you change your mind, it's not too late."

She put down the grapefruit knife and reached over like she wanted to stroke my hair, but I ducked away at the last minute and her hand landed on my shoulder, which she rubbed three times, like I was a lucky purple pebble.

* * *

Here's something I've wondered a lot. If I could go back in time to the day before I left for Grandma's, would I:

A. not go to the mall when Dallas invited me

B. go to the mall but leave her cell phone alone

C. do the same thing I did, but bigger—

 finally serving her the shit-steak she deserved

I wouldn't let there be any fourth choice (D. none of the above, fuck your life), because in reality that's what I chose.

DH was sitting in the mall food court again, thinking up jokes with Babyshits for a punch line, while I stared at the potted tree by the escalator, wondering if someone had dumped a bowl of fried rice on it. It was looking kind of greasy.

Dallas leaned forward and said her boyfriend's jizz tasted like warm pickle juice. I waited for the punch line as she smacked her lips, but instead she started showing Ella how she'd gagged on it, and I must have looked like I was about to lose my flap because Dallas pointed at me.

"Look at Babyshits. She's scared of dicks."

I wasn't scared of dicks. I stuck my finger in my pocket and touched the ruffled edge of a leaf. In less than twenty-four hours I'd be at Grandma's house, watching vampires. Until then, I had to let the burnt mud slide back down my throat.

"Ella, you've got to see this," Dallas said. She took out her cell phone and pulled her chair closer.

Their heads touched and they spewed laughter. I sipped my Coke and leaned over to see.

Dallas covered the phone with her hand. "Not you, Babyshits. This is adults only."

I was sure there was something about me on that screen.

"What is it? Kevin's dick?"

"Don't you wish you knew." She gave her bleachy hair a victory toss and I sat back in my chair like a very weak tree that's stood alone in a field through snow and rain for a hundred years and can barely hold up its last few branches.

Ella said they were going to the bathroom and I could stay behind to watch their bags. After they left, I looked at Dallas's phone on the table. It had spent thousands of hours under her fingertips, pressed against her face, dropped into her bag, hidden beneath her desk, and tucked under her covers. It was the first and last thing she touched every day, when she checked her power and leaked tongue cheese to half the world. But her phone was just plastic and silicon and chemicals, put together on an assembly line in a faraway country by someone who'd never imagined it would end up here on a table in a mall in a country they'd only ever seen on TV. I closed my eyes. I was dangling from a branch, and the air felt cool around my edges as I swayed in the breeze. I was either Double Hockeysticks or I was dead. I picked up the phone and started scrolling through her pictures.

Dallas's cats. Kevin. Someone's foot. Kevin at her house. Ella. My thumb swiped faster and faster.

Then Dallas, stripped and stupid, white as a peeled potato. She'd taken the picture herself in front of a mirror and she was triple-X, über-waxed. She'd arched her back and shoved up her boobs to make them bigger than they really were, and then her neck was bent to one side and she'd puckered up, showing off the biggest, puffiest fish lips I'd ever seen.

That's when I chose none of the above and fucked my life. I didn't put the phone down. I didn't select "send all" to launch the picture to all her contacts. I didn't even think about how it might look on her Facebook page. The multiple choice in my brain went into full hibernation and when the name Dad popped up, I clicked and hit Send. Then my life was over.

I would never be Double Hockeysticks again. When the ringtone on

Dallas's phone started playing a second later, I realized what they'd say: that I was a tit troll and a meat monster. A real grimy fuck. I stood up and walked to the escalator like a zombie. Was there a name for someone as brain-dead as me? Yup. Babyshits. A pile of yellow-green turds about to get squashed. By the time I got home, they'd sent me seventeen texts.

Babyshits gonna cry cry? Die bitch DIIIIIIIIEEEEEEEEEEEE!!!!

Pervy Mervy run away. Pervy Mervy fucking pay!

Every time the phone buzzed, my stomach jumped like I'd just swallowed too much mustard. I belched and put it on silent, but the buzzing didn't go away. It hummed in my head as I walked back and forth, slapping my hands against the trees behind the shed. Dallas would probably be in trouble for five minutes. Her dad would sit her down for a big talk, and she'd sell him some juicy story, and by the end of it, he'd think that I was the one who'd ripped off her clothes and taken the picture in the first place. And for the next four years, I'd spend my life getting crushed in new and more evil ways. DH was like a virus that would get stronger and meaner as I got weaker and sicker. I sat down on the grass and pressed my mouth against my knee. I was Babyshits. Babyshits was me. I tried saying it soft and shy. Then I spat it into the air. I coughed it and swallowed it over and over until I could taste it. I found a twig on the ground and stuck it in my mouth, chewing and sucking the dirty end. Chewed. Spit. Chewed. Spit. The pressure built up in my ears until the twig was gone.

That night I got a message from someone calling themselves Phoenix Drake. Her profile picture showed the Grim Reaper smiling out from under a black hood.

Babyshits

U got no friends u smelly little baby and I've been hired to burn your stinking ugly ass. Better watch out because I am coming to kidnap u and murder u. U R GOING 2 DIE.

I will keep u alive first and cut off your fingers, stick them up ur butt the way u like. Plug the poopie hole so u stop making a mess. You've been warned.

Phoenixxxx

Phoenix Drake's profile was empty because DH had just created her. They wouldn't let it get traced back to them. This was how they were starting, but I knew they would do much worse. I wished for a minute that Phoenix was real. Then she could come and cut me to pieces and finish me off. I wouldn't have to worry about what was coming next. The biting and gobbling and pulverizing that would be more painful every day.

I didn't write back to Phoenix. Instead, I Googled "emphysema." If I learned enough about Grandma's disease, I could help her and she might let me stay permanently—change to a new school. But what I read gave me the grinds. People didn't get better without a lung transplant. The Google image showed a pair of lungs like an upside-down tree in a man's chest. Each lung had its own set of pink branches. The sick lung was different. It was gray, with rotten black leaves, thick and blobby, crowding the end of each branch. As I stared at the black leaves I was breathing harder and harder and it felt like I was going deep and deeper and deepest all over again.

* * *

"You seem quiet," Rebecca said, on the way to Grandma's house. "Are you sure you want to go?"

I said I was looking forward to it *extremely,* and then Rebecca pulled out her strawberry ChapStick and rubbed it on her lips for the ten-thousandth time that morning.

"Teach me some Latin," she said.

Rebecca had signed me up for private tutoring with Miss Jarvis because someone told her it would help me get a higher score on the SATs. Rebecca thought I was probably going to end up somewhere like Yale, and she'd once driven me to New Haven to walk around the campus. "Imagine you're a student here," she said, as we looked up at the buildings made of lion-colored stone. "You're about to go to class. How do you feel?" I hated when she did this. She looked at me like I might turn into someone else, and I knew who she was thinking of, and I knew it wouldn't work. But I couldn't figure out how to tell her this, so I just said, "It feels fine," and kept going to the library to practice Latin roots with Miss Jarvis each week.

Rebecca tapped the steering wheel, waiting for me to speak Latin. "Come on. I want to learn," she begged.

"*Corpus,*" I said. "Body."

Rebecca nodded and repeated the word.

"*Oculus:* eye."

"Like octopus."

"*Manus:* hand," I said. "*Donum:* gift. *Laguna:* small lake."

"I know that one," Rebecca said. "And *caveat emptor:* buyer beware."

She waited for me to tell her some more, and when I didn't she started talking about passports. "I forgot again," she said. "I meant to get your picture so we could apply over the summer—I'd hate for you to miss out because I didn't apply in time. The high school does so many trips. I think they go to England, Spain, France. Maybe some other places, too.

I should probably get mine—you know, I've never even been out of the country. Wouldn't it be funny if they asked me to chaperone?"

I didn't say anything. She uncapped her ChapStick and rubbed on some more.

When we pulled up to Grandma's house the grass in her yard had grown really tall. If DH could see it, they'd say it was ghetto. Rebecca knocked and then opened the front door without waiting for an answer. We walked past an oxygen tank on the floor, and then into the living room, where Grandma sat in her recliner, watching TV, with a little tube in her nose. Grandma wasn't a hug-and-kiss kind of person, but I went over to her recliner, and she pressed an arm around my waist. Right away, Rebecca squared off.

"Bea, are you still smoking?"

"Nope. I quit."

"I smell it in the house."

"That's old smoke," Grandma said. "When you smoke for twenty years the smell sticks around."

Before she left, Rebecca pulled me aside. "It's really dangerous for her to smoke now that she has oxygen tanks in here. That's how fires start. The tanks could explode." Rebecca held on to my arm. "If she takes out a cigarette I want you to run out of the house and call me right away."

I said I would. Rebecca wrapped her arms around me and squeezed. "If you change your mind about staying, give me a call. I'll be in the area for a little while."

She hadn't told me she was going to Mom's grave, but I knew that's where she'd be. She couldn't get enough of it—but at least this time I wouldn't get dragged along.

As soon as Rebecca left, Grandma pulled out a cigarette. She'd been hiding the pack under a pillow on her lap.

"She really burns my ass," Grandma said, flicking her lighter. "She's been like that ever since she was born. Snotty little kid."

She sucked her cigarette and I couldn't take my eyes away from its hot tip. I didn't want to run outside. I wanted to watch it burst into a giant fireball—a red globe that would swallow me up. Heat and smoke like red planets and starlight in the fog. Death by fire. The end of my problems. I stayed put.

"Don't worry." She waved her cigarette at me. "I've been doing this a long time."

"I'm not worried." My cell phone was humming in my pocket and Dallas's name was on the screen. I breathed in Grandma's smoke and flicked a finger toward her pack. "Can I have one?"

I grinned as Grandma started laughing, but then the laughing turned into coughing and the coughing turned into gasping. I stood up and looked at my phone like that might help. "Should I call Rebecca? Or nine-one-one?"

Grandma shook her head at me. She was still holding the cigarette and I didn't know if I should take it out of her hand. Her whole body was heaving and I felt as evil as DH when they watched me drown, so I kneeled in front of her and put my hand on her bony knee. She didn't look at me; her eyes were squeezed shut. I thought she was dying. Her chest kept moving up and down, and her throat was making a hot, dry noise, and if I knew how, I would've tried to pull her back to the surface. But Grandma wasn't underwater, so I kept rubbing her knee and watching her face and then finally, a million years later, the coughing and gasping stopped, and Grandma brought the cigarette to her mouth and took a puff.

"Do me a favor," she said, her eyes watery. "Go get yourself a soda from the fridge, and bring me a beer."

I knew she wanted me to go away because she was embarrassed, so I took my hand off her knee and went into the kitchen. I wasn't thirsty, but I ran the cold water in the sink over my hands and then found her a beer and poured it in a glass.

I was going to do everything right that week—I wanted to make it impossible for her to live without me. So I started learning all the things I could do: Velcro her shoes, read the labels on her medicine, find her three inhalers. In the morning, when Grandma woke up and muttered, "Jesus Christ! My goddamn sacs," I knew that meant her lungs were bad, so I went to the kitchen and made her a bowl of yogurt with banana mixed in. I mopped the floor and scrubbed the shower, both without her asking. Grandma gave me a funny look when I washed out her ashtray and then I realized I was acting too much like Rebecca, who she hated. So to prove I wasn't a fuzzy-perfect blah-blah I started doing Rebecca impressions for Grandma. I went stomping around the room, pretending to look for dust under the bed, and then running my finger along the windowsill and screaming in horror that it had plaque buildup. I put on a gushy voice and said, "Hon, there's so much bacteria in the world, but if you work hard and floss six times a day everything will be awesome and cavity-free." I didn't sound anything like her, but Grandma laughed anyway.

Then I told her how Rebecca liked to pretend everything was so perfect, always saying "Life is good," but that I heard her crying in the bathtub at night.

"Fucking Enforcer," Grandma said.

Sometimes I didn't check my phone for an hour. I'd be watching TV or washing the dishes and I'd forget about it for a few minutes, but after an hour I always got the jiggles. Even though I knew it would make me feel worse, I had to go check. Sometimes I'd try to hide it from myself in my room, but I'd just end up running around until I found it. I had to know. What were they thinking, what were they saying, what did they want me to hear? Afterward I would feel like my guts had been scraped out with a knife. I was brown and green and dripping. A fat sweaty blob, made of dirt and rust and ashes, hanging upside down and waiting to drop.

When Rebecca called, I said the things that Grandma had told me to. We'd been eating mostly cereal and yogurt, watching TV all day long, but I knew how to lie.

"We just had spaghetti and salad," I told Rebecca, "garlic bread on the side."

"Are you getting out at all or are you just cooped up all day?"

"We drove to the mall. We get out."

We didn't want Rebecca to know how bad Grandma was because she'd probably overreact and force me to come home. Grandma ran out of breath even walking to the bathroom, so we sat in her living room for two days, watching the vampire series, and every once in a while when I heard the click of her lighter the hairs on my neck would stand up, but then I'd tell myself, *No, it's okay to die.*

In four days, we went out in the car only twice. Grandma dressed up in her jean jacket and puffy cap, and tied her stringy gray hair in a low ponytail. She said I could take whatever I wanted from her jewelry box, so I picked out a pair of dangly skull earrings so she'd know I liked her style. I helped carry Grandma's portable oxygen to the car, and then I sat in the waiting room while she saw her doctor. Another day, we went to the supermarket, and even though we parked in a handicapped space, by the time we got inside, Grandma was wheezing and pressing her chest. I put her oxygen tank in the top of the shopping cart, and we stood near the vegetable section, waiting until she felt better. I didn't care who looked at us. They could stare at Grandma's tubes all day long and neither of us would care. I'd made myself leave my phone in the car, and when Grandma and I started walking slowly along the aisles, I felt just as good as I used to with DH. She didn't give a damn what anyone thought and neither would I. Grandma dropped a bag of starlight mints into the cart, and she let me get two boxes of Cocoa Puffs cereal. "I love staying with you," I said. "You understand me so much better than The Enforcer."

"Don't get me started on her again," Grandma said.

"I bet if I lived with you I could help a lot."

"Oh, yeah?" Grandma asked. "You wanna be my slave?"

She pointed to a box of Raisin Bran that she wanted me to reach, and I plucked it off the shelf, dropped it in the cart. "Sure," I said. "Yes, master!"

Grandma didn't laugh. She turned away to look at something else, and by the time we got home, I knew she was mad. After I put away the groceries, she said I should go outside and get some fresh air. She told me she wanted to take a nap, and she made it sound like she wouldn't be able to if I was around. I wanted to stay inside, but I couldn't risk annoying her.

I left Grandma in her chair and went out to the garage, where she said there was a bike I could ride up and down the street. The bike was prehistoric, like something you'd dig up from the bottom of a lake and then put in a museum. It was crusty and dirty, the tires were flat. It might've been green once, but it also could've been blue or red or silver or black. There was a bar down the middle and I realized it was probably my dad's. Grandma never would've ridden it. I wasn't even sure if I should touch the ganky thing, but I knew if I was going to live here I'd need a way of getting around. I could even use it to pick up food or Grandma's medicine—that's what I could tell her. I found a pump and filled up the tires. Then I pushed the bike out to the street and held it upright. It wobbled some, like it might shatter into a thousand rotten parts, but then I pushed the pedals and it started to go. The wheels rolled and I held on to the worn rubber grips.

I rode back and forth, getting used to the trees and bushes and side-walks and streets. Pedaling faster, I breathed in crystal fuel and began to taste the secret history of this place.

Before my dad, before the telephone poles and painted signs, every-thing was quiet. Ice Age, Stone Age, birds lifting into the sky. I erased houses and cars and people and lawns. There was just forest, moss, the smell of stones. Something leaking out into the universe and telling me I could stay. This would be my place. Giant trees. Frozen lakes. A woolly mammoth with thick fur crusted in ice. No language, just silence. Soft as the flapping sigh of a moth's wing.

My cell phone sang out and I hit the brakes. Rebecca wanted to know how I was doing. It was the second time she'd called that day. I knew that when she found out I was staying with Grandma she'd cry for so long that her eyes would swell up and her nose would get red and then mine would, too, and I wouldn't want to leave her. But I'd have to do it—escaping was all that mattered now.

"I ran into Dallas," Rebecca said. "I think she really misses you. She said she couldn't get you on your cell so I told her I'd ask you to call. I thought it might be nice to bring her and Ella along when I pick you up."

"That's okay," I said, swallowing. "You shouldn't do that."

"Dallas just sounded so lost without you. She can't wait for you to get back. I thought it was sweet."

"Is that it?"

"Is now a bad time?"

"I'm just outside. I'm riding a bike."

"Do you have a helmet?"

"Uh-huh."

"Is everything okay with Bea?"

"Yeah. She's great. I really love it here."

"Good, sweetheart. Well, call me later."

After I hung up with Rebecca, I rode back to Grandma's house. When I put the bike back in the garage I read the latest text from Dallas.

You can run but you can't hide. Dead Babyshits leaves a stain.

Grandma was asleep in her chair, so I sat down on the couch, breathed in the smell of smoke and medicine, and told myself that this was home. The long wrinkles on her cheeks reminded me of ant trails, and I must've been staring when she opened her eyes.

"Why are you looking at me?"

I looked down at my phone. Maybe I could show it to her. If she saw their messages she'd have to let me stay. Either that or she'd wonder what I'd done to deserve it. Then I'd have to explain about Robyn, and DH, and the naked picture I'd sent. Grandma might look at me like she smelled Babyshits, too.

"I was just wondering," I said. "Do you think people who have trouble sometimes deserve it?"

Grandma made a face like it was a stupid question. "Nobody deserves anything. What happens happens. That's life."

She was still wearing her jean jacket, and I thought about the black leaves floating in her chest.

"What if everyone started calling you a name that wasn't yours? Like if everyone called you Jennifer instead of Bea."

"What do I care about that? Some of us have real problems in the world."

The phone was starting to sweat in my hand. I had to find a way.

"Do you ever wonder about what would happen if I lived here? In Cansdown?"

"I can't think about that, because you don't. Now do me a favor. Quit theorizing and go find yourself some dinner."

I ate my Cocoa Puffs without mentioning it again, but that night I couldn't sleep. The bedroom used to be my dad's, but Grandma redecorated after he died. The walls were plain white and all his things had been thrown away. Even if there were real traces of him in the room—dandruff on the mattress, toenail clippings in the rug—they were too small to see. And I was glad because I didn't want to imagine things that weren't true. Like if there was a baseball glove, I might think he loved baseball—I might even imagine him pitching in a field. I'd walk around every day thinking my dad played baseball until I believed I'd really seen it and it was true. Then one day someone might come up to me and say, *Actually, your dad hated sports and the baseball glove was just a thing he had.* Then I'd have to admit I was fooling myself, and I'd promised I wouldn't do that anymore. When Rebecca had told me how he'd left me, *committing suicide,* I said I never wanted to hear about him, ever again. Grandma had his ashes in a box in her closet, but I didn't want to see that either.

From: C.Mckenzie@chronomail.com
To: R.Doblak@sparkon.com
Subject: (no subject)
Date: Wed, Aug 26 2009, 23:47:05

Robyn

I never told you this before, but my dad killed himself when I was five. When I asked them why he did it they told me he was sad. I used to think that was a bullshit excuse. Über-pathetic. Like just because you're feeling shitty doesn't mean you have to die.

But I've been thinking about it more now and I'm starting to get it. Like there was this girl Autumn Sanger who drowned at the beach. She disappeared one day and everyone thought she was kidnapped, so they blamed all these different people, and Autumn got more and more famous. But she was only trying to escape and I think I can understand that. We're the same, you know? I need to escape, too. C

* * *

I waited until after breakfast the next morning. Grandma sat in her chair, watching a talk show and sucking a cinnamon drop. There were only four days left until high school started and if this didn't work, my life was fucked. I doodled the number in my notepad. FOUR. I drew little red flames shooting off it, and then I scribbled it out. The commercials came on and I had to do it now.

"I've been thinking I could stay here with you," I said. "I know you don't need my help, but I could stick around just in case."

Grandma was still looking at the TV. The commercial showed a hulky man holding a laptop.

"I'm sick," she finally said. "You can't live here."

"It's just . . . I'm having some problems with my friends, so I don't want to leave. I can't go home." I looked down at my notepad; the words wobbled on the page.

"I've got twenty percent lung function, which means eighty percent doesn't work," Grandma said. "So your friendship dramas don't mean a lot to me."

"Are you on a lung list?"

"What?"

"To get a new lung? A transplant?"

Grandma made a face and brought a tissue to her mouth, spitting out her candy. "I don't go on those lists. They're a load of crap."

I watched her begin to search for her cigarettes. She ran her fingers along the side of the cushion she was sitting on.

"They call me Babyshits," I said. "My friends."

Grandma pretended not to hear. She put a cigarette in her mouth and flicked the lighter. I watched the flame. *Boom,* I thought. Let us both go up in smoke. We deserved it. A fire wiping out the last of our family. Heat like a wave. I would become ashes and rain down on the trees. And Grandma, with her cigarette, would be a murderer.

Grandma blew out smoke. "I'm terminal, you know? Do you know what *terminal* means?"

I nodded and I started to cry because I was terminal, too.

"Jesus Christ," Grandma said. She looked at me and I knew what she thought. *Big surprise they call you Babyshits. You are one big baby.* I stared at her cigarette. *Boom,* I thought. *Boom.*

I wanted to be nothing, just mud underground.

I wished I'd been with my mom that day.

No wonder my dad killed himself—with a mother like her.

I was thinking it, but I was also saying it, and then I had the grinds so bad I couldn't even see her face. I ran out to the garage, sticking my notepad down the back of my shorts, then I grabbed the bike, threw my leg over the bar. I was pedaling blind, my eyes so blurry that I might've been in a bright place underwater, straw and kelp catching my eyelashes.

I wasn't supposed to be here. I could feel it inside my skin, all the way down to my smallest bones and my racing heart. I kept pedaling, but I wasn't going back in time; I was just a body on a bike, passing houses and a gas station. I hunched my shoulders and pumped my legs until my throat hurt, until there weren't as many houses, just buildings and fences and auto repair shops and I wouldn't be able to find my way back, but maybe I could change my name, cut my hair, throw away my phone.

Then I could lie down and sleep, practice the stillness of being no one.

I realized where I was when I saw the trees up ahead. Mom's cemetery. I'd never been there on a bike and I always went with Rebecca, but it felt like the first time I actually wanted to go inside.

I pushed my bike through the gate and up the road. There were so many trees, and all of them were unlucky. They'd been planted here and they could never leave. Day and night, they lived. Swallowing tears and eyelashes, giving shade to no one. Roots that grew too deep touched the dead, tangling with buried hands and feet, hanging them in the world below.

At the edge of the parking lot, I dropped the bike, and suddenly I could smell myself, the dusty sweat that coated my calves, the wetness of my back. My shorts were bunched up, but there was no one around, so I tugged the damp fabric as I walked to the stone engraved with my last name. I didn't sit down or say anything to her. After two seconds, I was ready to go. But there was nowhere for me to go. I would have to stay here with the trees and the stones and the dead.

And I hardly remembered her. Except she had long hair that tickled me like feathers when she leaned down for a kiss. And when I stuck my tongue out to lick her stubbly knee, she smelled like milk, and patted my head, saying, "Good little cat." I rubbed my hand over the grass on Mom's grave and started feeling sick. I'd never know her and she'd never know what I'd done to Robyn. I remembered the way Dallas and Ella had coached me after I squirted the paint.

"Just tell everyone Robyn said something sheisty."
"Say she was going to kill you!"
"No, Ella. She should say something realistic."

It was the most realistic thing I could think of and it felt true after what I'd done. *My mom died so she wouldn't have to look at me.* I opened my notepad just to see how the words would feel.

> *Your daughter hurts people. She threw the paint and sent the*
> *picture. Callie deserves to die like you.*

There was an ant on the ground, and I got him to crawl onto my hand. I couldn't even feel it as he crossed between my fingers, up my wrist, and toward my elbow. But I knew he wasn't scared. We were the same. Together our two tiny hearts were beating, and underneath us my mom was dead. It felt like nothing as I slid the paper under Mom's stone. The ant crawled away and I heard a lawn mower. When I looked up there was a man cutting the grass. I started to walk back to the bike and then I saw all the messages on my phone.

When I got back to Grandma's house, Rebecca's car was parked out front and I wished I was a nun. Then I could take a vow of silence and never speak again.

Rebecca was sitting on the couch while Grandma watched TV. But when she saw me, Rebecca jumped up. "Where the hell have you been?"

When Rebecca started swearing, you knew it was serious. I told her I'd been out on the bike, which was true at least. Her face was purple, and I wondered what Grandma had told her. But luckily for me, Grandma wasn't a snitch.

"You're too much for me," Grandma said. "I'm not up to kids anymore."

She didn't say it like she was sorry. She just wanted me out of there. And the stuff I'd told her about Babyshits was probably the last thing on her mind. Rebecca gave me a moony sad face like she was oh-so-sorry and for just a second I wanted to break Grandma's TV. Smash it with my fist into a billion smithereens. But instead I went to my room and packed.

I didn't say anything to Grandma, and when I followed Rebecca out to the car, she put an arm around my shoulder.

"You okay, Callie?"

When I didn't answer, she gave me a squeeze. "I know this is hard, but you shouldn't take it personally. You know she's in pain and she's not a happy person."

The car was like an oven, and Rebecca shut me inside. I felt myself dissolving into nothing more than a slug: a lazy sleepy slug whose icky, sluggy insides started jiggling all sick when we pulled onto the road. My arms swelled at my sides, and my head bumped the window and then I tried to remember, was it salt that killed slugs? Could I sprinkle it on my arms and watch them shrivel up in front of me?

There were words in the oven, too cheerful and sharp. The lady was talking to sluggy.

"Why don't we stop and get ice cream somewhere? We can cool off in a diner for a while."

The slug oozed slime. It wanted somewhere dark and quiet. No to ice cream: too sugary and cold for its slippery belly. No to diners: too bright for its squinty, sluggy eyes. Everyone would stare.

"I'm just trying to be nice," the lady said. "I've been looking forward to having you back."

The slug sank deeper into the heat, where all thoughts were single words. *Yes. No. No. Yes.*

But the lady wouldn't shut up. She wanted to shove the slug into a space where it didn't belong. A space full of gym clothes and notebooks, band practice and bleachers, lip gloss and tights. Only three and a half days left. The sluggy slug curled up inside itself. It could try and cover its soft spots, but all it had were soft spots.

* * *

The first day of high school. Headband, earrings, ring. Ankle boots. Eye shadow and mascara.

None of it would help, but maybe DH hadn't told everyone yet. Maybe nobody would care.

The sluggy reality:

Outside the school, on a patch of grass, where everyone waited for the double doors to open, I couldn't find a place to stand. I wandered from the bike racks to a spot under a window and then over to the bushes, where I pressed my arm into a branch. If I kept moving, crablike, they might not notice me. But there were already a thousand boundaries I couldn't cross. Arms, necks, tongues, teeth, hair. Aliens. Familiar faces twisted into hectic shapes. If I got too close to anyone I would shrivel up and die.

"Squishies," a bunch of girls shouted as they hugged each other. Two prinks we used to eat lunch with laughed and wrinkled their noses when they saw me. My sluggy insides started to dissolve.

I looked at my phone. There was a new message from a number I didn't know.

Warning! Babyshits poops her pants. GET A FUCKING DIAPER.

I ignored the text and played Mythical Maze on my phone, focusing so much I forgot where I was. When the doors opened, I followed the crowd to the gym, where a big blue-and-white banner hung from the ceiling. WELCOME CLASS OF 2013. My schedule was on the *M* table, and I grabbed it, then sat on the edge of a bleacher, feeling the vibrations of everyone else through my body. When I saw DH, my tongue curled at the back of my throat.

Ella noticed me first with a skeezy smile.

Dallas puckered her blister-pink lips. "Babyshits!"

I looked at the schedule on my lap.

"Babyshits! You know I'm talking to you!"

I started walking to the exit, but I knew what I wanted to do. I wished I had a knife so I could turn around and stab them. I wished they had asthma so I could empty their inhalers and lock them in a room with no air.

A boy near the door hissed, "Sleeping bag," as I went past.

I didn't know what he was talking about, but I saw later that afternoon. Dallas had updated her status on Facebook.

> So f'ing nasty. Going to have to burn my sleeping bag after lending it to Callie McKenzie. Let's just say someone needs a diaper. Smells rank.

Under that, Ella had written:

> Babyshits!!! Strikes again!

Dallas had 582 friends. I wondered what I could write back. THE RUMORS ARE NOT TRUE. But I knew it wouldn't make a difference. Her words had already left a stain. For 582 people the shit was in the bag.

At school, a girl wouldn't stand behind me in the cafeteria line. A boy with emo hair crashed my chair as he walked past. Someone else pretended to flick chocolate pudding on my ass. Each time it happened, I could feel something swelling in my chest that left no room for anything else. I made my eyes like a slitty snake's, and told myself I wouldn't cry. I tried to keep my mind focused on one thing. Like a gun. Would Dallas and Ella shoot me if they could? Would I shoot them? I knew in an upside-down world, I'd be the one laughing and waiting for me to cry. I'd be laughing and planning what to do next.

The toilet paper on my chair in biology? I could've done that. And when Babyshits turned red and tried to hide the roll under her desk, I would've watched while the class burst out laughing. Everyone was laughing—even Lily Trager, whose brother has Downs and is supposedly the nicest girl in our grade.

It could've been me who brought the black Sharpie to the girls' bathroom on the second floor of B wing. There was a mural of dancers in there, spinning and leaping across a rainbow background, and one day, someone drew black turds coming out of one of the dancers. I might've watched Dallas draw the arrow that labeled the dancer Babyshits. Or maybe I would've done it myself.

Every time I saw them in the hall, I felt like a wild dog. Ella's arms danced in the air as they shouted my name, and my whole body shook. I wanted to jump the fence, rip their throats, howl at the moonless sky. I scared myself. I wasn't like my mother. I had a dark center, the blood of a killer. And as I ducked away to hide in a lavatory stall I wished that Dallas had a nut allergy so I could swipe her with fingers covered in peanut oil.

In Spanish class, Señora Vallsay showed us a slideshow on the whiteboard. She'd gone on vacation to Mexico and wanted us to see her eating the food, walking the streets, standing in front of museums. Under my desk, I opened the note that someone had dropped in my bag. It was a quiz: "Are you the school's biggest loser?"

Please circle.

Everyone calls me:

a. amazing

b. beautiful

c. Babyshits

When I need a shit, I:

a. do it in my pants

b. do it in my diaper

c. sit on a toilet and remember to flush

Congratulations, you are officially the school's biggest loser. Why don't you die?

I didn't know why I didn't die. I waited for my breath to stop coming and my heartbeat to end. I was nothing. I watched the changing pictures of Mexico and wished I was anything else. The blankness of a sheet of paper. The lime-green of a fallen leaf. A plastic watch ticking on a boy's wrist. The Mexican burro with empty eyes who stood alone in the slideshow.

After the last picture, Señora Vallsay switched on the lights and said we'd introduce ourselves to the class in Spanish. I could suddenly picture myself saying the wrong name. I got ready for the snorted giggles, and the echoed hoot, but when I opened my mouth I could hardly speak. My throat clogged with mud, and for a moment Señora Vallsay looked in my eyes like she was reading me. Her eyes were clear to the bottom and they knew me, my suffering. She was half smiling, but she was also knowing me. And I finally whispered, "Me llamo Callie."

After the first few days of sitting by myself, I stopped going to the cafeteria at lunch. The school library was open, and I played games on the computer, plugged in my earbuds, and pushed myself far, far away. Sometimes when my stomach rumbled and no one was around, I pulled a twig from my pocket and sucked its dirty end. I held it like a cigarette and wondered about Grandma. I knew which shows she watched every day, and I imagined I was there with her, sitting on the sofa, eating a bowl of Cocoa Puffs. Sometimes she looked over and said my name. Other times I held her hand, and then she lit a cigarette and we died together. I didn't know if she hated me because of what I'd said. I hadn't told her good-bye that day, and I realized I wanted to talk to her.

I locked myself in a bathroom stall and took out my phone. "Grandma?" I said, when her answering machine clicked on. "Grandma?" I was giving her time to hear my voice and pick up. "It's Callie."

She didn't pick up, so I kept going. "How are your sacs? Are they okay?"

I sat down on the toilet and took out my leaf, balanced it on my thigh.

"I just wanted to say I'm better now. I'm sorry about what I said."

I wondered if she was sitting there, listening. I touched the leaf and waited. "I didn't mean it and I shouldn't have said it."

I gave her one last chance to pick up, and then I told her I had to go. Then I took a red pen out of my bag and looked at the smooth, clean walls around me. I could write anything. I could tell the world that Dallas was a fat-chinned cannibal who ate penises for breakfast. Or that Ella was a defective scarecrow. I could draw pictures of them both, burning at the stake—but instead I lifted up my shirt. There was only one word that I wanted to write. Babyshits. I wrote it on my stomach first. Then I unzipped my pants. Each thigh took the ink. I pulled down the neck of my shirt and wrote it on my shoulder. The pen tip was cool as I pressed it into my skin, finding new places. It would be my word now. It was the one thing I had.

From: C.Mckenzie@chronomail.com

To: R.Doblak@sparkon.com

Subject: (no subject)

Date: Thu, Sept 3 2009, 19:22:14

Robyn

Today I woke up so happy because I forgot that you hate me.
For 10 amazing seconds we were friends again. You told me to
watch cartoons and eat some cereal and when you said my
name I opened my eyes and smiled.

It wasn't real. I'm alone again. C

＊ ＊ ＊

Rebecca was excited about the first Friday of the high school year. "School
spirit Friday," she reminded me. "Do you know what you're wearing?"

We were supposed to come to school dressed in blue and white, our
school colors. There was going to be a pep rally and freshmen were expected to try the hardest, painting our faces and arms half blue and half
white. It was supposed to make us love our high school, and love each
other, but I knew it was a lie. Under the paint I would still be Babyshits.
Even if I could transform back to Double Hockeysticks, it wouldn't
mean a thing. It was empty. It meant nothing, and I told Rebecca what
I thought.

"But don't you want to show you support your school teams?"

"The color I'm wearing won't make any difference."

"It might make a difference to how you feel," Rebecca said. "Like, when I was a kid, I used to get these chain letters in the mail. The message always started the same way: THIS IS NO JOKE. It usually said it had been around the world at least seven times, and promised that believers who forwarded it on would have good luck, while people who broke the chain might die or lose money. And Callie, I knew it was probably all made up, but I always went and got a pen and started copying it out, which took a really long time. And it wasn't that I believed a piece of paper could have all that power, but while I was writing it, *I* felt powerful—like the things I did might make a difference. And I liked to believe that I was part of something bigger, and could maybe help the people around me by taking part." Rebecca put down her spoon and looked at me for a second.

"I mean, you guys nowadays are a lot less gullible than we were. There aren't even chain *e-mails* now, are there? I knew this one guy who thought he was going to get ten thousand dollars in the mail, just because he'd sent five dollars to a name on a list. He told me he was going to throw a big party on the beach when the money came, and of course, it never did because it was all a scam. But for a while, he felt rich."

"That's the stupidest thing I've ever heard. He must've felt ultra-stupid."

"Maybe." Rebecca closed her eyes for a second. "Maybe he needed that lesson. I guess the point is that some rituals can be good for you, even if they don't make a real difference to the eventual outcome. Even if they don't give you the thing you think you're going to get."

I looked at her and realized she wanted me to be brain-dead, like her and everyone else. We'd all be zombies doing brain-dead meaningless things together. That was what life was.

At school, I started paying attention. When the bells rang everyone jumped. At pep rallies, everyone screamed. In homeroom, we stood up when the loudspeaker told us and put our right hands over our hearts. The principal said the Pledge of Allegiance, and some kids mumbled along while others mouthed the words. One boy at the front shouted the whole thing, and he stood up so straight you could've chopped him right down. I looked at the raggy flag hanging over the door and wondered if people were feeling something right now. Were they believing? Was the principal really thinking about what each word meant? Or was this just another zombie habit? Something we'd all memorized in kindergarten before we were old enough to decide what we really believed. I knew it was wrong to think this. But what if nobody felt the things we were supposed to? What if everyone was pretending? And what if one day there was a completely different flag at the front and nobody minded at all?

The recording of the national anthem played over the loudspeaker and everyone sat down before it finished. Nobody sang along. Mrs. Dobbler looked at her laptop and rubbed lipstick off her teeth. We were all basically brainless.

My algebra teacher gave me a detention because I was late.

"Miss McKenzie, you will be staying after school."

He looked proud of himself. He was enforcing a rule. Everyone in class was copying an equation from the whiteboard, and I sat down in my seat and opened my notebook. But I couldn't do the next thing. I couldn't copy the symbols. The X's and Y's. I couldn't pretend that they had meaning to me. That the letters were numbers—variables that might change at any second. Lose value, go negative, shrink to nothing at all. Everyone else would try to solve it, but not me. I broke the tip of my pencil and looked at my wrists.

If a number could disappear, how would you prove it existed in the first place? How small could it get before it vanished completely? In real life there was no coming back. X couldn't equal –1,000 one minute and then rise back up to 64. Once you lost your value, everything else did, too. And maybe all those things you thought had value had been empty all along.

After school, I texted Rebecca to say I was going to Ella's. I walked to Shabby Maggie's on Main Street and wandered around the store, touching all the things that people had thrown away. I knew that when I got home I'd find a new message from Phoenix Drake. The night before, the picture of the Grim Reaper appeared, and I'd read what DH wanted me to see:

> Babyshits! Are you happy that you're still walking around, fouling the earth, making a mess wherever you go? Your smell makes us sick. Your clothes look like garbage you found in the trash. You're a dirty fucking cockroach and I'm going to crush you.

Dallas had more than six hundred friends now. She was friending new people from school, while at the same time, my friend list had gone down from 356 to 322. And of those 322, most of them hated me, and none were my friends. Everything I'd been was gone, and even though I looked the same and dressed the same, I was someone else now. I was Babyshits.

I picked up a T-shirt from the men's rack. There was a picture of a black man with an Afro on the front, and the shirt was the color of babyshits. It felt soft and worn out, so I held it in my hands, wondering where it had come from and why. The sleeves had held someone's arms and then let them go. Now it was here with me. I bought it for three dollars, and when I got home I put it on before checking my computer.

Phoenix hadn't sent me any messages, and Dallas and Ella hadn't written anything new. I rubbed the soft sleeves of my shirt—they smelled like fabric softener—and then said my name. Babyshits. I felt like a wild dog again. I wanted to sink my teeth into something. I started writing a message to Phoenix Drake:

Dallas & Ella. I know it's you. Love, Babyshits

A few minutes after I sent it, I got a notification. Dallas had invited me to join a new group. It was called "HAVE YOU SMELLED BABYSHITS?"

I clicked on the group. In the left-hand corner there was a picture of me from last June, dancing at Ella's house in my green pajamas. My hair was frizzy and my mouth was hanging open and it looked like I was either panting or trying to take a shit.

This group is for people who have smelled the most ass bad smell around—Babyshits. Share your photos and experiences here.

Phoenix Drake was listed as the group creator. There were seven people in the group, and Kevin Brunetti had written a comment.

Smelled her today and it smelled like dung. ROFL

I looked at the picture of me again and then the air stopped working. My chest was moving up and down, but the air wasn't going in. I grabbed the front of my shirt. Something wasn't working. It was the air or my lungs. Swirling or spiraling away. Like black leaves. No. Yes. Yes. No. I pushed myself onto the floor and waited for it to be over. For the colors to strip away. Clear. Deep. Stranglified.

The door was knocking. I breathed.

"Callie?" she said. "Why are you on the floor?"

A zombie.

"Hon? Are you okay?"

There was a yellow sock under my bed; I reached for it and held it.

"Looking for my sock." The sock told me to stand up, so I stood, very shaky.

"You've got your own personal Bermuda triangle in here." The zombie picked up a jacket and hung it on the door. "You'll have to clean up this weekend. Dusting and everything."

I dropped the sock on my bed and moved to my desk. I clicked so the screen went dead. The zombie was watching me.

"Hey, where'd you get that shirt?"

"Shabby Maggie's."

"I'll put it in the wash for you. It might not be clean."

They had made a group about me and it was only going to get bigger. The shirt wrapped me in its arms and I shook my head no. It didn't want to be clean. It wanted to stay the way it was, exactly how I'd found it.

When I woke up the next morning, I held my breath before checking. There were eleven members in the group now. I'd slept in my new-old shirt and it told me, *Don't change.* My unbrushed hair felt right, and then my skin said, *Please don't touch.* So I left my foundation and eye shadow on the sink.

"What's with the new look?" Rebecca asked, when I walked into the kitchen.

"Emo," I lied.

"Emo? We used to call that 'hippie.'"

Before first period, I saw Dallas and Ella coming down the hall. If I screamed at them, they would laugh. If I asked them to stop, they would throw my words back in my face. I tucked my hands inside the hem of my shirt and made my face as smooth as blue water.

"I think someone's very proud she used the potty," Ella called.

"What a good girl, Babyshits," Dallas said, clapping.

I didn't think I would make it to homeroom. My legs couldn't understand why they should walk me to that place. They thought I should run away, take off into the woods, and when I didn't, they told me they were going to collapse. They said I'd have to lie there in the middle of the hall while someone called an ambulance, and then what would I do? I pinched them, and they kept going.

As I walked through the hall, I felt them moving around me. All the zombies who hated me, all the empties who would join in killing me. I was a tree in the woods, and they were the villagers, circling me with axes and knives and switchblades, ready to stab me from every side. They'd seen the word carved into my skin, and it made them want to take me down. I let my shaggy leaves hang over my face and walked fast, looking at no one.

When I got to algebra, I heard a gagging noise. The teacher wasn't there yet and everyone was watching me. "Smile!" Ashton Davies held up his phone. Click. Click.

"Beautiful." He turned the screen so his friends could see and I put my head down on the desk while more phones clicked.

"Babyshits," a voice whispered, and I knew they were waiting for me to creep along in the mud and pose for their photos with a sluggy smile. I pressed my head into my arm. I heard Mr. Gimble come in, and when he turned on the whiteboard and said "square roots," I lifted my head. I couldn't stop picturing it all of a sudden. Square roots: like boxes under a tree. They could be red or black and filled with seeds, or leaves, or shrunken people. And maybe square roots weren't just under trees but were also inside people. Like a box behind your ribs that held the smallest thing that was you, multiplied by itself. I drew the square-root symbol in my notebook and put Ella's name underneath.

Inside her box was a pair of sharp sticks. Hockey sticks or toothpicks. But if I pulled those out, I wasn't sure if her box would be empty. I remembered how she'd cried when we watched *The Boy in the Striped Pajamas* and the way she'd carried my bag around after I sprained my ankle in sixth grade. She'd given me my favorite earrings, and turned vegetarian for a while after I told her that pigs were as smart as four-year-old children. But if her square root wasn't just evil, what was the solution?

And now that my hockey sticks were gone, how could I solve myself? The root inside me was tough to understand, but sometimes it felt like a twig or a brown slug or a smooth stone with a name on it. Or maybe it was something I couldn't yet see. Something brighter and smaller. A word. A claw. A shiny black seed that would grow into something new and real.

There were fourteen members of "HAVE YOU SMELLED BABYSHITS?"when I got home from school. I scrolled through the new comments on the wall.

> Smelled her today and almost puked. Raw sewage dipped in menstration.
> Worst smell eva—rotten eggs and diarrea 😨
> DIRTY BEAST LOL.

The more they wrote, the less anyone would know. I clicked on Phoenix Drake's profile and thought about square roots. Words and passwords that could crack the code. Then I took out a notebook and wrote a name at the top of the page. Dallas Yardley Price. I knew lots about her, and somewhere in all those facts I might find the X or the Y. The solution to all the empty boxes that were crowding around me.

Dallas's birthday. Her favorite brands, food, music, and movies. Nicknames and secrets. Her lucky number. The names of everyone I knew in her family, including her cats. Her e-mail addresses—I would need those. Her favorite color and favorite animal. The names she gave her breasts, and all the stuff she'd told us about Kevin. When I finished with Dallas, I turned the page and wrote Ella Abi Brooks. Then I made a list for her. I wouldn't be able to start testing my solutions until later, so I went into the living room. Rebecca was sitting on the couch with the red photo album on her lap. I'd forgotten it was that time of year already. Usually, I remembered sooner. There was more crying in the bathtub and sometimes when you said things to her, she didn't hear. But right now, she was smiling.

"Come have a look at these photos, Callie."

Rebecca's square root would always be Mom. I sat down next to her and let her turn the pages. The pictures started from when they were young. Mom was prettier than I would ever be. She was small and grinning and loveable, and now she would never change. There was nothing new to discover, but Rebecca chuckled as she turned the pages, like she'd never seen any of this before. She and Mom had dressed up in costumes one night. They'd wrapped themselves in silky robes and covered their faces in white makeup. Mom held a fan in front of her mouth and her eyes peeked over the top. In another picture, they had pulled their sweatshirts down on one side to show their shoulders, and covered their eyelids with blue shadow. Next they smiled and posed in pajamas, then they made monster faces at the camera. Something popped into my head that I'd never thought of before. Who was taking the pictures? Was there a third friend who was too ugly to be included in any shots? Had they invited her along just so they could have someone to watch them?

"Who took these?" I asked.

Rebecca turned the page and didn't answer for a moment. "Your dad took some. When we were young."

"Why isn't he in any?"

"I guess because he was the photographer."

"Too bad for him, huh?"

Rebecca pulled the album closer. "You know, I was thinking about what we talked about the other day—about school spirit," she said. "And

I didn't mean to give you the wrong idea. I don't think you should do pointless things just for the sake of it. But I do think that sometimes you need to join in with things, so you can feel like a part of something bigger than yourself." Rebecca let her finger glide across the page. "I want you to enjoy your life and your school and your friends—and you have to get involved to do that."

I looked at the pictures of my dead mom, flat and frozen, with her endless smile that would never change. I could get involved, but I wouldn't enjoy the things she wanted me to. It was too late to become anyone else.

That night, I took the laptop in bed with me and started getting involved. On Facebook, I typed one of Dallas's e-mail addresses into the username box. Then I looked at the Dallas page in my notebook and began to try different words in her password box. Jaguar. Maury. Tif-Tif. DH95. Prada. Twilight. I knew there could be hundreds or thousands of combinations. Letters and numbers mixing together. Every time "the password you entered is incorrect" popped up on the screen, I made an *x* next to the word I'd tried from my notebook. After a while, the website locked me out. So I tried to break into her e-mail account instead. After six tries, that website locked me out, too, so I went back and started trying combinations for Ella's account. I knew it might take a long time, but I had to stay positive. None of the websites locked me out forever. And as I worked my way through the lists of words, I imagined how Dallas and Ella would look after they'd both lost their hockey sticks.

Dallas first. She would try and hide on the edges of crowds, hunched over like she was trying to cover up the pit in her middle. She wouldn't be able to laugh or smile. Her mouth would drop open when she saw someone she usually shouted at, but nothing would come out. She'd pull on the edges of her mouth, scared, and stare at her feet. *Alone,* she'd say to herself. *My new name is Alone.*

Ella would be shivering in a bathroom stall, afraid of being seen. She would understand that the girl she'd been was gone. Her arms would have lost their swing, and she'd be scared to get in the water because she'd know she'd sink. Ella would wrap her hands around her shoulders and say her new name. *Gone,* she would say. *My new name is Gone.*

As for all the rest—all the empties who had joined in so that they could feel like they were a part of something bigger—I would become part of their boxes. I would be the piece of square root that they could never get rid of. Every time they tried to laugh or thought up a prank, I would be there inside them, hard and choking, making them double over in pain.

I didn't crack any passwords on that first night of trying. I still had to get up in the morning and go to school with things the way they were. I wore my new-old shirt and listened to boys blow wet farts when I walked past. Sixteen members of "HAVE YOU SMELLED BABYSHITS?" I collected leaves behind the shed in our yard and carried one in my pocket. Nineteen members. In homeroom, the girl on the desk behind me had a bottle of Coke. I sat down and waited to feel the cold, sticky spray on my back. When I stayed dry, I put my head down on the desk. The morning announcements started, and when they told us to all rise, I didn't move. I pressed my forehead against my arm and closed my eyes as Mrs. Dobbler started to shout, interrupting the Pledge. "Callie! Callie, stand up!"

Someone poked my shoulder.

"I think she's crying," a boy yelled.

The National Anthem began and nobody sang. Chairs scratched the floor and Mrs. Dobbler's voice was close.

"Come speak to me in the hall."

My hair hung so far over my face that I didn't have to see anyone as I followed her out.

Mrs. Dobbler thought that there was something wrong at home. When she said "home," she sounded like a cooing pigeon. Home, home. She had little bows on her shiny shoes and I knew what would happen if I told her. She'd feel sorry for me, but she'd also blame me. I tried to imagine Rebecca meeting with Dallas's parents. They'd destroy her and she wouldn't even know what happened. Then Dallas would get teary and say she'd been bullied by me—I'd sent out a naked picture of her and she had proof. Then everything would only get worse because I'd blabbed.

"I don't feel well," I told Mrs. Dobbler. "My stomach."

I wrapped my arms around my shirt and she said I could go to the nurse. I thought I'd get to lie down for a while, but the nurse wanted to know what I'd had for breakfast. Her bangs were clipped back with kiddie barrettes and her skin looked scratched.

"It's very silly not to eat something for breakfast," she said, pouring me a Dixie cup of juice.

"I felt too sick to eat."

"You're giving yourself low blood sugar. Do you always skip breakfast?"

I sipped the cup of juice and she tried to give me an energy bar, but I didn't want it. "Can I just lie down for a while?"

She took my temperature and then said I could lie down if I tried to eat the energy bar. I unwrapped it in front of her and started nibbling the edges. Forty minutes later, when the bell rang, she said I had to go back to class.

On Saturday morning—the morning we were supposed to visit Mom— "HAVE YOU SMELLED BABYSHITS?" had twenty-four members. Twenty-four empties who shared rotten thoughts and pinprick hearts. Davenport

Henshaw had posted a photo of dog doo in the grass, and Megan O'Leary responded, "Noooooooooooooooooooooooo! Babyshits? LOL!"

I didn't want to go to the cemetery; I wanted to stay home and test out new passwords. Rebecca's little ceremony was dicey and pathetic. She always told stories about Mom and checked my face like she was waiting for me to cry. Even if my eyes got itchy I wouldn't let myself touch them because then she'd think I was wiping away tears.

When I told her I was sick, her hand landed on my forehead like a fruit bat. Warm and moist, it quickly flew away. She went to get the thermometer and stood with her hands on her hips, looking around my room. Then she brought in a tray of food and started saying how she'd have to stay home with me. She was talking about doctors and hospitals and how I wouldn't miss going unless I was really sick. Then I wanted to screech and caw and scratch my talons on her face. She wouldn't force me to go; she'd just make me regret it. I imagined a slim white bird, standing on one foot. It opened its long beak and poked me in the bed. Egret, regret. Egret, regret. Regret. Regret. Regret.

"I'm sure that missing it *this once* won't be the end of the world."

She would never stop pecking. I held the hot tea in my mouth and thought how I could spray.

In the car, I told myself I wasn't even there. It was only Rebecca in her striped sweater and earrings, driving alone. She wore flowery perfume, and tilted her head, glancing in the rearview mirror as she left Pembury. Every time she shifted in her seat or tucked hair behind her ear it was exaggerated, like she was saying, *Watch me! Pay attention to me!* But the car was empty; I wasn't there. When she looked at my seat, her voice went up and down, talking to herself, but I could tell she knew that her audience was gone. She was alone in the car.

When she turned off the engine at the cemetery, I knew I had to leave her behind. She opened the trunk, and I was sicker than ever. My square root filled with fat brown turds and I could barely lift my legs. They weighed thousands of pounds each—and I swallowed the stinging seeds crawling up my throat. When I got to Mom's grave, I touched my shirt and tried to get used to the idea of never taking a shower again, of always wearing the same thing forever. I picked up the shovel and started digging a hole. This was my grave, full of chunks of dirt. I would tunnel down forever and dive in headfirst.

Rebecca started doing this gaspy thing. Ah-ah-ahh. Ah-ah-ahh. I saw the paper in her hand and almost dropped the shovel. The flittery jits were jumping from her to me, from me to her, and she was holding the page I'd left for Mom.

Your daughter hurts people. She threw the paint and sent the picture. Callie deserves to die like you.

I felt her circling. Bare-necked, she turned from side to side.

As I collapsed to the ground I felt her hand on my back. Now she would see me and know me and there would be nowhere left to hide. I was a hermit crab without a shell and she was looking at my body. How had she missed this ugliness before?

"I'll go to the police," Rebecca said. "I won't let her get away with this."

After we got home I went to bed and let Rebecca baby me. She brought in cold drinks and soup, and called me sweetheart in a runny voice. It gave me a swampy feeling, but I was too weak to struggle. My bed was a raft, and the water and quicksand were pulling me under, and I knew if I didn't try to swim, soft bubbles would rise from my lips, and I could let go. When Rebecca asked to wash my new-old shirt, I said okay. I was letting go. When she asked me if there was anyone else who could've written the note, I couldn't tell her the truth. Then Rebecca said maybe Robyn deserved to be bullied because she gave off a bad vibe.

From: C.Mckenzie@chronomail.com
To: R.Doblak@sparkon.com
Subject: (no subject)
Date: Sat, Sep 12 2009, 14:51:45

Robyn

What if I could become you and teach myself a lesson, tell everyone the truth about Callie, show them her messages? I'd teach the others too, show them what they did to us. Make sure that they remembered and never did it again.

Remember that girl I told you about, Autumn Sanger? After she drowned people remembered her for the rest of their lives. Rebecca didn't even know her but she still talks about her 20 years later. And I was imagining what would've happened if Autumn left a note. What if she blamed her bully and said that she killed her? Or what if she was a bully and admitted what she'd done? Would our lives be different now? Do you think one person can change things? I'm changing all the time now. I'm changing into you. C

* * *

By Sunday night, there were thirty-one members of "HAVE YOU SMELLED BABYSHITS?" and I made myself throw up so I wouldn't have to go to school on Monday. The next morning, after Rebecca left for work, I put on my new-old shirt and sat down at the computer. I looked up "how to hack passwords" and watched videos on YouTube showing how to download programs that would break into your friends' accounts. Other pages gave advice on how to guess passwords and claimed that if you really knew a person, you could figure it out. I'd never downloaded a hacking program before and I wasn't sure if it was a scam that would infect my computer with a virus. So I decided I'd give myself a deadline. I'd keep trying to guess their passwords for a week, and if I couldn't crack any, I'd take a chance on downloading one of the hacking programs.

I drank cans of Coke and cracked Life Savers between my teeth while I tested different passwords on their accounts. I looked up the names of famous swimmers to try with Ella's. For Dallas, I typed in places she'd been on vacation: Mexico, Paris, California, Hawaii, Colorado. I wasn't hungry, but sometimes I made myself get up to walk around the house and open the refrigerator. I'd be staring at a container of soup and a new word would pop into my head, so I'd rush back to try it. I didn't feel like myself then; I didn't feel like anybody. It was like I was an investigator, or a scientist. I thought that if I tested enough words, I'd find the one that worked. I filled my notebook with pages and pages of them, marking them off when they didn't work. My phone buzzed sometimes and I didn't even bother checking what they said anymore—that was how I knew I'd changed. It didn't matter what they said about Babyshits now, and the hundreds of texts they'd sent would become evidence later— after I'd cracked the password and wrote the messages that would arrive at our school and the newspaper.

I started thinking about some other people, too. I called Grandma's house, but nobody answered. I spoke to her answering machine for the third time. I Googled "Alex Penders" and then "Josie Dixon." They both had online profiles I could send messages to, but what would I say to them? I'm sorry? Their pictures looked normal. Alex had straight brown hair and you could see his dimple. Josie's lips curved in a shy smile and she'd made sure there weren't any hairs growing out of her face. Was I really sorry now that I knew how it felt? My dad knew what it was like to grow up without a dad, but that didn't stop him from ditching me twice. First when I was born, second when he died. But maybe he had been sorry. Maybe that's why he killed himself: because he knew how bad he was. Or maybe I was tricking myself again and he didn't have a conscience at all. Some people were born without one, and others got one at the last minute.

I remembered the way I used to laugh, and then Googled "Irene Lutz." Nothing came up, so I checked the website of our middle school and found an e-mail address for the school office.

I could send messages to all three of them—to Josie and Alex and Mrs. Lutz—telling them I was sorry and promising that Dallas and Ella would be sorry, too. They might not believe me, but after they heard the news they'd know I'd been serious. I just needed to find the password first and then I could write my apologies.

When it was five o'clock I closed my laptop and got into bed so that Rebecca would think I'd been sleeping all day. She was wearing her work clothes and she sat down on the edge of my bed, putting a damp wash-cloth onto my forehead. She smelled like dental floss, and I kind of felt sorry, thinking about how she might sit here in the future.

"Do you think you can eat something for dinner?"

I'd hardly eaten anything all day and suddenly I was starving.

"How about mac and cheese?"

I heard my stomach purr. Mac and cheese was my favorite, and Rebecca was actually a pretty good cook. Food that seemed boring, like a lump of potato, turned ultra-delicious when she cooked it. She'd throw in salt and pepper, cheese and chives, buttermilk and butter, and you'd be trying to lick off every little molecule on your fork when you took a bite. I was embarrassed to be so hungry, but by the time I sat down at the table, I was practically drooling. I could smell all the cheesy vapors pulling me closer. She'd made it extra-gooey and it slipped under my fork—all that soft white salty cheese—and I thought about how much I'd like to dive in and swim around for a while.

"Callie!" She knocked back her chair, almost landing on top of me. "What's wrong!"

I was bathing in cheese, letting the warm creamy glue wet my sleeves and my hair and my chin, and when I saw how scared she looked I almost laughed. Then I stuck out my tongue to lick off the tangy sauce.

"Are you okay?"

I smiled at her. "Uh-huh. Yummy."

I was getting silly, and I tried swallowing my giggles when I saw her face. I wanted to tell her it was magic cheese, miraculous cheese. I started eating it off my hair because I didn't want to miss the tiniest bit. Rebecca looked at me like I was foaming at the mouth—*I was foaming at the mouth*—and I started laughing out loud. I was making a mess, and I didn't care, and it tasted even better, and then she was laughing, too. Everything went away and it was just cheese and laughing and I forgot what I'd been planning and what I'd spent the whole day doing, and for those two minutes I felt like my old self again.

I knew it couldn't last. When I checked my computer after dinner, there were thirty-four members of "HAVE YOU SMELLED BABYSHITS?" All I had to do was think about going back to school the next day and it was easy for me to puke.

* * *

By Tuesday morning, when Ella's e-mail account finally opened for me, I'd spent almost twenty hours trying different passwords, but it had taken me less than a week. The password she'd used wasn't even hard to guess, and I wished I'd tried it sooner. It was *credit*. When I looked at her inbox, I realized I'd gotten lucky. I could make my plans even bigger now. This wasn't Ella's main e-mail account, but it was the one she'd used to register Phoenix Drake, and her inbox was full of unopened notifications. Every time someone posted a comment on "HAVE YOU SMELLED BABYSHITS?" Ella got a message, letting her know. Ella was Phoenix, Phoenix created "HAVE YOU SMELLED BABYSHITS?", and now I could control them both. *Credit,* I thought. *Fucking credit.* I logged out. Everything could go fast now if I wanted it to. But I felt shivery and I wasn't as excited as I'd expected. I wasn't running around and falling all over myself with happiness. I knew that Ella almost never changed her passwords, so if I wanted, I could wait. I could give myself a little time to think about it and prepare.

I knew I couldn't waste the rest of the day inside. I put on a sweatshirt and jeans and looked at my hair for the first time in days. I watched myself brushing it and didn't tug the knots. The smooth wood of the paddle brush was solid in my hand, and I took my time, lifting my elbow and watching the strands pull away from my scalp before dropping back down. I tied it in a ponytail and then opened the front door. This day reminded me of a thousand other days when the sky was white and the leaves swished on the trees. I could see the telephone poles and electric lines, and I remembered watching snow fall in the street from this spot on our balcony. When school was cancelled, Rebecca would make me put on snow boots and a coat over my pajamas and then we'd stand right

.

here, watching the white drifts covering up the driveways and lawns and bushes. I wished I could see it all again today. Snow and hurricanes. Thunderstorms smashing the sky.

I went back inside to count my money. I had almost two hundred dollars saved up. I looked up the number for a taxi and called to ask how much it would cost. Twenty minutes later I climbed into the backseat of a plain gray car.

"They didn't tell me you was a kid," the driver said. His eyes slid from my face to my jacket to my bag. I snapped on my seat belt while he kept on staring. "So what's the deal? You running away?"

"I'm not running away. I have to get to my grandma's. They told me it was forty-five dollars. I can pay you right now."

"Your grandma's or your *boyfriend's*?"

"My grandma's," I told him, and then I mentioned her illness. "Terminal," I said sadly, pulling the money out of my purse.

He took my cash. Then he apologized and started driving.

Grandma's car was parked in her driveway, and someone had cut her grass. I walked up the cement steps and began knocking on her door. The taxi waited by the curb as I knocked, and I wished he'd go away. I wanted Grandma to smile when she opened the door. *How the heck did you get here?* Then I'd tell her I was worried about her sacs. And she'd say, *What are you thinking about that for? Don't waste your time.*

Then I'd say I was sorry. It wasn't her fault about Dad.

"Grandma! It's Callie!" I yelled. "Grandma, are you okay?"

I knocked until my knuckles twanged. I kicked the door three times. "Grandma, Grandma, Grandma, Grandma!"

The taxi was still in the street and the driver motioned to me with his hand. I tried to wave him away because I wouldn't leave until I'd seen her. I could wait in the backyard or climb in through a window. I could use my library card to pick the lock or sleep under the bushes.

Maybe she couldn't hear me knocking. Maybe she was sleeping. Maybe she'd fallen down and needed my help. Her car was right there, so she had to be inside. I looked around the yard, trying to figure this out. Then I walked over to the raggedy bushes under the front window and saw that her curtains were open a crack.

When I stood up on my tiptoes, I saw right inside.

Grandma was there. She was sitting in her chair. And she wasn't getting up because obviously she hated me. She didn't return my calls. She sent me home last month. She'd seen what I was like and it was absolutely pathetic. This had been my last chance and now my decision was made. *Thrash! Crash!* I wanted to smash through the glass window. I would scream and bleed until everything went dark. I lifted my hand to do it and I saw she wasn't alone. There was a woman standing with her, and my hand slapped the window. The woman stared at me with surprise—like I was a snapping, snarling pit bull—and then Grandma was looking, too, and she shook her head at me.

The woman walked over to the window, and she raised her hand like she might wave. Instead her hand flew out, pulling the curtains closed.

I let myself fall. I lay on the ground. The seconds ticked by as I waited for someone to come. The earth tilted and the clouds drifted and I waited to hear the door. I waited, but they didn't come. Nimbus, nubes, cirrus, cumulus. I closed my eyes and imagined a flock of birds. Curved feet tramping lightly across my shirt, wings tickling my neck. I would be so quiet that they wouldn't fly away. They'd think I was just like them—a large, calm bird with no thoughts beyond air and trees and water. Take me, I'd say. And they'd lift me from the earth, so that this house and this town and our state got smaller and smaller, and we'd finally stop on a stony mountaintop where the air was so thin that I'd forget my name, and my language, and I'd only speak in cheep-cheep-chirrups. Eating berries, scratching dust.

I walked to the taxi in slow motion and slid into the backseat. Chirrup, chureep. It was good to be a bird, to have no more thoughts. Peep peep. A hundred bird years later, I heard the man's voice.

"You ready to go home?"

"Take me to Saint Benedict's cemetery."

I wrote the letter in the car. I wanted her to know I was coming. I needed to tell someone exactly why.

> *Nobody cares or understands me on this fucked-up planet and what if I wasn't meant to be here and everyone saw I was a mistake? Every day I walk around listening to them laugh and laugh and all of us know that I should be dead. I was a shitty mistake and I'm ready to be erased. I want to look up and the sky will be DIRT!*

I asked the driver to wait in the parking lot while I ran to Mom's plot. I ripped the page out of my notepad and left it beneath her empty stone.

Grandma answered her phone that night after the sixth ring. I could hear the sound of her lighter, and then the suck of her breath.

"I saw you," I said. "I know you were home. I saw you and that lady. Why wouldn't you let me in?"

"You came at the worst possible time," Grandma said. "I was getting my treatment."

Her voice sounded fake, and right away I didn't believe her.

"What treatment?"

"What do you think? For my breathing. My lungs."

"Who was that lady?"

Grandma coughed like she'd swallowed a volcano. "What were you doing here, anyway? Why weren't you in school?"

"I was home sick," I said. "Who was that lady?"

"Home sick! I bet The Enforcer doesn't know you were out."

I told Grandma that I didn't care; she could go ahead and tell her. Then I asked her again who that lady was.

"My nurse," she said, and somehow I knew it wasn't true. I knew my grandma. She never wanted a nurse.

"You're lying," I said, and I got ready for more lies. Let us both be buried under an avalanche of lies.

"If I tell you something, you can't tell The Enforcer I told you," she said, and then I really couldn't breathe. The truth was hot lava.

"Your dad was engaged to someone else when your mom got pregnant. He was engaged to that woman you saw at my house. They got married before you were born. I haven't seen her for a long time. But that's who she was—your dad's wife."

My brain was dry as dust, and everything was crumbling, but I tried to follow the words coming out of Grandma's mouth. My dad had an affair. That was with my mom. That woman was his wife. They'd never told me.

"Your dad wasn't a bad man. He was just in a lot of pain. You don't need to be a bad man to do what he did."

To do what he did. I knew and I didn't know. I understood how it could happen. It was happening to me, too.

I found Rebecca in her room and thought about blurting out what I knew. That my dad was married and she'd lied to me all these years. I always just figured my parents were dating, and she'd let me think that. I didn't know they were cheaters, which made my birth a cheat, too. Then I saw what she had in her hand. A plastic bag. She'd gone out that afternoon after my doctor's appointment, acting so secretive I thought maybe she had a date. But no—she'd gone to the cemetery. I saw the outline of my note.

I was a mistake, just like I'd written, and I *wasn't* meant to be here, but I didn't want her to know—to find out like this. She must've checked Mom's grave, found my message. The worst timing ever. Then I remembered my way out.

"Did she come back?" I asked, and Rebecca *had* thought it was Robyn. She didn't recognize my handwriting. It was Robyn she pitied.

"I think everyone can be helped," Rebecca said, and I felt half brain-dead.

On Wednesday, I had to go back to school. My doctor had told Rebecca I was fine, so I left my new-old shirt under my pillow, then I put on makeup and pretended that I was still DH because Rebecca was paying attention. I hoped school would be easier now that I'd found a way out, but by the time I got to first period, I was a mess. Everywhere I went they found me. Rancid grins, plagues of laughter, deadly words I didn't understand. On the wall outside my homeroom there was a poster on the wall: DALLAS PRICE 4 FRESHMAN CLASS PRESIDENT.

Credit, I reminded myself. *Credit*. I wished I'd done it yesterday, then I wouldn't be here today. I walked down the halls and imagined I was sinking. Water filled up my chest and it felt so good.

In social studies, they were waiting for me. Their phones were ready to record every last moment of my life. I went to my chair and saw the diaper. Something rattled inside me. Then water was rushing into my ears and I felt the choke in my throat. A brown mess had been rubbed across my desk and I could see them grinning but I couldn't hear them laugh. My legs took me out of there. Miss Laing shouted something at me as she came in and I broke inside.

"Fuck off." I ran down the hall. I ran outside. I headed toward the trees. Then there was a hand on my arm. I looked at the man in a sweat-shirt. "Fuck off," I said.

He walked me back inside, down the hall, to the principal's office. People said things to me. They told me to sit in a plastic chair and I sat there looking at my wrist. My veins were like roots I was ready to cut. Purple branches in the shape of a Y. Equations, symbols, values. On my wrist, under my skin, I'd found the answer. There were no more questions. I looked at my wrist and knew it was the same thing my dad discovered. A square root. Equations, loss, and an answer. It was the first true thing I'd known about him.

They said I'd smeared the chocolate on my desk and I went along with it. The principal wanted to know why I'd sworn at Miss Laing and I couldn't tell him. They explained I'd have to write an apology and spend the rest of the week in in-school suspension, and I tried not to smile. I couldn't have planned it better. I would have my own vacation for the next two days. I'd just given myself a little more time to work out the details.

After school, I headed back to the trees. As I walked, I remembered the things I learned at camp when I was younger. Leaves created the sugar that kept the tree growing, and then in the fall, the tree had to let the leaves die and drop off. One of our counselors told us how Native Ameri-cans used trees, and then he made us stand in a clearing with our eyes shut. He told us to imagine we were living through all the seasons as a tree, with our roots reaching out twenty feet below us. There was the hot sun on our bark and the sap in our trunk and the cold rain on our branches. We were supposed to rock back and forth when the wind hit us, and when he said our leaves were turning colors and then getting torn off, I felt each perfect creation falling to the earth around me like it never meant a thing. Then it was spring and we had tiny buds growing, and all the animals and bugs came back to live in us. "You create half the oxygen in the world," he told us, and afterward he asked how we felt. Some of the kids said "tall" or "strong" or "beautiful," but for me, it was different. I felt sad. It had something to do with the leaves. I didn't want to have let go of them so easily. I wanted to crouch down and collect them from the ground, like each one of them was still a part of me, alive—and I knew this was stupid. Trees had to drop their leaves because they would die if they didn't. They couldn't understand what they had lost, and even though I knew this, the more I thought about it, the sadder I got.

Now that I was older, I understood it wasn't sad. You could see the true shape of a tree only when it was stripped clean, standing naked in the wind and cold. I'd been stripped the same way, and I saw what I was. Calm, pure medicine. The antidote to their poison. I'd found credit and I was going to change everything.

I followed muddy footprints along the path, and decided to collect leaves one last time. I held them in my hands and stuffed them in my pockets. Small sharp ones like fallen stars, and soft broken ones like skel-etons. I didn't have to go home or do anything yet. I carried more and more and walked farther and farther, filling myself up, holding on to everything I touched.

———

That night, Rebecca sat me down for a big talk. There was a grapey flap of skin on her lower lip that I wanted to peel as I answered her questions. I said I'd got lost and had run outside by accident. I told her the swearing had come out of nowhere. She kept talking and talking, with the grapey flap hanging there, and I wasn't tempted to tell her the truth. Telling would feel good only for a second, like a hug in a heat wave. Arms closing around you, snuggling close, your head drooping: *Poor baby, you needed my help!* She'd take me into her heart and I'd be trapped there forever, weak, pitiful, a little loser bullied at school.

"Well, do you think one of Robyn's friends could've left it?" she asked. "That girl Lucinda?"

I started scratching my arms and I thought of Evil McFrenzy, how she changed what everyone saw. A little blond girl turning into a monster.

". . . you're allowed to make mistakes," Rebecca said, "but this isn't like you."

She had started rubbing her Mom tattoo and it made me sick to my stomach. She kept everyone too close, and she held on too tight. A tree that couldn't let go of its leaves would die eventually. I needed her to stop clinging—I wanted to fall like my dad.

"Stop pressing that," I told her. "I know what you're thinking."

She took her hand off her chest and looked at me like I was crazy, and then I was turning into a beast, the rawest sewage draining away.

"I'm not like my mom!" I shouted. "Maybe I'm more like *him!*"

I knew that everything had a limit—love included—but Rebecca was still following me as I ran into the kitchen. I pushed my hands under the faucet. My nostrils were streaming. Her love was never mine anyway—she loved me for someone else.

"I smashed the chocolate because I *wanted* to. Not everyone does things for a reason. Sometimes we just DON'T have a conscience."

Rebecca still hadn't walked away. I could hear her breathing behind me, and I hated how she wouldn't leave me, how she always had to be there. She'd taken care of me for so long without knowing anything about me. Without knowing what I could do, the hurricanes I could make. She followed me into my room and I heard her voice trying to help me, and I hated that this was how I had to throw it all away. But I didn't have a choice. There are limits to everything. And even Rebecca couldn't love me past a certain point.

From: C.Mckenzie@chronomail.com
To: R.Doblak@sparkon.com
Subject: (no subject)
Date: Wed, Sep 16 2009, 23:10:07

Robyn,

It takes 7 minutes to drown, I read that on the Internet, but it's hard to do it on purpose because your body tries to survive. That's probably why Autumn Sanger got drunk—so her body would be relaxed. It wouldn't start fighting back and she could sink the way she wanted.

I wouldn't want to be alone. I wish you could be there with me. I'm alone all the time and now I know how it was for you. It's like nobody can hear you and you're sinking deeper and deeper and there's so much pressure that you have to let go.

I feel like I'm disappearing and you're the last one who can see me. If you're there, just say something—just let me know. C

* * *

In-school suspension was in the C wing at school, and I signed in with the teacher who sat at the front of the room. There were three students sitting in different corners, and the teacher pointed at a desk in the empty back corner where I would spend the day. He handed me a folder with work from my teachers and I sat at the desk. There was a sign at the front of the room.

NO TALKING WHATSOEVER.
NO GUM, NO FOOD, NO DRINKS, NO PHONES.
IF YOU NEED TO USE THE BATHROOM, YOU HAVE TO
WAIT FOR A CHAPERONE.
NO LEAVING UNDER ANY CIRCUMSTANCES.

The other students in the room weren't working. They had their heads down on their arms like they were sleeping. In the other back corner, a boy with spiky hair looked at me without raising his head. His eyes met mine and I looked away. I put my head down, sniffing the clean Clorox smell, looking at the dried water marks where a sponge had swiped the desktop in half-circles. I would give myself until Sunday: Sunday night. In the meantime, I'd go along with everything. I'd do whatever it took to avoid getting caught. I'd plan out my messages and write a letter of apology to Miss Laing. Maybe I'd even call Grandpa Pat—my mom's dad—to say good-bye.

The boy looked at me again and I wondered if he knew about Babyshits. I hated that any stranger could see what was happening. Every day more people were joining in the fun. There were hundreds and thousands, soon there would be millions. Watching and laughing, disgusted by me. I'd even had one message telling me to report it. The girl's picture showed praying hands that glowed with white light. *You don't know me, but I saw the page they wrote and I think you should report it. Friendship & peace. Lana Hebe.* I wished for a second that Lana was Robyn. If she told me to report it I'd do it for her. But I knew you couldn't just report it and escape that easily. Even if you tried deleting it, it would pop up somewhere else. Things on the Internet followed you for life. All our teachers had warned us: if you tried to get a job, your employers would Google you. If you applied to college, they checked your pages online. If I moved to another state, another country, another planet, I'd still be in their trap. Somebody there would know.

I looked at the skin on my elbows. It was dark and wrinkly like an elephant's hide. Even if I escaped, I wouldn't forget what they'd done. If I let them keep their sharp sticks, they would go on forever. They'd attack harder and faster and never stop. Dallas would be elected class president and Ella would lead the swim team, and they would go on destroying lives just because they could. I was the only one who could stop them and I had to make them pay.

There was no stress in in-school suspension. When the bells rang, we stayed in our seats. After the regular lunch period was over, a teacher walked us to the cafeteria, which was quiet except for the sound of the lunch ladies, pushing around rolling trash cans and wiping up splattered food. We bought our sandwiches, and then the teacher put us each at separate tables. I ate my cheese sandwich in silence.

That afternoon, I started planning out my message for Josie Dixon.

Hi Josie

Do you remember when you were in 7th grade and some girls were assholes to you? I was one of those girls, but I'm not anymore. First, I want to say sorry. You didn't deserve what happened. Your face was fine, you were a pretty girl, and there was no good reason for what we did.

We were trying to make you feel like vomit, and now I know how you felt. I learned how it is to be left behind because everyone's joined up against you. They do it because they don't have a conscience. Or because they want to feel like they're part of something bigger. Or because they think you don't matter.

But everything matters. You matter a lot. I want you to have a happy life wherever you are and I don't want you to end up like me.

Most of all, I want you to know that Dallas and Ella and all the other kids who hurt you are going to regret it. They're going to change, because I changed. I think people without consciences can get them, because I didn't have one and now I do. You're part of my conscience, and I hope you understand what I mean.

Credit,

Callie McKenzie

I folded the handwritten draft so I could type it up later. Then I looked at my wrists and thought about my dad—how I'd hated him all these years, when he'd been in pain just like me. He didn't like who he was—a liar and a cheater—but he'd found the solution and I finally understood it. The bells rang, nobody moved, and when I looked at the spiky-haired boy at the back of the room, he opened one eye and looked back at me. There was pink in his eye, and a scratch above his nose, and I waited for him to mouth *Babyshits,* but he didn't. So I kept looking. He left his head on his arm, and I looked into his eye, and he looked back into mine, and I let him.

After school, Rebecca and I met the principal in his office. I had to explain again how I'd got lost, and then Rebecca started spewing about everything. "Her mother passed away. And we just marked the ninth anniversary this weekend." She couldn't resist talking about Mom, even now. I listened to her explain how sad we were and I felt his powerful blood rushing through my veins.

"You forgot my dad," I said. "My dad's dead, too."

Saying his name made me buzz like I'd just drunk twenty cans of Coke. Or like I'd brought someone into the room with us who had pink eyes and a scratched face and bruised, bloody fists. They didn't say anything.

Take that, I thought.

I imagined him pacing back and forth, punching holes into the plaster walls for the rest of the meeting. He wiggled his butt in their serious faces, and when they kept talking, he let out a long, smelly fart. When Rebecca stood up, I followed her and he came with us, sneering and kicking at the ugly air.

When we got into the car, I turned to her.

"Was it because he killed himself?"

She looked scared. I imagined him gnashing his teeth outside the window.

"You love telling everyone all about Mom, but never Dad. Was he so evil?"

She shook her head no.

I stared into his eyes and he stared back at me. He nodded, and I knew I had to say the thing I'd always tried not to let myself think.

"Did he kill her? Did he kill my mom?"

I watched him press his ear against the window as she began to talk. "It was a car accident. You know that. Your mom was hit by a car."

He closed his eyes and I glared at him. My mom had been hit by a car. She'd died and he still left me.

"So he slit his wrists?"

He backed away from the car. Then he turned in a flash and ran for the trees. I knew that I shouldn't have asked. He'd already shown me the truth. The X's and Y's. I wanted to call him back and say that I finally understood, but he was getting smaller and smaller and then he was gone.

* * *

COULD SOMEONE PLEASE GIVE THE DOG A BATH?

Dallas posted this comment on "HAVE YOU SMELLED BABYSHITS?" at 3:23 p.m. on September 17.

There were forty-two members of the group now. I took screenshots of their comments and saved them in a folder named *evidence*. Late at night I retested the password for Ella's e-mail account and it still worked; she hadn't changed it. Then I thought about what Rebecca had told me in the car, and how it wouldn't change anything.

She said Dad didn't slit his wrists, he killed himself with pills. I knew I'd been tricking myself and it didn't even matter. Pills or razors or guns: they all cut through the X and the Y. Rebecca tried to say it was impossible to know exactly why he'd done it, and that anyone who pretended to be sure was lying, but I knew she was wrong. I understood: not the beginning, but the end. Not the cause, but the release.

On Friday, when I walked into in-school suspension, the spiky-haired boy was gone. I took my seat at the back of the room and began planning out what I would say in the rest of the messages that I'd send on Sunday night.

To Alex Penders, I promised that the girls who threw berries at him and called him Piggy Kibble would finally pay for what they'd done.

To Irene Lutz, I apologized for laughing and screaming at her on the last day of school. I also told her that I was going to make sure that we never did something like that again.

For Rebecca, I wrote one last note from Robyn:

SUNDAY NIGHT, 1 A.M., BRIDGE OVER FLINT STREET, JUMPING.

I decided that I'd wait until late on Sunday night, then I'd begin the first of the eight steps I'd planned. I went over the steps in my mind, to make sure nothing would go wrong, and when I was sure it would work I put my head down on my desk and listened to the school bells for the rest of the day.

After school on Friday, I sat on the couch, eating carrots. I'd put the note from Robyn on top of the mail, and I was waiting for Rebecca to come home and see it. I was also thinking about that morning in eighth grade when I saw Robyn in the cafeteria. That must've been the moment. The moment when the universe could've changed. I wouldn't be grounded right now. There wouldn't be a suicide note on our sideboard, and bullets would just be the stuff you shot from a gun. I would've walked over to Robyn and left DH for good. I just needed to wave back. I needed to call out her name.

On the far end of our couch, I imagined Papa crawling on Robyn's lap. Robyn reached for one of my carrots and held it up like a cigarette. "I keep meaning to quit, but they're super-addictive."

"Vitamin C," I joked. "You must not resist."

Since that morning in the eighth-grade cafeteria, Robyn and I had been best friends. We slept over at each other's houses, and she showed me pictures of her dad. I showed her some of my mom, too, and I told her what I remembered. And she said I shouldn't feel bad that I'd forgotten so much.

When Rebecca walked in, I gripped the pillow on my lap. I was back in the wrong dimension and Rebecca was carrying a strudel. A strudel? What for? What did we have to celebrate? Celebrate that I was going? Or celebrate that I was gone?

"Robyn left something for us," I said. And then I watched her read my note.

If there was one thing Rebecca couldn't resist, it was a girl in trouble. Someone who needed to be saved, a victim to make her a hero. I needed her to go to the bridge on Sunday thinking she could finally be a rescuer, then she'd be out of the way and I could start my plan. Rebecca pressed her hand into her hip. She started asking me questions. But she was mostly worried about me, getting harassed by Robyn. She didn't think Robyn would really jump. She was unsympathetic as DH.

I started stress-eating the strudel, wondering how I was going to convince her. She called Robyn's mom and gave her a warning, but this wasn't the old Rebecca. I'd never seen her give up on someone, so I tried making her sorrier for Robyn—telling how there was nobody else who really cared. "Her mother won't help her," I said. "She sent *us* this note." Rebecca's eyebrows crinkled like I was overreacting. "We don't know if this is real," she said. "Or if Robyn even wrote it."

"Who else?" I said. Then I saw what I had to do.

"I know because—because of what I did."

Rebecca covered her mouth with her hand like she was about to throw up.

After Rebecca rushed out, I went in my room and took off all my clothes. The inky places where I'd written Babyshits had faded. I pointed my toes, wiggled my fetus feet, and then I ran my hands over the smooth spaces that gave me the jiggles. I knew what clothes I'd wear on Sunday night: my new-old shirt that someone threw away, my good jeans, and my favorite earrings that Ella had given me. I would brush out my hair that Rebecca said was just like my mom's, and I would give her a kiss good-bye because I knew she'd remember it for a long time.

I lay down on my bed and felt a weight sinking my mattress. Robyn pulled a handful of chestnut hair across her mouth, giving herself a mustache.

"What are you doing here?" I asked, eyeing her on the end of my bed.

"Keeping you company."

"I don't want company."

Robyn let her hair slip and then I pulled up my sheet. I needed to shave my legs and I didn't want her to see.

"Are you sure you want to do this?" she asked, chin in her hand. She was imitating Miss Baranski's serious tone.

"Yes. I'm sure."

"Very interesting." She tapped her fingers against her cheek. "And how do you think Rebecca will take it?"

"I don't need a psychiatrist, so why don't you leave me alone."

Robyn nodded like we had some special agreement. "Okay," she said. "But just answer the question: How do you think Rebecca will take it?"

"She's going to be fine. I can't worry about her right now."

"You didn't worry about me either," Robyn said. "That's always your problem."

"I worried about you, you just didn't know it. And as far as Rebecca goes, she's going to be better off."

"We weren't better off after my dad died."

"That was totally different. Your dad had leukemia. Everyone loved him."

"My dad had to die. You get to choose."

I pressed my face into my pillow, and then her face was close beside mine. There was a spray of red droplets across her nose and between her eyes.

"Why do you still have that crap on you? Are you trying to make me feel worse?"

She rubbed her hands on her cheeks in circles. "It doesn't come off."

"Get some soap and a sponge," I told her. Then I jumped out of bed and ran over to my desk, grabbing the page I'd been working on. "Why don't you read this?" I said. "I wrote you a letter."

I shoved it in Robyn's face and she held it limply in her hand.

Robyn

I think the end will be like the beginning. I'll feel you waiting beside me, and I'll answer all your questions and wipe away your tears. You'll wear your silver headband and hum along to "Frosty" and I'll want to stay with you but it'll be time for me to go. One kiss to never forget, and you'll whisper in my ear, "I forgive you. I love you." Then you'll watch me go under. The sky will burst open as I wash away our names and then I'll turn into the rainbow that finally ends the storm. Up in the sky, I'll watch them changing, losing their sharp sticks, and the world will be safer for people like you.

Please forgive, don't forget. Callie McKenzie

Robyn dropped my note on the floor. "All of this is bullshit."

For the next hour, Robyn haunted me. When Rebecca came in my room to talk to me, Robyn slithered under my sheets. "I read your letters to your mom," Rebecca said. Then she showed me something I'd written. It was about how if Mom could see me from heaven, I'd be this big disappointment. And I didn't want to look at Rebecca, to see how much I'd let her down, too. I knew I couldn't take anything back, and I'd probably already reached her limits. But Rebecca was so sure I was wrong, saying that mom would never regret me, and I knew she meant well, but it was too sad—to see her still trying.

Then Rebecca was trying to keep it together as she asked me about Robyn, and I realized why people confessed right before they died. The crying was a release. Like flushing a lake out of my body. Dirty water flowing out until I was empty and wet. Rebecca mopped my face, and Robyn hid by my legs, and then it all came out like a burp, filling the air with its stench. I had squirted the paint. There. It was done.

"If that had been you," Rebecca asked, "how do you think you'd feel?"

I was still crying as I answered. It was the easiest question in the world. I'd feel hopeless. Ruined. Like everyone hated me. Humiliated. Awful. Like I wanted to die. Rebecca seemed satisfied and I saw Robyn peek out at me. She rubbed her soft cheek, but the paint was still there. Nobody would ever know how much Robyn and me were connected. There wouldn't be any record of our friendship if Robyn wanted to forget. I wondered if she'd already deleted our messages, and unremembered our first meeting. Maybe when she looked at Papa she pretended she'd bought him herself. "We were friends," I told Rebecca. "Me and Robyn."

"All My Interactions with Robyn Doblak," I wrote. Rebecca had agreed to let me write it as long as I told her everything, and now Robyn leaned over my shoulder as I stared at the empty screen. I couldn't remember the first time I'd seen her—it must've been in seventh grade, but she didn't stand out to me, not until I heard about her dad. That was when *everyone* noticed—the girl whose dad died. I typed #1 at the top and started with the first time we talked—almost ten months ago, right before Christmas. I could hear her humming "Frosty the Snowman," and then I smelled strawberry perfume, and when I looked around we were back in middle school. There were foil trees stapled to the walls, and Miss Baranski was running late. We were waiting outside her office and I was about to take off. Robyn spoke to me first. She was looking at my wristband. "Pit bull awareness?"

I turned to the ghost in my room. *Why did you talk to me?*

She flipped up her hands: *Who knows?*

She looked in my eyes as I repeated my ten-month-old words.

"There was once this pit bull who saved thirty peoples' lives. But all anyone thinks is they're these vicious crazy killers."

You were nicer than I expected, she said. *I knew about DH.*

I remembered how she touched her headband and told me she wanted a dog. She cried so openly, but I didn't know what to do. She came closer and I saw her mascara, running down all over her cheeks. I knew I couldn't change the past; I could only do what I'd done already. I raised my hand to her face, using my sleeve to wipe under her eyes. Her skin was hot and I didn't want to move. But I knew I had to go soon. There were only two days left.

She seemed really thankful, I wrote.

I was embarrassed, she whispered.

"She seemed really thankful, but embarrassed, too," I wrote.

By the time I got to my tenth interaction, Rebecca had made about a hundred phone calls. She'd called Robyn's mom and the police and this guy named Danny she'd met at the cemetery. I'd let her read our first five interactions, but I was saving the rest for after. I wanted to disappear before she found out we were more than just friends. Right now, Rebecca only knew that Robyn was depressed last Christmas, which made sense to her with all the notes. But it also made her calls to Mrs. Doblak sound more and more crazy. I imagined Mrs. Doblak eagle-eyeing her daughter. *Why does this weirdo think you're going to jump off a bridge?* I hadn't meant to mess with her life again, but it was the only way this would work.

I looked at my screen and typed #10 as Robyn chewed gum beside me. She popped a big bubble right next to my ear. *Don't lie,* she said. *This is your last chance.*

"After Dallas spread it around, everyone started calling Robyn Bullets," I typed.

After YOU spread it around, she hissed.

No, I only said it that once!

Robyn cracked her gum and looked away as I kept writing: "I couldn't apologize because I couldn't get through to her, and I couldn't catch her eye in class because she wouldn't look at anyone."

I felt my chair jump. Robyn had kicked me. *You said it at least twice. Probably more.*

Okay, twice. I wish I could go back.

Robyn hunched over, like she was sitting at a desk, and then I smelled paint and looked down at my hands. I held a paintbrush in one hand and Ella was sitting beside me, dabbing yellow dots on her papier-mâché mask. The windows were open and I could hear a PE class yelling outside, and when Adam Liebowitz did a pratfall, Miss Dimmock pointed at the door. I was painting lips on my mask, wrinkly red lips, and when Miss Dimmock walked out of the room, I glanced over at Robyn. She wasn't wearing her coat that day—it was a warm April afternoon—and her wrists were bare in her summery white top.

"Bullets," Ella called. "Ooh, your bullets are so hard."

You looked so lonely. I wanted to go over.

Robyn pretended she couldn't hear me and I heard Ella screeching. I could only repeat the past now. I had to do it all over again.

"Why are you such a bitch?" I asked Ella, and then I got out of my chair. My legs felt like rubber as I started stumbling forward, and Robyn was a million miles away, but also closer than ever before. I knew I was losing DH. I already knew what they would say. But all I wanted was Robyn and I thought she wanted me.

Bullshit, Robyn snapped. *You weren't coming over to be with me.*

Yes, I swear. I told you before.

I stopped in front of her table and I was ready to change things. I could leap over mountains, bend the rays of the sun. I breathed in Robyn's air and I wanted to stand there forever, looking at the top of her head, watching her move her brush.

What were you painting? I asked.

A dog, she said. *Duh.*

Two guys shouted something and I glared back at them. I needed to get a chair. I would need someplace to sit. But Robyn still hadn't seen me.

Maybe she didn't know. "Robyn," I said louder, and then the hairs on my arms stood up.

Her eyes were cold and wet, and her mouth was sort of open. I could see some of her teeth as her lips moved. Then my face was burning and my insides were exploding and I felt the bullet hit me and start tearing me apart.

"Total odium," I wrote. "I saw it on her face."

That's not right, Robyn said, knocking my hands off the keyboard.

You hated me, I cried. *I saw it in your eyes.*

No, she stared back at me. *I was totally scared of you.*

I found Rebecca in the kitchen. "Has her mom answered yet?"

Rebecca hadn't talked to her and I realized this was my chance.

"But I have to tell her I'm sorry," I said. "I need to see her before it's too late."

Robyn sat behind me in the car on the way to her house. Then she floated around her front step and laughed when nobody came out.

"OMG. We went away for the weekend!"

"Are you okay?" Rebecca asked me. "You look a little pale."

"Fine," I said.

Rebecca put her arm around my shoulder like she understood everything. Then I felt Robyn pinch me with her sticky fingers. "She has no idea. Don't you feel bad? You made her think *I'm* the creeper jumping off a bridge."

———

Late on Sunday night, Rebecca came into my room, ready to drive to the bridge over Flint Street. She was wearing light pink lip gloss and she kept patting my shoulder because she didn't want me to worry that Robyn might die. And I wasn't worried. Robyn was safe. She was leaning against my window, holding Papa in her hand.

"Are you sure you don't want me to come?" I asked.

"Yes. I'm sure."

Rebecca patted me again and I sat up quickly and gave her a kiss. She'd be free of me soon and could live a normal life. No more meetings at my school, no more fights and crying. No unthankful kid, dragging her down.

"Callie, are you okay?"

"I just wanted to thank you," I said. But then I was almost crying because I couldn't list all the things she'd done. Giving me milk shakes when I got chicken pox, working so hard to support us, pulling back her covers and sharing her bed when I couldn't sleep. She used to throw me these crazy-themed birthdays—she once bought ten sombreros—and she always forgave me. She thought I would make her proud.

"I won't let anything happen to her," she said, kissing me back.

Rebecca waved as she left my room. I hadn't thanked her for anything. Robyn didn't wait; she got right up in my face. "Did you see her eyes? She's really worried."

"She's not worried about me. She's worried about you."

"Because you tricked her. Don't you know what this will do to her?"

We heard the front door shut and it was time to begin.

First, the messages for Alex Penders, Irene Lutz, Josie, and Robyn. Robyn leaned over my shoulder as I pressed send. "You're not doing this for me," she said. "Don't pretend you're doing it for me."

The second step came when I logged in to Ella's e-mail account and changed her password. I imagined how she'd type in "credit" again and again, confused and then growling with frustration when it didn't work.

"It might not work out the way you imagined," Robyn warned.

Next I went to the site where Phoenix Drake destroyed me. I typed in Ella's e-mail address and then I clicked "I've forgotten my password." When the link arrived in Ella's account, I reset the password to something she would never guess. Then the screen opened and I saw the profile for Phoenix Drake along with the picture of the Grim Reaper.

I pinched my cheeks. It was all working the way I'd imagined. Robyn shook her head. "It might not make any difference."

I took a final screen shot of the group "HAVE YOU SMELLED BABYSHITS?" along with the names of the forty-six members and put that in my folder marked evidence.

"People forget quick," Robyn said.

"I didn't forget you."

As Phoenix Drake—group creator—I could change the name of "HAVE YOU SMELLED BABYSHITS?" and I did. The next morning, when the forty-six members of "HAVE YOU SMELLED BABYSHITS?" logged in they would find a message telling them that the group had changed its name. They were now members of **"I Killed Callie McKenzie"** and they would see the following post:

> This is not a joke. By joining this group you have committed murder. A girl died tonight because of you. Callie McKenzie—who you called Babyshits—was not nothing. Her life wasn't meaningless. But you decided to kill her anyway. Ella Brooks and Dallas Price led you here, but you still had a choice. You could walk away or you could stab her with lies, steal her name, make every moment of her life a burning hell. And you know what you chose. You can try to say you didn't know what you were doing, but we know that's not true.

You took her life. And now she's going to live inside you—right behind your ribs, where you were empty before. Every time you think
about hurting someone else, she'll be there. She'll feel like a choke,
or a thick swallow, and you'll remember her and stop.

P.S. It's too late to remove your name and try to get away with
murder. A list with all forty-six of you has already been sent to the
powers that be. Credit.

I felt okay then, seeing what I'd written. There were just a few more
steps left.

I went back to my e-mail and began writing our confessions. I sent
Rebecca the last five interactions I'd had with Robyn, and apologized to
her one last time. Then I opened Ella's account and started writing. Ella
admitted to trying to drown me, to sending hundreds of threatening
texts, to starting a war against me with Dallas. She included the evidence
I'd collected—the screenshots of "HAVE YOU SMELLED BABYSHITS?"—
and she explained how she and Dallas had got away with this kind of
thing their whole lives. She told about Alex Penders, Mrs. Lutz, Josie
Dixon, and Robyn. Then she signed her own name and sent the message
to the e-mail address list I'd prepared: everyone in the school, the principal, the local newspaper. She would take responsibility now; I knew how
a dead friend could live inside a person.

Then there was only one thing left for me to do and I had to do it
quick.

I rubbed my arms and put on my new-old shirt. I picked up the leaves
like stars and skeletons and memories, and stuffed them in my pockets.
My blood felt cold and slow as I wrote one last note to Rebecca, and left
it with my phone on the floor outside her room. Then I tiptoed out of the
house.

"You didn't ruin my life, if that's what this is about," Robyn yelled.

"You're not even real," I told her. "So how do you know?"

She made a face and pretended she wasn't coming, crouching down by the side of the road. There wasn't a cloud in the sky and it was chilly as we walked to Ella's house. The hairs on my arms stood up, and the green air cleared out my lungs, and it was easy to listen to the crunching sound of my soles on the street, and the snowy-shush that my thighs made as they brushed together. Overhead, I could hear the trees. At night they were like us. They breathed in oxygen and exhaled carbon dioxide. We breathed together, still growing, a little while longer. Robyn didn't speak as she walked beside me. Then suddenly she fell behind, and when I looked back she wasn't there. At one point, I turned around quickly and squinted into the shadows. Was that someone's face? "Robyn!" She disappeared. I could still feel her following me, and sometimes I heard her footsteps, but when I stopped to wait for her, she hid behind the trees.

At dinner that night, Rebecca had blamed Robyn's mom. We were eating vegetable stew—the last thing I'd eat. I crunched an ice cube between my molars as she talked about Mrs. Doblak, saying she should've taught Robyn how to handle her problems. Like if Robyn knew how to cope none of this would be happening. Like adults could control everything, including how their kids thought.

"You guys can't protect us from everything," I said. "You can't control our minds."

"We can protect you from a lot. If we're careful we can."

"But what if Robyn doesn't want to cope?" I said. "It's her choice, not her mom's."

Rebecca stared into her bowl of stew like it had turned into cold jelly.

"If I was her mom I'd sleep in her room tonight. I'd chain her down if that was what it took."

"But what if she convinced you that she wasn't going to do it?"

"She wouldn't be able to. I'd know that she was lying."

I stirred my stew and picked out a soft round potato for my last bite.

Ella's house was dark. I stood on the lawn and stared up at her empty bedroom window. It was hard to see as I passed along the side of the house, but I'd walked here so many times, I knew the way. I stuck my hand in my pocket and pulled out a handful of leaves, dropping them as I went. I didn't feel sad as they disappeared in the inky air, so I kept moving forward. When I was in the backyard, where the wooden deck overlooked the lake, I couldn't even see where the water began. My feet squished in the mud, and I listened for the sounds. A frog belching. A fish singing. Green leaves flapping in the breeze.

"Robyn?" I whispered. "Robyn?"

It was so dark that the earth and water and sky turned into a single thing—a confusing muddy ball—so I closed my eyes. The black behind my eyelids was thick and familiar, and as long as I didn't open up, I could be anywhere, forever. The icy water started seeping into my shoes, numbing my toes and biting my legs. It sloshed and sucked at my body, rinsing away the last of Babyshits, rising to my waist. Eyes closed, I leaned back and felt ice and water and body like a single edge and I wanted to let go. Then, when I opened up, I would see everything. Stars bursting in the sky, the world cracking open, rings and rings of history spreading out like ripples around me. The water would turn warm, and I'd see the yellow flash of eyes from under the pines, along the banks, at the muddy edges of the lake. A girl collecting moss, wild horses listening to my watery splash, an ancient fox peering from under the trees. My parents would be there. And there would be children from the future, watching me with their hands over their hearts. They would stand in the shadows, and I'd wonder: *Are they sorry or are they thanking me? Are they pressing their hands to their chests because they can't breathe or are they hiding something?* A pledge they can't understand; words that lost their meaning.

I opened my eyes and it was dark. Empty, visionless. This was it. Nothing more to see. Opening my mouth and swallowing cold water, filling my lungs. Ice and silence. A body sinking in a lake. No stars, no kiss. Nobody waiting for a rainbow. They could press their hands over their hearts and unless they felt something it would all be for nothing. Indivisible, liberty, and justice for all.

I was shivering and they wouldn't understand. They would go on and on and I would turn into a secret history and it wouldn't mean a thing. For a second I forgot their names. It was the future and they were gone, and I could only hear my own breath. My branches stirred in the wind, and the ground around my roots began to thaw. My numb hand reached for my chest, and I pressed it to my thunking heart.

Good little cat, Good little cat, Good little cat.

A silver whistle blew and I heard a voice calling. *Callie, you have to swim.* She watched me by the shore. And I wanted to but I couldn't. Everything was heavy. My head, my arms. My legs were asleep. And I wanted . . . I needed . . . my body was dissolving. I closed my eyes and re-membered about the mud. The mud swallowed everything in this watery waste, the fish bones and bird bones and mold and dust.

REBECCA

The lake behind the Brooks' house had become thick with weeds over the summer. Waxy clusters of leaves floated on the water, forming dense tangles that swayed like rafts. Ali Brooks had once told me she *needed* to live on the lake. "If it was up to me we'd live on the boat." In her living room there were sliding glass doors where she could watch the sunset color the water each evening, and as I looked at the doors in the darkness, I thought I saw movement inside. I had called on my way over. I'd left messages asking her to check the lake. But the glass doors weren't opening, the lights stayed off, and the police, who I'd begged, still hadn't arrived.

The cold wind snapped and rushed as I switched on my flashlight. Then I stumbled down the slope, catching myself in the mud. I was here because of Dallas—what she'd told me on the phone. I knew she might be lying, but I had no other leads.

"You stupid bitch," she'd said in greeting. "I knew it was a joke."

I'd been calling on Callie's phone. She'd left it on the floor. I was still standing in our hallway with the red-inked note in my hand. *Sorry Rebecca. It was me. C*

It was me who threw the paint? It was me who wrote the notes? It was me, not Robyn. Had it never been Robyn?

Callie's handwriting tilted across the page, giving me an answer.

"Dallas, this is Rebecca. What joke? What's going on?"

As soon as she realized it was me, Dallas's voice softened. She attempted a babyish coo, which turned my stomach. She could transform so easily, without missing a beat, and everything was tilting toward a sharp, queasy drop. The notes weren't what I'd thought, and this girl wasn't, either.

"Callie's gone crazy," Dallas said. "She sent out all these messages. She said that we killed her, but I don't know what she means."

"Do you know where she is? Please tell me."

She sniffled and gasped, and then she started to cough.

"Dallas! Come on! What do you mean she said you killed her?"

"She says we drowned her. In Ella's lake."

I had begun skimming my beam across the shore, across the trees and the black sky. The left side of the lake was cocooned by countless gray trees. On the right, there were small docks and large houses, some with little porch lights. I imagined those white lights leading kids back home from moonlit swims and trips out in a canoe. Barefoot and dripping, they ran back to their houses, drying their feet on the carpet and leaping into clean beds. Then their parents came in to check on them, kissing their damp brows good night.

Sweet dreams, sleep tight. I'll see you in the morning.

Curtis swallowed his pills. Callie kissed me good-bye.

A pale buoy bobbed in the water and I caught my breath. Then I started to call her. Again and again. The reeds rustled, the water lapped at the rocks, and I listened for her voice, a splash, a sob. My voice echoed back at me, desolate and empty, and I started screaming louder, not caring who I woke up. Then I was grappling for my phone because what if she was trying to reach me, but it wasn't where I thought, I must've dropped it in the car. I was racing so quickly, I'd done everything wrong. I couldn't even remember turning off the engine. I'd just needed to find her. But what if she was elsewhere? She could be anywhere else: at the bridge or on the road. I was blind sometimes. So stupid and blind. All those notes. That slanty red writing.

I aimed my flashlight down and saw all the markings.

In the mud there were shoe prints. They were small, like Callie's. I followed them to the water and saw they didn't come back out. And I was gripping my stomach because I was going to be sick, but there was no time to be sick, I had to follow them in. My breath got short as the water soaked my pants, and this couldn't be happening, she wasn't in the lake. Those footprints were old, Callie wouldn't do this. She'd always refused to go swimming, even on the hottest days of summer. She lay on her pink palm-tree towel, sweating in the sun. She said she hated the feeling of cold water on her skin. I could hear her perfectly. This didn't make sense. My whole body was numb, and I remembered Dallas's voice.

She said we drowned her. In Ella's lake.

Her logic escaped me. All of this escaped me. But there must be some kind of progression, a sequence I could follow. I kept my arms high as I walked in deeper, casting my beam along the moving surface. The rafts of leaves, the pale fingerlike flowers, the distant rope that floated on the surface. She had thrown paint on Robyn. She had written those notes. She'd asked me about Autumn Sanger over and over again. She'd said that Autumn was bullied and her bullies killed her. She'd wondered if Autumn drowned herself because her life would never be good. *I was a shitty mistake and I'm ready to be erased.* I kept forgetting to breathe; my chest contracted. There was something gold in front of me, something like hair. I opened my hands and my flashlight started sinking. Then I saw what it was, coiling around my fingers. Not hair, just grass. My flashlight was gone. I grasped at the water and my hands came up empty.

I screamed Callie's name and a light blinked on in the distance, then I sloshed deeper into the lake, deeper into this nightmare. I couldn't feel my legs, but they didn't matter. As long as they kept moving, I wouldn't lose my mind. As long as I kept screaming, this panic wouldn't beat me. And then I'd see her on the shore, waving sheepishly. Because she wouldn't really go in, no matter what she told Dallas. The footprints were just a joke. Part of the whole plan. "Oh, Rebecca!" She'd shake her head. "Why are *you* here?" And I'd tell her she was grounded, and I'd keep hold of her, tight.

Something strange was happening. Maybe it was shock. The temperature in the lake was suddenly warm. I was still screaming, but I couldn't hear my voice, and then blue and red patterns started flashing across the water. I took a moment to watch them. Neon flowers. I couldn't feel my body and I was staring at the light. And that was when I saw them, on the far side of the lake.

There was a woman carrying something. I saw what it was.

"Ali!" I screamed. "Ali! Thank God."

Then somehow I was running, or trying to run, and then I was falling, the weight of my clothes pulling me down.

"Ali! Is she okay?"

Had she heard me? She kept walking. Then she turned her head. And as I saw her profile I realized my mistake. It wasn't Ella's mother. It was somebody else. Her body was more swollen and her hair was too long. She moved slowly, out of the water, flinching against the light, turning her face away. I watched her stumble and catch herself, carefully cradling the thing she held. Clutching tightly, the way a mother holds her baby.

There were sirens now, a flash of white skin under the lights. A flash of copper hair as she turned my way.

Did my husband call you? Is Curtis there?

Men's voices were rising and she looked right at me, eyes panicking, the way they had when she couldn't speak. Mouth clamped shut, our eyes connected, and I was moving toward her as she quivered under the lights. She was no longer tall and goddesslike, but I wasn't dreaming. She had returned with her arms full, a brutal reminder of the past. People were joining us in the water, splashing in their haste, and I screamed one last time because I knew who this was.

Lara Shanley was holding Callie. Her body was in her arms.

Callie wasn't wearing shoes. Her arms hung loose and her feet were slick with mud. The paramedics were rushing around, and in the confusion I fell again in the water. Then I was dragging myself out, dazzled by the light. Callie's eyes rolled open as they set her on the ground, and I crawled behind them, undone by visions. Where was my vision? Where was Lara? We had to stop her. Please, fast. Someone was holding a penlight over Callie, and streaks of water trickled down her face. She didn't move. She was completely limp. They tilted her head to one side, and then they tilted it back. I saw the blue rubber gloves touching her skin and I saw how she didn't gasp. Lara was already gone. Lara had vanished.

"What's her name?" someone asked.

"Callie!" I was screaming. "CallieCallieCallie."

"Callie! Can you hear me?"

"Nonononono!"

"Starting compressions!"

They started pumping on her chest, and the pressure of their hands

made her body jump, then voices were blooming and lights were exploding and as her body flopped forward, the water rushed out.

* * *

We spent our first night on the fourth floor of the Kinney Trust Hospital,
in a small room where nothing seemed solid or real. Not the blue folding
curtains or the shining speckled floor. Not the walls or the window or
the bed where she lay. Over the sheet, I traced her shoulders like delicate,
breakable eggshells. Her chest was sunken and inky black streaks were
smeared on her skin. Callie's chest went up and down and I counted into
the hundreds, then I counted into the thousands. It still wasn't enough.
I needed more—more breath, please, more life. Proof that there would
always be more.

I kept my hands in her hair, anchoring her to the earth. It was tangled
and dirty and still smelled of the lake. I worked out the knots, crumbling
mud between my nails, and every once in a while, a nurse would come
in. She would pad over to Callie's machines, check her oxygen level,
say something incomprehensible, and then pad back out. There was a
chair in the room where I was supposed to sit or sleep, but I'd decided I
wouldn't sleep. I would stay awake forever. If I closed my eyes she might
slip beneath the sheets, transform into air, evaporate like steam. I was
going to stay awake, guarding her like this. A doctor came in. A nurse
wrote on her chart. My mother arrived, spoke words, and then left. I'd
been given a pamphlet telling me how to cope. The word *suicide* was on
the cover and it seemed like nonsense. A word like *sclerosis* or *sumac* or
sunrise, maybe. It was a word that could mean anything, anything but

that. I looked at the tips. Hide your household poisons, lock up your pills, throw out your razors. I was trying to understand, but my brain was flooded. Had I really seen Lara? Was she saving Callie? Had Callie been doing what they said in the lake? Had she planned it all out and thought it all through? Or was it just a joke that could change our lives forever?

Why did anyone do anything? That was the real question.

I watched a small brown spider crawl across the speckled floor. If Callie were awake she'd crouch down and scoop him up. "A pholcid!" she'd exclaim with childlike awe. Then she'd deposit him somewhere safe, unharmed and free. The spider paused, lifted two legs, and then continued onward. His reasons for being here were as incomprehensible as ours.

You can run but you can't hide. Dead Babyshits leaves a stain.

Warning! Babyshits poops her pants. GET A FUCKING DIAPER.

BETTER DO WHAT YOU SAID BABYSHIIIIIIIIIITTTTTTTTSSSSSS! DIE BITCH GOODNIGHT.

I looked at her texts for the second time that night, trying to understand the bitter jumble of information. Her friends had sent these—their names were on them. Nauseating words that seemed irrational, repulsive. I wanted to lie down on the floor, press my face against the cold vinyl, and be sick down there until something made sense. I had never looked on her phone—I thought that she would tell me. Why didn't she tell me? How couldn't I know? The answers seemed impossible and my regrets were useless. The only thing that made sense was Callie's moving chest. It went up and down and I started talking.

"Let's get out of here," I said. "Let's get in the car. I'll give you the map and you choose where we're going. We'll go anywhere you want, Callie, anywhere you can imagine. I'll roll down the windows and put on some music."

I watched her chest rise and fall. I put my hand on hers.

"Do you want to go to Iowa? I've never been there. We'll get on the highway and drive for a while. We'll watch the states flashing by, the fields and valleys, the wide-open plains like you see on TV."

I looked at the tubes covering her nose and mouth. The respirator hissed, loud and relentless.

"I think we'll live on a farm. It'll have a bright shining silo, and we can start raising animals, whatever you want. You won't have to go to school. We'll spend the day outside. We can learn to milk cows, and you'll tell me about your plans. . . . Maybe you'll decide to travel the world, learning different languages. Or you'll go work in a rainforest so you can discover new species. You might want to stay up all night, just dancing, in your socks. . . ."

I stroked her smooth forehead and touched her hair.

"You can still do anything. Callie, you can."

Callie had sent me a message. I noticed it around dawn. An e-mail with the subject line "Sorry Rebecca." I squinted at my phone's small screen and managed to open it as I trembled.

> Rebecca I'm sending you my last five interactions with Robyn so
> you can know the whole truth. I also wanted to tell you I'm really
> sorry again. Love, Callie

It was excruciatingly intimate, the details of those interactions. Callie's friendship with Robyn had changed in the space of a few weeks. They had become so close that it felt like love—or maybe it really was love—and this was more astonishing and difficult than either of them expected. Callie was ashamed and afraid and she hadn't wanted anyone to know. She'd hidden it from me and then their love had gone sour.

I remembered my feelings for Joyce—how I imagined walking into the ocean when she ignored me. When you were thirteen or fourteen years old it seemed like a reasonable reaction. When things felt so wonderful and awful your life could shrink in a dizzying moment . . . and then you couldn't see all the moments still waiting in your future. Callie had been hiding behind a mask, thinking she was too messy and complicated. And I'd been hiding, too, hoping her life would be easier than mine. But easy wasn't real. Love was powerful because it could hurt you. Love hurt now; I could've told her that. It was messy and graceless. It went wrong, it even died. But the thing she needed to know was that it didn't have to destroy you. It could resprout and grow again; it could still come back.

*

A police officer came by the hospital on Monday. He introduced himself as Gary Gatewood and carried a manila folder full of computer printouts. As I looked through them, he stood patiently beside me, like a notifying officer in military shoes. There was a picture of Callie beneath the words "HAVE YOU SMELLED BABYSHITS?" and I wasn't surprised when I saw Dallas and Ella's names. I wanted to kill them, but I wasn't surprised.

Officer Gatewood showed me the e-mail Ella had sent out late on Sunday night, where she bragged about how she and Dallas got away with bullying. There was a list of her victims, and she described what she'd done to Callie. She'd tried to drown her in the lake, she'd heck-led her at school, and over the past month she'd repeatedly threatened to kill her. Ella sounded shamelessly triumphant as she recounted her crimes, and I wished, for a spiteful moment, that it was her in the hospital instead. "We've talked to Ella and she claims she didn't write this," Officer Gatewood said. "We've got reason to believe Callie hacked her account."

He showed me another paper that looked like the group I'd seen before, but then he pointed out the headline.

I Killed Callie McKenzie

This is not a joke. By joining this group you have committed murder. A girl died tonight because of you. Callie McKenzie—who you called Babyshits—was not nothing. Her life wasn't meaningless. But you decided to kill her anyway.

I started to shudder. I pictured them gathered around her in the lake. But there hadn't been anyone there. Just Callie and Lara.

Every time you think about hurting someone else, she'll be there. She'll feel like a choke, or a thick swallow, and you'll remember her and stop.

"Does this sound to you like something Callie would write?"

"Yes," I admitted. "It sounds like her."

Then I asked him if the woman who carried her out of the lake had been found.

I made the call from the hospital lobby, just inside the sliding glass doors. Every few seconds the automatic doors opened and closed, shoop-shoop,

shoop-shoop. A regular doo-wop as people came and went. I was calling my mother to find out what she knew.

"Did you know that Lara's out of prison? They let her out early."

"What happened?" She sounded groggy. "Is Callie okay?"

"Callie's the same. But it was Lara at the lake with her. Lara was in the water. I thought I was dreaming."

"Lara was there?"

"Yes! She was carrying Callie!"

"Okay. Just stay calm," Mom said hurriedly. "I'll see what I can find out."

There were things that I needed to do. I started telling Danny my plans. He'd showed up at the hospital after texting me, carrying a bag full of doughnuts. First, I would get Callie out of here. Second, we would move far away. Then I would find a place with a really good oven so I could bake Callie bread. Cinnamon loaf brushed with melted butter. Herb bread laced with thyme and parsley. Great chunks of hot cornbread that would crumble on her tongue. I'd brush the crumbs from her bed and bring her loaves full of walnuts and raisins. Maybe I could even sell it. Start a new life making bread.

I watched Danny play with the collar of his T-shirt, his long, blunt fingers searching the neckline for holes. He listened in his decent way, but I knew I sounded crazy. His gray eyes steadied mine and I wondered what else I could do. Insanity was the only thing that made sense right now.

Danny cupped his chin in his hand, rubbing the sharp, sandy bristles. He'd talked to the police about Robyn and reassured me that she was okay. She'd been at home the whole time. Callie was just using her as a cover. I stared at her in the bed and reminded myself of the bread. We'd devour it by the fistful. Sourdough and cheese bread.

"Is that made with cheddar?" Danny asked, and I looked at him gratefully.

"Sharp cheddar cheese," I said. "And two tablespoons of honey."

That afternoon, I watched as my mom and Aunt Bea shuffled through the sliding doors. Bea looked like a patient who had come here to die. She had an oxygen tank on wheels, and she stood with a hunch, like she was shielding from bad news. Her skin was the color of mushrooms, and Mom gripped her by the elbow as if she might collapse on the floor. Mom handed me granola bars and bottled water in an old plastic bag. "I brought you some clothes." She held out a pink jogging suit. I looked down at what I was wearing: gray sweatpants and a sweatshirt. They weren't mine, and I couldn't remember putting them on. I must have peeled off my wet clothes at some point, but I had no recollection.

They took two seats in the lobby, but I didn't join them. I didn't want to sit down—I needed to keep moving. Bea wore a pair of acrylic pants and a cheap yellow sweater. She fiddled with the clear oxygen tube in her nostrils and her expression was tense.

"So," Bea said. "I heard the EEG was normal."

"They say she'll wake up soon, Rebecca, isn't that right?"

I nodded and looked at my mom. I could hardly recognize her. She pressed her eyelids for a moment and then told me to sit down. "We talked to Lara," she said. "We went to see her after you called."

"You sat down and talked to her?"

"Yes, and your aunt has something to tell you."

Bea rubbed her fingers fussily across her scalp, and then frowned at the wall. "Lara saw Callie at my house."

"What! How?"

"Lara visited me last week and Callie peeped in through the window."

"She didn't let them meet," Mom said. "Callie didn't meet her."

I turned on my aunt. "You let her in your house?" I felt like dropping to my knees, grabbing her wrists and screaming. She'd hated me since Curtis died, and I wanted to know how this could happen. How could she hate me and let *that woman* into her house?

"I never planned it this way," Bea said, then she told me about Lara's letters—the apologies and pleas, postmarked from York Correctional. Lara had written that she wanted to trade. Her life for theirs. She said she would die in Curtis's place if she could figure out how to go back.

"I told her to rot in hell." Bea winced. "I wrote the nastiest things. All I wanted was for her to suffer." Bea pinched her thighs as she spoke, hard little tweaks for punctuation. "I knew her since she was fourteen years old, but that was a whole other person."

When Lara wrote back to my aunt, she agreed with all of Bea's insults. So my aunt responded with more and worse: Lara was poison. Unfit for society. A terrible wife to Curtis. She couldn't have been a mother. She deserved every one of her miscarriages.

Bea looked at me and her expression was awful, like she'd been dipped in ice water, the color draining out of her lips. "She agreed with that, too," Bea said, "and then I couldn't do it anymore."

Those babies—Bea's grandchildren—she and Lara had mourned them together. Bea couldn't wish those children away, and Lara's suffering wasn't helping. Bea was as miserable as ever: her son wasn't here. Neither one of them could do anything to change that. When my aunt finally picked up her pen, she knew exactly what she wanted to say.

Dear Lara, Bea wrote.

I understand how you feel.

When Lara was released from prison, she went to visit my aunt, and when they were together in Bea's living room, Lara started to cry. She said she wouldn't have made it without Bea's understanding; Bea's letters, no longer hateful, had helped Lara to survive. Bea had wanted to tell Lara that she still couldn't forgive her, but before she could say the words, she heard someone banging on her front door. "Grandma, Grandma, Grandma, Grandma!"

"She took a taxi," Bea explained. It had happened last Tuesday. When Callie was supposed to be home sick, she had seen her through Bea's front window.

Lara saw Callie, too, and she had always wondered. Now Curtis's daughter was right in front of her like some kind of sign. She looked at the piercing green eyes, the chin like her father's, and she planned to Google Callie only once, but then she ended up on Facebook. She clicked on Callie's friends' profiles and then she saw the page: "HAVE YOU SMELLED BABYSHITS?" Just like Officer Gatewood had showed me.

Lara started scanning the web compulsively, watching for new comments, clicking the report button as the filth built up. She even sent Callie an anonymous message, suggesting she ask someone for help. "Didn't she think she should tell you?" I asked Bea. "Or call the police?" But Lara was in a precarious position, spying on her husband's daughter. And she didn't know how it would escalate in just a couple of days. Late on Sunday night, as I was driving to the bridge to meet Danny, Lara spotted the page "**I Killed Callie McKenzie**." And as I waited on the road for Robyn, believing I could save her, Lara was driving to our house, thinking it was too late. She thought Callie's tormentors had already killed her. She didn't know Callie had written it herself. Then she saw Callie walking down our steps and out into the night.

"She followed her," my mother said, and I couldn't help choking.

"In a car?"

"No. On foot. She thought someone might hurt her."

I closed my eyes and remembered the shock I'd felt when Lara hit Joyce and Curtis. She'd been a normal woman—how could she be a killer? How could anyone transform themselves so completely? And how could she change again now, coming back to save Callie's life? I knew there was no such thing as mind-reading. The ESP we once dreamed of was fantasy. Lara had checked online at the right time; she saw Callie leaving our house. It was just timing, luck, chance, circumstances. She wasn't a hero; some of us never would be.

* * *

If I'd seen her on the street I might not have noticed her. She wasn't a striking figure; she looked mild, harmless. If I hadn't recognized her I might've guessed she was a middle-aged waitress, or a cafeteria worker, taking a much-deserved break. Her skin was pale and doughy, her dark red hair had faded to blandness; even her eyebrows were too sparse to give her face any definition.

The hospital's cafeteria was clattery and dim in late afternoon, a large, smelly place full of plastic chairs and tables. Families came here to eat tasteless food in the midst of tragedies and miracles. The scent of ketchup and tater tots contrasting with the jumble of emotions. She didn't look up when I sat down across from her, and I was surprised that my hands weren't twitching, that I wasn't grabbing for her throat the way I'd imagined thousands of times.

"I'm not here to bother you," Lara said, staring down at the table. "I just wanted you to know I was only there because I was worried."

Her face was so stark that I wondered if she'd learned this in prison: how to make herself appear so distant, fully absent from reality.

"I also wanted to tell you I'm sorry," she said automatically. "And I hope she's doing okay. But you don't have to worry, I'll stay away after this."

I heard the cash register dinging, the scrape of knife and fork against plate. I looked at the elderly couple sitting near to us, sharing a bag of chips. Lara tugged her sleeves, glanced at the paper cup on our table. I realized with disgust that she had bought herself a cup of coffee.

"How's the coffee?" I asked, a greasy tang at the back of my throat.

"The coffee?" she asked uncertainly. "Do you want me to get you a cup?"

"I can't drink anything right now," I said harshly. "I don't want anything."

I stared at her cup, willing her to drink. Willing her to display her most inhuman qualities. She folded her hands together. Her nails looked pink and healthy, and her skin wasn't rough or chapped. She'd been taking care of herself.

"Callie doesn't know anything about you," I said. "I never showed her your letters. I couldn't let her find out what you almost did to her, too."

"Rebecca, I w—" Lara stopped and pressed her lips together. I knew the drill: she was holding back her stutter. "I wouldn't," she finally managed. "I didn't mean to."

"Imagine how she would've felt," I said. "If she had to think about that." I waited for Lara to absorb this, to taste the bile in her throat. "Callie always had a vivid imagination," I continued. "She would've imagined it. After Joyce died, she used to wait for her every night. She would see her in her bedroom. She thought her mom would come in to visit, and they'd talk about the dirt in her grave, the dirt that Joyce had to sleep in."

Lara still hadn't given me her eyes. She watched the table like it might turn into an exit, an escape route right out of this conversation. I noted irritably that her wrists were unblemished. Her neck was unmarked. There were no signs that she'd ever been suicidal.

"So what changed?" I asked meanly. "Why are you still here?"

I think Lara understood what I meant. I wasn't asking about the cafeteria. This was about the rope, the noose, the opportunities she must've had. Her lips crumpled. I thought of Bea's letters. Making her suffer might not help, but it felt good at the moment.

"You shouldn't have been at that lake," I said. "You should've called the police."

"Rebecca, I know. I didn't realize until later."

"I didn't realize at all," I said bitterly. "I never do until it's too late."

Lara's eyes when she raised them were watchful, serious. She held my gaze, unblinking, and it was me who had to look away. "I wouldn't hurt her," she murmured. "I regret everything. I think of Joyce and Curtis every day. I know . . ." She paused. "What we lost."

It was too much. I couldn't let her.

"There's no 'we'! Don't lump me in with you. What I lost—what Callie lost—is completely different." My hand shot out, but it didn't strike her. Instead, it sank down like a stone in the water. Lara looked up in surprise as my fingers landed on hers: the fingers that grabbed Callie as she disappeared under the surface. Lara's hand was cold as I clutched at her spotted knuckles. I hadn't got to the lake in time; Callie wouldn't be here.

"I know," Lara was saying. "I didn't mean—"

Our hands were one mass on the table. I wasn't letting go. Callie's body in Lara's arms. Callie gasping for breath. I finally pulled my hand away and rubbed the wetness around my eyes.

"What was it like?" I asked. "Out there with Callie?"

"Well," Lara began. "It was a shock when she went under."

"But you didn't hesitate to go in after her? You didn't stand there watching?"

She tried to appear unrattled. "No, I just went in."

I thought of our last game of hyacinth girls, when I'd pretended to be Lara, stuttering my good-byes as I watched Autumn drown.

"Callie was asking me about Autumn Sanger," I said. "I think she was looking for inspiration."

"Autumn?" Lara touched her loose hair like she'd forgotten a bobby pin.

"I shouldn't have told her," I said. "I didn't make the connection."

"I think Autumn was different from Callie." Lara began tracing her fingers over the table. "Autumn didn't leave a note or anything. She was kind of resigned to how things were." Her fingers stopped moving, and she seemed to be gathering her thoughts. "Autumn used to meet me every morning at school, and I'd see these bruises on her ankles. She had these really skinny legs and her dad kicked her wearing his work boots. My dad had a temper, too, but he mostly went after my brothers, so I thought I understood, but I couldn't, really. So one day, Autumn comes in and she goes, 'You wanna see something?' She pulls up her shirt and there's purple bruises all over her ribs. I was like, 'Okay, this is too much. You gotta tell someone.' And she's, 'Nah, forget it. That's just the way it is.'"

"Her dad beat her." I felt wary. "Are you saying he killed her?"

Lara shook her head. "She just gave up."

"But you told us Mr. Hort—"

"Autumn was really unhappy. But I wanted to think she got kidnapped because she didn't leave a note. I thought, if she was going to do it, she'd at least try to get her dad in trouble."

Lara looked at me directly and I stopped brushing my tears away. "She was different," she insisted. "You saw what Callie wrote online?"

I tried not to sniffle as I nodded my head.

"Think about what she wanted."

I thought of the darkness of the lake, the vast span of the ocean. The starkness of her message, claiming she'd been killed.

"She wanted to make them sorry," I said, hesitating. "She thought she could change things."

"She wanted to have a voice," Lara said, "so that people would listen. She didn't give up the same as Autumn. That could be hopeful, don't you think?"

CALLIE

When I was little, death was something outside me. Not as far away as the moon, but only sometimes nearby. It was the smell in the street when I saw fur in the gutter. Or the cars rushing by when a hand suddenly squeezed mine. It was the shoe in the grass that lay there for weeks, filling up with worms and rain when nobody came back.

Death was a warning, a sharp voice, a door slamming. It was spiky and heavy like a bomb in a dream. You were scared it would fall on you, but you wondered what would happen. Then it surprised you by exploding right inside your house. You looked for your mom, but they wouldn't tell you where, and that was when it changed: it became something you searched for.

A magnet getting stronger. A planet sucking you closer. You were orbiting around it, like a loose feather in the air. You wanted to touch it and understand what it was. So you jumped off a swing at the very top— you closed your eyes and let yourself fall. It was a dare, a joke. A fantasy funeral. You laughed yourself sick until one day you learned.

It had been growing inside you, branching out, getting stronger. It was the thud of your heartbeat, more powerful than you thought. It was the beast who said "Freak!" and then whispered, "Come." It was a cage with the door open and a voice telling you, "Fly!" You flapped your arms, but then a new voice interrupted. Someone was calling you. She knew your name.

Here's how it could've happened when I woke up in the hospital.

There's a pile of cards, zillions of stuffed animals. Get-well balloons sway in the corners of my room. Rebecca begins reading the apologies from kids at school. There must be at least a hundred. They sound super-sincere. But most important, when I try to remember, everything is clear, my head isn't clouded with fog, I know who I am. It makes sense. Perfectly. Then I turn my head and see her. Her mascara is running the way it did once before. When she says my name it's like kittens purring, pink velvet noses pushing against my skin. She knows me by heart, like multiplication, and she quickly finds my hand under the covers. Then visitors start to arrive, everyone wants to see me. Teachers and friends, reporters and TV crews: they all start to clap and tell me I'm brave. The light isn't too bright and then weirdly smoky. And when I blink again I see them, my mom and dad.

And none of this was actually true. It didn't happen like this at all. There weren't any cards or balloons when I opened my eyes. Rebecca couldn't read their apologies because there weren't any apologies. My brain was so wasted I couldn't fit words into a sentence—they disappeared like gnats when I tried to catch them in my mind. There weren't zillions of stuffed animals, and the only people who visited were relatives: Grandma Bea, Great-Aunt Gina, and Grandpa Pat. They weren't smiling or clapping or telling me I was brave. I couldn't remember or think. Robyn never came.

Plus, there was the frostbite. My feet felt radioactive. It was like they'd been trapped in a cage deep inside the sun. My blisters looked disgusting, like tiny pink mushrooms, and when the doctor snipped them off, I needed the plastic bowl to vomit.

But how was I here?

"It was a miracle," Rebecca said.

"Did I swim out of the . . ."

"A miracle," she repeated.

I didn't feel like a miracle. I felt unbelievably blank. Like at long last I was supposed to see this movie and ended up staring at a black screen. I was just spectacularly glazed over, my mouth hanging open, a dull-brained baby, numb and confused. *Why am I watching this? What happened? Why isn't it starting the way that I thought?*

"I just can't understand it," Great-Aunt Gina said. "Such a beautiful girl."

"What kind of meds is she on?" Grandpa asked. "Is that why she's acting like this?"

"What do you want me to say?" Grandma Bea said. "It is what it is."

And then there was Rebecca, who was always there. Looking into my face, repeating my name like a code. She talked and talked, and I didn't know how many days had passed, and she was talking about bread and then I thought I heard her say "Papa."

"I know what happened with Robyn," she said. "All of us love you."

It was more than I could hear right now. I stared at the black screen.

One day someone brought in gigantic hot pink slippers. Rebecca wiggled them on over my bandages and offered me her arm. Then I was supposed to try and walk, but my toes didn't stop me from tipping over. There was a complete disconnect between my brain and my feet. I was going home. I gripped Rebecca's arm and wondered how I was even moving. I couldn't hold my own weight. Below my ankles was just floppy burning meat. I hobbled up the stairs to our house, clutching her, while she talked me to the top.

"Three more. Two more. C'mon, Callie. Almost there."

It was like crossing the finish line when I finally made it to my bed. Rebecca piled pillows under my feet and explained that there would always be someone here. It would be her or Great-Aunt Gina or Grandpa Pat or Mrs. Romero. I was embarrassed I needed babysitters, but I was too tired to argue.

"Think of us as your bodyguards," Rebecca said. "We're making sure you stay safe."

Then I lay in bed, trying to sleep as much as I could because when I was awake I started thinking. *What did I do? What happened?* My brain burned when I remembered too much. Sometimes, to distract myself, I pretended that I was holding a lighter to different parts of my body. I held it against my knees until I felt the shooting sparks. I waited for my fingers to sizzle. The hairs on my neck crackled and singed. When each part was feverish, I imagined snowflakes. They fell in mounds on my stomach. They cooled my lips and my tongue. They made my ankles shiver and my heartbeat slow. Finally, if I was still awake, I imagined a silky feather that tickled me everywhere. It slipped across my thighs, under my chin, inside my ears. I let it roam all over my body, but I never let it touch my feet.

They were swollen and stiff, like cavewoman feet, and every few hours they woke me with the throb of a second heart. Three toenails fell off. Rebecca fed me painkillers and unwrapped my bandages. Underneath, my skin was blue, gray, and poisonous purple. Rebecca dabbed on the special ointment and I wished she wouldn't look. But then, when she was about to leave, I gripped the side of her arm. I was grabbing at her leg, wiping my face on her shirt. I was crying so intensely, just incredibly needy. *Don't give up on me. What if you give up on me?*

"I won't give up on you. Callie, I promise."

"No! Go away!" I shrieked. "Leave me alone!"

And when she shifted the littlest bit, I started to wail. "Please don't leave me! Why are you leaving?"

Rebecca didn't leave. She stayed by my side. And even though I didn't mean to, I started telling her things: I was a freak, a pathetic baby. I'd been trying to hide it my whole life. But now everyone knew and how could she stand to look at me?

Rebecca let me clutch onto her as she tried to untangle the things I was saying. She said our whole family loved me. Things were going to get better. I wasn't the things they said I was, my mind was just mixed up. I could start over fresh and be anything I wanted. I didn't have to be anyone except for myself. I was trying to believe her, but then my brain was burning. I had to look at Rebecca and remember what I'd done. If I'd left her like that . . . if she'd had to sit here without me . . . I never loved her enough; I hadn't understood what would happen at all. And I wished I could still hate how she was always here for me, loving me without limits, forgiving my heartless heart—but I couldn't hate. I gripped Rebecca's sleeve tighter. It had been her voice calling my name; she was the one out there at the lake. "You saved me," I said.

Then she told me something impossible.

"The person who pulled you out—that was your dad's wife."

I let go of her sleeve. I stuffed my head under my pillow. Then I pressed it into my mouth like I could swallow it whole.

"I don't want to keep secrets anymore. I want you to know the truth."

I pressed my fingers into my eyes, sinking underwater. Rebecca said I needed to listen. Then she told me about my parents.

My dad used to visit me, once a month, at the beach. He kept it a secret from his wife because she didn't want us in contact. She was jealous because he'd cheated on her with my mom right before their wedding.

And then she thought they were still cheating, but my dad was only visiting me. He had visited me. He'd bought me ice cream, hugged me, and kissed me. He carried me in his arms. He'd wanted to know me. I kept trying, but I couldn't remember. "Why didn't anyone tell me?"

"His wife thought your parents were cheating," Rebecca said. "And she came to me, threatening suicide. So I told her the truth about your visits, thinking it would help."

But instead his wife went to the beach and saw us, and she hit my parents with her car.

"It was so horrible, Callie. We didn't want you to imagine. Or to remember any of it—even though that meant leaving out your dad."

The woman I saw at Grandma's—my dad's wife—had killed my mom. Mom was murdered, and Dad killed himself not long after. I felt a blankness stretching over me, like a sheet pulled tight, blocking out the light, the air, the feeling of being alive. I couldn't remember it at all, but I saw their faces changing. I saw the fear in their eyes. I saw the way their lips stretched. I hadn't known why my parents died or remembered my dad's visits. I thought my mom's life was perfect, but with just a few words they both were changing.

What about a bath? they asked. *It'll make you feel better.* But the idea of getting in the tub seemed totally impossible. First, I would have to get out of my bed. Put my feet on the floor. Find a way to stop crying as I staggered down the hall. Then there would be soap and undressing and my feet wrapped in plastic bags. They weren't supposed to get wet. I'd have to keep them out of the water.

"Let me open your curtains," Grandpa said, but I wanted it dark.

"I brought you some juice. Just have a little sip."

I sipped like a newborn baby, starry-brained and speechless. I was learning how to speak—each word felt like a stone. Mom, Dad. They didn't mean what they used to. When I closed my eyes they lay heavy inside my stomach. Mommy, Daddy. I tried curling up around them, sticky drool drying against one cheek. I wanted to pull them close, feel them with me, decide if we were the same by the way their names sounded on my tongue. But they were always too far away. They weren't here when I needed them. And when I cried out their names new words came raining down. Murdered. Victims. Babyshits. Bullets.

"They're just labels," Rebecca said. "Nobody's just one thing."

I felt the words heaping up on me in a tall stone pile—a thousand colored stones—ready to crush. She was murdered. A victim. They rolled and shifted. She was a hero, Evil McFrenzy. They pressed down on my chest. *Your parents were so much more than what happened to them.* I was supposed to be more, too. Mom's murderer had given me that chance.

Lara, Rebecca said. Murderer, killer. *Not just one thing.* The woman who saved me. But who had she saved? Who was the girl who tried to die in the water—who looked for an answer in the lake and came up cold and empty? That girl had wanted to change her own story, but she missed the most obvious thing: after you died, your story wasn't yours. The things you'd left behind—your notes and actions—could all be misunderstood, forgotten, ignored. My dad had loved me, but I couldn't remember. My mom suffered, but I'd seen only perfection. The words I'd had for my parents were as wrong as the ones I'd been given at school. And the words I gave Rebecca . . . I looked at her again.

Raspberry-tea-drinking guardian. Falls-for-everything hygienist. Turtleneck-wearing softie who couldn't understand. She held my hand as she sat on my bed, and I tried to really see her. If she knew me now, I wanted to know her back. She had never asked for a title, she wasn't

Momma R or Auntie, even though she raised me and loved me the way a parent would. Who was she? What words? I dropped my head onto her shoulder. Then we sat there for a while, feeling the things I couldn't name.

It happened one morning, I still don't know why, I opened my eyes and something was different. My feet weren't screaming. The second heart had stopped throbbing. My arms were light and the pile of stones was gone. Babyshits, murderers. I tested them carefully. Mom, Dad. I looked at the window and sunlight was coming in. The cane beside my bed was white like Christmas candy. I put my fingers around the handle and waited for the idea to wear off. I would lie back down in exactly two seconds. Three, four, five, six. I wasn't lying down—I wanted to get up.

Push back the blanket. Shift feet carefully. Don't go too fast. Take your time. Someone had opened my window. I could feel the cool air. A bird was cawing outside. Sounded like a crow. Then my feet were on the floor, and my legs were all wobbly. But it didn't hurt too bad, and I kept holding my cane. Then like a miracle I was leaving my room.

Grandpa Pat was sitting in the living room. He was working on his laptop. When he saw me coming in, he stopped typing. He didn't say anything as I continued unsteadily forward. But he looked at me like I would burst into flames. Was I going to escape? Try to kill myself again? Start sobbing like a maniac? My grandpa didn't know.

Then my foot went wrongward and I tumbled to the floor.

Grandpa crouched beside me. I could see the wet comb marks in his hair.

"Gina!" he yelled. "Gina, can you get in here?"

My great-aunt came in and then they moved me to the sofa. They put pillows under my feet and checked my pulse. Grandpa covered me with a blanket and then they both stood together. Mom's dad, Rebecca's mom. Watching me like I was a broken doll.

"I'm okay." I waved one hand to reassure them.

"You sure like to make an entrance."

Great-Aunt Gina rubbed her forehead. "Callie, I'm making eggs. Can you eat an egg?"

An egg? I thought about it. Yes, I could eat an egg.

Great-Aunt Gina brought me a glass of juice and a handful of pills. She held the glass to my lips. "Can you take a sip?"

I sipped, I ate the eggs, and then I asked for more. When I asked Grandpa what month it was, he told me October.

By the time Rebecca came home they'd been keeping me company for hours, and I felt relaxed, alive, actually laughing. Grandpa kept saying hilariously stupid things. He said he was thinking of becoming a nurse. Or a professional darts player. "But playing darts is thirsty work," he said. "You have to drink beer the whole way through."

"How can you hit the target if you're drunk?" my great-aunt asked.

"You'd be surprised. Sometimes it actually helps."

Rebecca opened the door and saw us cracking up on the sofa. She looked surprised at first, like finding aliens in the house. She didn't take off her coat; she was in such a rush to get to us. Then she kissed each of our cheeks, one by one.

When I was a lot better, Rebecca told me about the billboard. She'd put a picture of my face up on the road near my school. She said she'd tried calling the parents of the kids on my list, but they hadn't wanted to listen to the truth about what happened. They didn't believe her and they had all kinds of excuses. "I guess I can understand that," she said. "I was the same about you." She said that some of the parents had even threatened to sue us. They sent her letters about defamation, and that was when Rebecca decided to get the billboard. She wanted them to remember, and to think about who they were, and she was showing them they couldn't intimidate us again.

My principal sent out an e-mail while I was still in the hospital, after the first articles in the newspapers started to appear.

Dear Pembury High Families,

I'm writing today to inform and reassure you about a recent event that has affected our community. It may be upsetting or confusing to many of our students, so your support and understanding is invaluable at this time.

This morning we learned that one of our students is recovering from serious self-inflicted injuries. We were stunned and disturbed by this news, as well as by the student's allegation that a number of our students were involved in harming her. The police have since confirmed that the student acted alone, however, we are investigating whether unreported acts of bullying may have occurred prior to the incident.

Bullying, hazing, or harassment in any form, physical or verbal, is prohibited at Pembury High in concordance with state and federal laws, and will not be tolerated under any circumstances. If you or your child is concerned about any act of intimidation, I'd urge you to contact me immediately. At Pembury High, we pride ourselves on working hard to create a safe and inclusive learning environment for all our students. We've been involved with the anti-bullying league for over five years, and our own student group against bullying has been a growing success. On the rare occasions when harassment does occur, we respond swiftly and vigorously, and encourage all our students to report any incidents they have witnessed.

Counselors and teachers will be available to support and reassure our students in the coming weeks, and we ask for your patience and understanding as our community gets through this difficult time.

James Wattis

"What happened with the investigation?" I asked.

"You're going to be disappointed."

"Nothing changed?"

Rebecca put her hand on my shoulder and then closed the laptop. "I wish I could tell you that everything's all better. That your school really cracked down and your classmates became nicer. But I'm not going to lie to you—change is rarely that fast."

It turned out that no one was suspended. Or arrested, for that matter. The kids who joined the Babyshits group had to sign a contract about their online behavior. I never found out if Dallas was elected class president. Or if Ella kept swimming for our high-school team. Sometimes I wondered if they'd gone on with their lives like I'd never existed. Would they ever change? Would anyone be different? If they called some kid Meatball could he turn around and say, "Murderers"? And would that remind everyone what might happen? Or would they laugh and laugh like it was the greatest joke? I didn't know. Maybe I never would.

After we moved out of Pembury I started paying more attention, and I noticed something about bullying that hardly anyone mentions.

It's not just teenagers. Or bad little kids. It's everywhere, in everything, it's adults as much as us. On TV. In the movies. Politicians. Comedians. The guy pushed off his feet will always get the biggest laugh. When a singer gets called a hag the talent judge is "honest," and when a congressman calls the president a liar the whole world wants to see. It's drama. It's insults. It's enjoying humiliation. The adults pile in to comment on the girl who twerks on TV. *It was pathetic. It was gross. I feel bad for her mom. She turned out to be such a joke. I bet she wishes she was dead.* I had once wished that I was dead, but now I wondered if I could even blame them. If it was everywhere in everything, how could they resist?

I resisted. I changed. I remembered my humiliation. And I found words that made more sense when I thought about myself. I was real, kind, living, alive. I was the daughter of two people who had been those words, too. They had been breathing, red-blooded, not perfect people. And their stories changed my own as I carried them inside.

There was one other story I carried as I found new ways to be different, to fight against the tide of doing the same as everyone else. It wasn't that Robyn was perfect, or even perfectly different, but I missed who we'd been together. I'd liked the people we were starting to be. We'd been connected, wanting to know each other, understanding and not judging. We'd shared stories about our parents that nobody else knew. I remembered how we'd sat on the floor in the library, and she'd wrapped her arms around me, her warm hair against my face smelling like fruit. *It feels like this,* she said, and her body was like my shell. And when we imagined holding hands in our bedrooms, we wanted it so much. She said she thought about me thousands of times, and now I thought about her, too: when my alarm clock went off, when I brushed my teeth, when I opened my window and looked at the sky.

We were friends back then, and maybe someday, I hoped, again.

From: R.Doblak@sparkon.com
To: C.Mckenzie@chronomail.com
Subject: Hi
Date: Fri, Jan 1 2010, 17:48:19

Hi Callie

So I'll be 100% honest. I didn't think I'd EVER write you because
1) what you did to me was EVIL 2) I didn't trust you. Everyone
said you were a psychopath. My mom thought you might
try blackmailing us, and when a reporter called our house
she practically burst his eardrum "We DON'T know Callie
McKenzie!!!" & she was right, huh? All those times we talked,
I still don't know who I was talking to. Was it you or who you
wanted to be or just a really bad liar? My friend says people like
you do it to get you under their power, and if that's what you
were doing, congratulations, I guess it worked. I felt all the things
you wanted me to—I really fell for it—and then I felt like such an
asshole for being so dumb. I don't know how I could've known,
but when I found out I wanted a hatchet. *Chop-chop-chop*
until you told me the truth.

So let's start with that first day I met you. A day when my life felt
extremely shitty. Inside I was Endless Doom but I was trying to be
Miss Perky. There I was acting all sunny, humming along with the
chorus, asking you about pit bulls like there was nothing else on
my mind. And that Xmas song was actually so sad. "Frosty the
Snowman." About this kid who meets a great friend who ends
up melting away. It made me think about my dad and I was
like ROBYN, KEEP IT TOGETHER!!! Then you told me about this pit
bull, and all of a sudden my fakeness popped. Was that story
true? About the pit bull saving those people? I don't know why

it matters now, but I kind of feel like it does. Anyway you were
nice to me that day. You pulled me out of the quicksand and
then we were talking together online and you know all the rest.

I don't know how much of what you wrote was just lies and
stories. I read through all our old mssgs and there's a lot I want to
believe. I know you lied about the ketchup, but did you lie about
how they watched you, after your parents died, and you felt
like you couldn't be you? Was it a lie when you gave me Papa?
When you said you dreamed we slept under a tree? And what
about when you told me that you *felt* it, too? All the stuff you
wrote me after makes me think you felt *something*. But by then
I was in a new school, and I was trying to be someone different.
I decided what happened between us only happened in my
mind. How could I love someone I didn't even know?

So here's the thing, when you started e-mailing me about
Babyshits and everything, I swore I wouldn't change my mind
or let myself feel anything for you. I thought the old Robyn was
dead and the old Callie was never real, and how did I know
you weren't tricking me again? But then I heard about what
you'd done and I wished I'd tried to help you. I was sorry you
got so lonely and I never wrote you back. I know how it feels
when you want to die, and what it's like when everyone hates
you. I didn't want to chop you with a hatchet or find out you
had drowned. I talked to my mom and we decided it was too
risky for me to ever write you. But here I am, risking it, wondering
when you'll write back to me. Wondering if it could be different
this time if we can figure out how to be real.

xoRobyn

Acknowledgments

I want to start with Lizzy Kremer, my agent at David Higham Associates, whose early belief and long-enduring patience has sustained me for many years. Also, to Harriet Moore, Alice Howe, and the team at David Higham—thanks! I'm also massively grateful to Allison Hunter and Kim Witherspoon at Inkwell Management for seeing where the book needed to go and giving me the expert guidance to get it there.

I couldn't have asked for a better editor than Christine Kopprasch at Crown. Her sympathetic ear, boundless enthusiasm, and awe-inspiring professionalism make her a force to be reckoned with. Not to mention that her e-mails never fail to cheer me up. I'm so thrilled to have worked with her, as well as the whole team at Crown.

I've been lucky to have some excellent feedback from readers who I also count as friends: Megan Bradbury, Emily Midorikawa, and Gayle O'Brien all read early drafts of this book and have inspired me, motivated me, and acted as role models. My sister, Jane Frankel, gave me amazing insight into Callie, and was willing to listen to me ramble long-distance about plot points on numerous occasions. Most of all, I want to thank my mother, Leslie Frankel, for her invaluable feedback on later

ABOUT THE AUTHOR

LAUREN FRANKEL received her BA in English from Vassar College. She has worked with young people, as both an educator and a librarian, in the US and the UK. She holds an MA in Creative Writing from the University of East Anglia, where she won the David Higham Award. Born in Connecticut, she now lives with her family in England.

drafts. Not only is she a great mother, but she's also a serious reader, and she was always willing to offer her unvarnished opinion.

My friends have played a big role in my life as well as in my writing, and I wish I could mention everyone who's given me support and inspiration. Special thanks go to: Dana D'Auria, my best friend since '88, a girl who's happy to fly 3,000 miles just to pop out of my laundry room as a surprise; Stephanie Litos, whose advice on the High Line kept me going for longer than she imagines; and Laura Fowles, a girl who's still always up for a game of "make me laugh."

Also, big thanks and love to all my family: Bob and Deborah Frankel and all the Frankels, the Kramers, the Seldens, and the Howards. I couldn't have done it without you.

Finally, to my husband John—the funniest, most fun, and kindest guy. The one who's been there every step of the way, with otherworldly patience and love. I couldn't have dreamed you up. You're the best, for real.